SHERLOCK HOLMES:
LORD OF DAMNATION

SHERLOCK HOLMES:
LORD OF DAMNATION

Simon Clark

Trade Paperback Edition

Text © 2022 by Simon Clark

Cover art & interior art © 2022 by M. Wayne Miller

Grateful acknowledgement to Conan Doyle Estate Ltd. for permission to use
the Sherlock Holmes characters created by the late Sir Arthur Conan Doyle.

Editor & Publisher, Joe Morey

Copy Editor, F. J. Bergmann

Interior design by F. J. Bergmann

ISBN: 978-1-957121-35-2

Weird House Press
Central Point, OR 97502
www.weirdhousepress.com

List of Illustrations

Chapter 1

For Sherlock Holmes, the journey was a pleasure cruise. I begged to differ.

"This is a voyage to hell!" I shouted above the thunderous cacophony that resulted from waves violently smashing into the flanks of the ship. "If we ever reach land again, it will be an absolute miracle."

"My dear Watson. You know my views on miracles." Holmes lounged back in an armchair in the ship's saloon, smouldering pipe in one hand, a book in the other, his long legs stretched out as if he relaxed in the comfort of his Baker Street sitting room, not in this tin can of a steamship that lurched upward violently before dropping suddenly in a dizzying, plunging fall into the sea again as the storm raged. "Miracles are random events that the gullible interpret as magical gifts suddenly bestowed upon them from Heaven. Just as a machine makes, for example, cigarettes, so rational men, such as you and I, must manufacture circumstances that are agreeable to ourselves."

"In that case, Holmes, we have assiduously engineered our own destruction by making this voyage. Ye gods! Just listen to that hurricane. I swear it's going to tear away the

1

entire upper-deck and leave us exposed to the elements."

Holmes stretched out a long, thin arm in order to tap the wall of the hull with the bowl of his pipe. "Inch-thick iron plates, riveted by Clydeside's finest shipbuilders. This vessel isn't merely robust; it is essentially a floating castle, impervious to choppy waters, and brisk south-westerlies."

"Choppy waters?" I exclaimed. "Brisk south-westerlies!" I staggered across the heaving floor to a porthole where I pointed out through the glass into that liquid hell. Yes! An aquatic Hades! A briny abyss! "Waves higher than the ship's funnel. The air full of spray. And the only reason I can see all this at midnight is because the lightning is … is constant!"

"We are in the tropics. Such interesting variations in weather are to be expected." Holmes made a languid gesture with his hand, quite unperturbed by the brutal storm that had attacked the ship for the last six hours. "I rather think I might go up on deck shortly and photograph the ball lightning that often appears during electrical storms in these waters."

"Do not go outside, Holmes. A wave will sweep you to your death."

Holmes tilted back his head and laughed at my anguish over his intention to go out onto the storm-lashed deck. His laughter appeared to me, at that moment, cruel and lacking in any appreciation of my heartfelt concern for his safety. Holmes and I have been the closest of friends for many long years. So often have I been at his side while he investigated mysteries that on so many occasions led to the arrest of all kinds of criminals. I confess, at that moment, I glared at my friend with a great deal of anger. How dare he have such disregard for my feelings?

Jets of the most intensely brilliant light shot through the porthole as lightning kept up its non-stop barrage. That light cast a shadow of Sherlock Holmes' head in profile upon the saloon wall. The resulting image was a famous one indeed—those sharp features and eagle-beak of a nose had often been rendered in silhouette in newspapers to the extent that millions of men and women would recognize the world's greatest detective from just a simple profile in solid black upon white paper.

At that instant, I felt a compulsion to drag him roughly to his feet before swearing most foully into that gaunt face, and then taking unholy delight in the expression of shock that would no doubt fill those deep-set eyes. In fact, I even took two steps toward where he sat, with the express intention of pulling him out of the chair by his jacket lapels. However, some instinct prompted me to stop dead in my tracks. A sensation of bewilderment then swept over me, for I realized that the ceaseless bouncing of the ship on mountainous seas had temporarily robbed me of my senses. Holmes had not been laughing cruelly at me. My friend had, in fact, merely chuckled pleasantly. No doubt he'd been only too aware of my anxiety about our safety in the storm-tossed ship and he had been endeavoring to lighten my mood with a jest about taking photographs of ball lightning, whatever the dickens that is. Obviously, photography was a pastime that Holmes would never have the remotest interest in pursuing.

Holmes patted the arm of the chair next to his. "Do take a seat, friend Watson. Your face is looking decidedly grey. Are you feeling unwell?"

"Thank you, Holmes." I sat down beside him. "It's this infernal up-and-down motion of the ship. Rather unsettles one's mental equilibrium, as it were."

Holmes gave a caring smile. "I will ask the steward to bring you a brandy."

"Oh, there's no need, Holmes. Sitting here for a moment will soon have me right as rain."

"As you wish, Watson."

We sat quietly, in the way old friends can. Neither having to speak, just enjoying each other's company, content at being in the presence of someone we have known for decades.

The day of the frightful storm occurred on the 29th January, 1907. We were the only passengers in the saloon of the steamship *Blue Star,* which travelled southward through that rather turbulent Atlantic, just fifty miles or so from Africa's Gold Coast.

All of which brings me to penning a few introductory words about this extraordinary case—made so, as much from its nightmarish elements that defy rational explanation, as the dangerous events that would confront Holmes and I in the coming days.

I confess that, initially, I asked myself whether I should begin this narrative back in London, in the civil service office of Holmes' brother, Mycroft, where the three of us met just before Christmas. That was the occasion when Mycroft Holmes sat behind his desk, resting those large fists of his on a map of world, and asking Holmes to embark on a lecture tour of a fair-sized array of foreign nations.

Mycroft had declared in that deep rumbling voice of his: "Sherlock. The governments of those countries have concluded that their police forces require improving their skills in the art of detection. Oh, the local police are competent at tackling poachers and locking up pickpockets, but they need to acquire the skills of the modern detective. After all, if they can learn one fifth of what you know, then they will become very adept police officers indeed."

Holmes had remarked drily: "If they absorbed even one hundredth of my expertise, then they would become the most efficacious police officers in the world."

Holmes hadn't relished the idea of touring a goodly chunk of the world for six months. However, I encouraged him to do so—mainly by the simple expedient of flattering his ego. This I did for the soundest of reasons, as both a doctor and his closest friend, because Holmes had worked tirelessly throughout the year, investigating dozens of intricate cases. The strain had taken its toll. Although his eyes still glittered with intelligence, they seemed even more deep-set than was usual even for him, while the skin beneath his eyes had formed black crescents. Holmes would often forego food when confronted by a mystery of enormous complexity. This lack of nourishment had made his stick-thin body even more slender until I could make out the individual bones of his hands through tightly stretched skin. Therefore, I endorsed Mycroft's proposal and heartily claimed that a lecture tour in sunnier climes would be a refreshing challenge to Holmes' intellect. As I spoke in enthusiastic tones, the doctor in me knew that a restful sea voyage would help restore my friend's well-being, while soothing his overworked nerves.

Yet, the story doesn't really begin in Mycroft's office, with its massive oak desk, book-lined walls, and marble bust of Sophia, goddess of wisdom, in its niche beside the window. Nor does the drama begin with our departure on the steamship *Blue Star* from Portsmouth. Nor is there any necessity that I should describe to you the rough crossing of the Bay of Biscay that confined seasick passengers to their cabins. Nor does it seem essential to go into detail about Holmes' first lecture in Gibraltar, when Holmes, while standing at the lecture-theatre window, identified a thief walking away from a goldsmith's office with stolen nuggets in a cloth bag.

No, I shall begin the actual narrative with a seemingly unconnected mystery, when our vessel happened upon a sailing ship. The vessel's masts had been smashed, its sails torn; they lay strewn either on the deck or hanging down the vessel's wooden sides. Naturally, our captain ordered his crew to investigate the derelict, which drifted in the manner of that fabled *Marie Celeste,* without, apparently, a soul on board. Accordingly, a boat was despatched from our ship. Ten sailors worked the oars, crossing the water to the schooner that was clearly in danger of capsizing, no doubt due to water leaking through its hull. Our sailors, upon boarding, soon discovered that the ship had been abandoned. Everyone had vanished.

Everyone, that is, apart from one man, found unconscious below-decks. The sailors from our ship had to carry him with great difficulty to the rowing boat, because he was a giant of a fellow. Eventually, they brought him onboard our vessel, to gasps of shock from the other passengers, and, indeed, crew.

One of the ladies muttered, "Dear Lord, that isn't a mortal man. It is a monster."

The man, dressed in rags, had not a single hair on his head. When I examined him, in my capacity as a medical man, I noted his eyes, when I raised the eyelids were blue—very bright blue. Almost the dazzling blue of electric sparks. To my surprise, considering the fellow's appearance of utter poverty, suggested by his ragged attire, his teeth were perfectly white, with no signs of decay; nor were any teeth broken, or even chipped. There were no tattoos, which is unusual for a sailor (and, at that moment, I did suspect that he'd served aboard the ruinous vessel that now wallowed astern of our ship). Holmes remained silent, albeit watchful, as I examined the man, giving no opinion about the giant, whatsoever. As my patient lay unconscious on the deck, I measured him with a yardstick and determined he would, when upright, stand fully seven feet tall.

After our brief diversion to investigate the derelict vessel, and rescue its sole passenger, the captain ordered his helmsman to steer our vessel toward its destination. As for the half-sunken ship, there was little point in attempting to tow the wreckage to port. Its salvage value would be minimal. Moreover, it probably leaked from a hundred or more points in its decaying hull. No doubt our captain was satisfied that the vessel would sink within a matter of hours anyway—perhaps he also considered a watery grave would be a fitting resting place for a craft as old and as decrepit as that one appeared to be.

Later that day, we learned that when the rescued man awoke, he became extremely troublesome, trying to attack those around him. Either he refused to speak or was mute, for he uttered no sound. However, he made clear his dislike for the people around him by the use of his fists. Ultimately, a considerable number of sailors were required to subdue him. After that, the survivor of the derelict was locked into a cage in our vessel's cargo hold— this was one of four cages that had been installed in order to house live lions on the steamship's return journey. For three days, that is where the wild man was held—behind stout iron bars. Because no one knew the fellow's name, the crew called him 'Brutus Bullman'—on account of his brute-like nature and massively strong bull-like neck that attached his bald head to his muscular body. The name Bullman stuck. Passengers would peer down through the deck hatch, when opened to allow fresh air to circulate, to catch a thrilling glimpse of Bullman. Still, he uttered no words. Yet his eyes spoke volumes. Even though I am a doctor, and have treated many a disturbing mental case, I have never encountered such eyes before in a human being. Bullman's eyes were blue explosions of fury. Such a description does appear bizarre; however, those eyes of his somehow contained ceaseless eruptions of violent rage and hatred.

Holmes, on gazing down at the caged man, had murmured, "I don't think we have to look far to discover what befell the sailing ship and its crew."

This brings me to the night Holmes and I sat in the saloon.

Thunder still rumbled. The ship still flew—and still plunged!—as enormous waves hurled the vessel through midnight seas. That's when the steward appeared at the door. Aged fifty or thereabouts, hair cut so short his scalp bristled iron-grey hairs, he was short in stature, and he always adopted the same posture: shoulders raised slightly toward his ears as if he stood out in the rain and hunched his shoulders in an attempt to stop the water trickling down his neck. Of course, despite the storm raging outside, all was dry within. In temperament, the steward was invariably calm and possessed the habit of his fellow Yorkshiremen of only speaking when it was necessary to impart some information. If he had no information to impart, he preferred to remain silent. He struck me as an honest and loyal fellow who served his employer well.

At this moment, as the ship plunged and bucked through heaving seas, the man clung to the doorframe to steady himself. "Sirs, do you require anything to drink before I retire to my bunk?"

Holmes replied, "Nothing for me, thank you. Watson?"

I shook my head, doubting if my stomach could successfully retain even so much as a teaspoon full of brandy.

"Very well, gentlemen," said he. "Then I'll bid you good night."

Holmes held up a languid hand. "Oh, Steward. Would you be so good as to answer a question for me?"

"I shall do my best, sir."

"Why did you exchange life below ground for a life on the ocean?"

During the voyage, I hadn't seen the steward's features alter one jot from a serene expression of unflappable calm. Now, however, his eyebrows rose, his mouth dropped open, and he gave a loud gasp of surprise. His voice rose in astonishment, too, as he exclaimed. "Blow me down, Mr. Holmes, how ever did you know that?"

"My eye observes, my mind deduces."

Despite being gripped by more than a touch of *mal de mer,* I stared hard at the robust little figure of the steward, trying to see what Holmes saw all too clearly, yet which I did not. Before me, stood a ship's steward in his smart uniform of black trousers and white jacket—signs of a subterranean profession? There were none. At least none I could observe.

"My dear Holmes," I said, baffled. "It maybe the effects of this dreadful storm dulling my senses to the point of ... of ... well, insensibility, but how on earth do you deduce that this good fellow worked underground?"

Holmes sat up straight, chuckling to himself, while rubbing his hands together—an action he tended to perform when becoming excited, or when my mystification amused him. He held out a hand in the steward's direction, as if he was a professor indicating a fascinating specimen in a laboratory. "The steward here worked for many years in a coal mine where he labored with pit ponies— the creatures that haul coal from the dark depths to the surface. The man still enjoys the company of animals, because he has two mischievous dogs called Jekyll and Hyde."

The steward's eyes protruded from his head in absolute astonishment. "That is true, absolutely true. Thirty years in the pit, I was, spending twelve hours a day in the company of pit ponies—such brave little souls, and as strong as beasts twice their size."

"But how do you know about the dogs, Holmes?" By now my head spun. I was in a daze, not knowing if it was the effects of being physically shaken by the storm or my friend's almost supernatural ability to peel away the surface of things, and then for that razor sharp gaze of his to plainly see what had once been hidden. "And what clue tells you the man's dogs are mischievous?"

Holmes gave an exaggerated shrug. "Ah, but it's getting late. I am detaining the steward from his bunk, and, after a long, arduous day caring for his passengers, he deserves a good night's sleep."

"Nay, sir," protested the steward. "Another moment or two won't break me. Please explain how you know about my life."

Holmes smiled, his commanding presence even making me forget how discomforted I'd become due to the rolling of the ship. "It's the essence of simplicity, really," said he. "You should bear in mind that the competent seeker of truth must observe the subject of their scrutiny with immense mental concentration, identifying anomalies in, for example, the formation of a human hand, or the distinctive wear in the heel of a boot. Once the anomaly has been identified and studied, without allowing subjective thoughts to distort what is actually scrutinized, then the investigator should interpret what they see by the careful application of knowledge. Do you follow what I'm saying, gentlemen? After all, a man might discover the words *Omnia Exeunt in Mysterium* engraved upon a golden chalice, but if he has no knowledge of Latin, he will not know that *Omnia Exeunt in Mysterium* means, essentially, 'All ends in mystery'. Therefore, the supreme investigator needs to accumulate a great deal of general knowledge about the workings of the world in order to reach an accurate deduction."

"So ..." The steward had to steady himself as the ship lurched before the onslaught of a particularly violent wave. "So ... you have studied my appearance, noticed certain details of my anatomy and so on, then calculated my history from that?"

"Broadly, yes." Holmes wriggled somewhat gleefully in the armchair, delighted that he had enthralled the man so much. Then, Holmes does love an attentive audience. "The skin on the back of your neck, between your collar and hairline, is speckled, here and there, with small blue dots. Those blue dots are not tattoos; they are caused when coal dust works its way into the pores of the miner's skin. It requires many years laboring underground to acquire that subtle mottling. However, for most of your subterranean career, you were not a miner."

"That's right, sir." The steward's eyes shone; he was delighted to be the subject of such expert scrutiny. "I never hewed a shovelful of coal in my life."

"No, instead of digging coal, you worked the pit ponies, meaning you had to get under the harness that connected a pair of ponies together. Invariably, you were bent almost double under the harness, as you guided the animals through the tunnels, while helping pull carts that contained a ton or so of coal. Am I not correct?"

"You are correct, sir. Absolutely correct."

"Years of such hard physical work, bent beneath the harness that yoked the ponies together and to the cart, resulted in the overdevelopment of muscles in your shoulders and upper back—hence your stature, which means your shoulders appear to be hunched upward. Indeed, the upper part of your back is somewhat rounded, too. That muscle formation is typical of men who work in the way you did with pit ponies."

"The dogs, though, the fact they are mischievous?" I was certain that this element of Holmes' deduction had to be a joke ... but then, is Holmes ever in the habit of making jokes?"

Holmes smiled—one of those knowing smiles that he employed when he knew that he was running rings around me. "Hah! On that occasion it was my ears that harvested a most valuable bushel of information. Upon passing the steward's cabin yesterday, I distinctly heard a loud voice shouting 'Jekyll. Hyde. Come here' in an exasperated way. In fact, in exactly the exasperated tones someone would use when calling dogs to them, and the dogs refusing to obey."

I threw out my hands in disbelief. "Surely the captain would not allow the steward to bring his dogs onto the ship?"

"No." Holmes allowed himself the luxury of a chuckle at the sight of my utter bafflement. "I am certain the voice belonged to a parrot, which the captain would, at his discretion, allow on board. Parrots tend only to repeat phrases that they've heard many, many times before. Therefore, we can imagine that when the steward is home, he repeatedly calls to his dogs, Jekyll and Hyde, and they invariably ignore his command, and consequently the man's pet parrot has learnt those pleas, which it now gleefully repeats at regular intervals as it sits on its perch in the steward's cabin. There ... now you have my deduction laid bare, and you will no doubt laugh and tell me how simple it was to piece those clues together to present a picture of this gentlemen, working in a coal mine with pit ponies, and who now owns two canine rascals and a garrulous parrot."

"Holmes, you astound me." I shook my head in awe. "If you turned your ability to making these deductions into a music hall act, you would fill the house every night and become a rich man."

The steward grinned with delight. "My goodness, it is like a magic act, isn't it? I'm going to write a letter to my wife and tell her how Mr. Holmes opened up my life story like it was a book." He chuckled. "Jekyll and Hyde are back in Bradford with my good lady." Then his chuckle faded away. "The dogs always obey the missus, though. Come to that, we all do. Because we get what-for if we don't."

Holmes acknowledged the man's praise with a nod and a smile. "Please forgive me, I have detained you for too long.

"No, I should be thanking you for your time, sir. I wouldn't have missed it for the world. Good night, sirs." As he turned to go, he suddenly remembered a message he needed to relay. "Oh, by the by, the captain asked me to tell you that we should make landfall at first light tomorrow."

I gripped the arms of the chair as a savage lurch of the ship threatened to hurl me across the room, "I heard that the storm might force our ship to anchor in one of the bays before docking in New London."

"Oh no, sir. We'll be arriving at New London tomorrow. Sure as eggs are eggs."

Holmes steepled his fingers together. "You pronounce the name 'New London' with a certain inflection, suggesting amusement."

"Begging your pardon, sir. It's just the crew never call it New London."

"Oh?" I began, puzzled. "Then the city has another name?"

"Not an official name," answered the steward. "But a much more accurate one." He paused for a second. "We call the place Damnation."

I laughed. "Damnation? A joke, surely?"

"Oh, Damnation's no joke, sir. As you'll find out for your good selves."

Before I could question the man about our destination further, a ship's officer suddenly appeared in the doorway. His face glistened with perspiration, and he had this look in his eyes. Fear, pure fear.

"Gentlemen!" he shouted. "Lock yourselves in your cabins!"

Holmes leapt to his feet. "Whatever's wrong?"

The officer quickly glanced back over his shoulder, as if expecting to be attacked, then he shot a frightened glance back at us. "It's Bullman! He's escaped!"

Chapter 2

Holmes led the way along the corridor that would deliver us to our cabins. Not to lock ourselves inside those cabins. Not to hide until that brute of a man had been recaptured. No! Because to retreat from danger is not the habit of Mr. Sherlock Holmes.

Holmes called back over his shoulder, "Watson. To your cabin, man! Collect your pistol!"

"Holmes, what is your intention?"

"To find that creature the sailors call Bullman."

Holmes is adept at unarmed combat; even so, the thought of him endeavoring to tackle that giant of a man, who undoubtedly killed the crew of the sailing ship, troubled me immensely.

"Holmes," I said as our vessel juddered before a fresh onslaught of waves. "Yes, by all means, find the man—just don't attempt to capture him by yourself."

My friend, Holmes, flashed a delighted grin back at me. "What a perfect battle, Watson. My intellect pitted against Bullman's formidable brawn."

The ship rolled from side-to-side to such a degree, that moving forward along that narrow corridor was extraordinarily difficult. Repeatedly, we had to steady ourselves, by clutching onto the brass handrail, fixed to the wall specifically for that purpose. Just ahead of us, stairs led down to the lower decks. That's where our cabins were situated. My plan was to rush down there, collect the revolver from my trunk, then hurry back upstairs to find Holmes—ideally, before he located Bullman.

However, before we reached the stairwell, a door to my right crashed open, whereupon a figure hurtled from the cabin to collide with me, sending me reeling backward. For a moment, I truly believed that Bullman had attacked me.

Yet the next moment I recognised the man as Garner, one of the ship's young officers. He was a pleasant young fellow with blonde hair, blues eyes, and the most gracious manners. Now, his blonde hair at the top of his head was wet with blood. Blood had trickled down his face into his mouth, so even his teeth were smeared with the red stuff that fills our veins.

Garner's eyes were unfocussed, dazed. When he swayed, I realized his unsteadiness wasn't purely a result of the rocking motion of the ship. The man had been suffered a fierce blow to the skull.

Holmes assessed the situation in a flash. He caught hold of Garner to save the man from falling.

Holmes spoke quickly. "I've got you, sir. There. Lean against the wall." He glanced at me. "Watson. Check the wound."

I did as he asked. "A nasty cut to the scalp. However, as far as I can tell, no damage to the skull, thank goodness."

Holmes helped the young man to remain on his feet. "Your attacker?" he began. "Bullman?"

Garner took a deep breath, wincing with pain from the wound. "Yes, Mr. Holmes. He broke out of the lion cage … just bent steel bars as if they were made from rubber."

"Do you know where Bullman is now?"

"No, sir."

"Did he attack you in the corridor?"

"No, he burst into my cabin. When I tried to restrain him, he hammered his fist down onto my head. One blow

... one blow did this." Almost marveling at the power of his attacker, he touched the bloody gash.

Holmes patted the young man on the arm—a tender gesture of reassurance. "Doctor Watson here will mend that cut splendidly. First, however, we must find Bullman."

Garner trembled. "Please find him quickly, Mr. Holmes. There are ladies onboard. If Bullman should attack them ..."

"Of course, of course. Now lie down on the bunk in your cabin. We'll return as soon as we have dealt with the wretch that did this to you."

Garner thanked Holmes in a most heartfelt way before mustering the strength to totter back into his quarters.

Once again, we hurried toward the stairs. This time we heard an eruption of terrible shrieks from the deck above the one we currently found ourselves on.

My blood ran cold. "Those are women's screams."

"Forget the pistol, Watson. The time's come to tackle this creature, come what may."

"I'm with you."

Holmes' sharp eyes darted toward mine. I saw his trust in me in that glance. We would fight side by side.

As we ran up the steps to the next deck, Holmes shot me a telling look. "Do you have that clasp knife in your pocket?"

"Yes."

"Then make ready with it. If we can't restrain Bullman, you know what you must do."

I gave a solemn nod.

We were soon in the corridor on the upper deck. There, an astonishing sight met my eyes. Pandemonium. Sheer pandemonium. Cabin doors had been smashed, as if they were nothing more than flimsy board. Splintered wood lay scattered on the floor. Ladies clad in their delicate white bedroom gowns filled the corridor. A dozen sailors—burly, courageous men to the last—had gathered on the far side of that colossus of flesh and bone that was Bullman (if I can make myself clearer:

Bullman stood in the corridor with the ladies before him and the sailors behind him). Those eyes of his—they were volcanic eruptions of blue fire. Explosions of savagery. Blazing infernos of hatred.

Passengers, both male and female, blocked our way forward to the man. So tall was he, that the top of his hairless skull bumped against the ceiling as he prowled along the corridor. When he reached a door, he raised his fists and smashed the wood to pieces. Then that large head of his, sitting on a massive bull neck, from which veins bulged, would be thrust into the cabin. Invariably, this would be followed by a flood of terrified screams from within the room.

Imagine the horror. You are lying in bed, frightened, because you've heard cries of fear from the corridor, then your door is smashed to pieces—following that, the ugly, monstrous face of the man looms through the doorway, and a pair of eyes that blaze MURDER fix on you. Terror, alone, would feel like a steel blade being driven into your heart.

Frightened passengers were solidly packed together by the confining walls of the corridor, and, at that instant, none appeared inclined to flee, undoubtedly hoping the old phrase still rang true: *that there is safety in numbers.* Then came a gap of ten paces of open floor between the cluster of men, and of women in their flimsy night attire, and Bullman, who was engaged in the savage business of breaking down cabin doors. Behind him, just four or five paces away, were the sailors. These men were, I surmised, judging the right moment to pounce. Another door splintered beneath Bullman's fists. He glared in through the doorway at its shrieking occupant before withdrawing that colossal head and moving onto the next door.

Pulling the lock knife from my pocket, I eased open the hinged blade. A doctor's Hippocratic Oath requires them to do no harm. Yet, there must be exceptions to this rule.

Bullman shattered another door.

Holmes glanced back to me. Above the passengers' screams he called out, "Watson! The brute searches for something—or someone!"

A sailor rushed the giant. And the giant flicked the sailor away, as if he was nothing bigger than an insect. The sailor fell back into his comrades' arms, blood gushing from his nose.

Holmes shouted, "Men, don't attempt to tackle Bullman one by one. We must attack him as a coordinated group."

I realized this would not be easy. The narrowness of the corridor would only allow two men to stand abreast at any one time, which meant that the sailors couldn't surround Bullman. What's more, Holmes and I couldn't approach him yet because of the press of passengers filling this confined space.

Holmes is a tall man. Therefore, his head was above all the heads in front of him—those belonged to terrified passengers that cried out in terror every time Bullman lurched in their direction in order to destroy another cabin door. Moreover, Holmes' considerable height allowed him to see the activities of that violent monster. Similarly, Bullman's seven-foot stature allowed him a clear view of Holmes.

And that is exactly what happened. Standing on tiptoe, in order to look over the ladies' heads in front of me, I managed to catch a glimpse of Bullman approaching another door, both fists raised, ready to deliver a hammer blow that would smash the panels. Bullman then glanced sideways. When he saw Holmes, he stopped absolutely still. Frozen. It appeared as if the huge man had been gripped by nothing less than instant paralysis as his rage-filled eyes locked onto Holmes' face.

Throughout all this chaos and screaming, I had not heard Bullman say a single word, or even grunt; all of which supported my belief that the fellow was mute. The sailors, on seeing Bullman freeze like this, must have thought this was the moment to act. They moved forward,

Holmes immediately stepped smartly back to avoid the blow.

each trying to grab hold of the monster, although severely restricted by the limited space.

Their efforts were in vain. Because, at that instant, Bullman surged along the corridor, his eyes locking onto Holmes in the same way a hunting dog fixes its gaze onto a rabbit that it craves to rip apart with its jaws. Even though the corridor was effectively plugged tight by twenty or more panic-stricken passengers—both male and female—the giant simply ran through them with the single-minded fury of a bull charging toward the object of its hatred.

Perhaps my next shout was unnecessary— nevertheless, I felt compelled to voice the warning: "Holmes! It's clear who Bullman has been searching the cabins for! The one he wants is you!"

Those in front of Bullman blocked his way no more effectively than slender reeds standing in front of a furious beast. The nickname 'Bullman', given to this terrible individual, was so perfectly judged at that moment, because that massive body of his knocked men and women off their feet. The monster then trampled over the fallen in his burning need to reach Holmes. The din of shrieks of pain and fear rose to the point I felt as if my ears would bleed.

I held the knife, ready to cut the brute's throat if need-be. Alas, such a violent remedy wasn't possible as several passengers tried to flee past me in the narrow corridor. So, mindful, that I might accidentally stab innocent people I held the knife down by my side, the flat of the blade pressed tight to my leg to avoid cutting anyone as they pushed by me in their desperate attempt to escape the lunatic.

Bullman raised clenched fists, clearly intending to bring them down with skull-shattering force on Holmes' head. Holmes immediately stepped smartly back to avoid the blow. And as the huge fists came down, Holmes delivered jabbing punches to Bullman's face. Holmes is an expert in the art of boxing. Even so, those well-aimed punches that struck Bullman on the jaw had no discernible effect.

Bullman attacked again—both fists clenched, swinging down. Veritable hammer blows. I'd witnessed the way those cudgels of flesh and hard bone had devastated wooden cabin doors; therefore, I had little doubt Bullman could easily despatch a human being into the hereafter if the fists successfully found their target.

During this pandemonium, the ship still bucked wildly in the storm. Indeed, it was a powerful lurch of the ship that saved Holmes. Losing his balance, he stumbled sideways, leading to Bullman's fist missing my friend's head, yet striking his shoulder a glancing blow. I saw Holmes grimace with pain as the knuckles connected with his body.

"Holmes!" I yelled. "Let me through! I have the knife!"

Even as I shouted, a young lady stumbled against me, and I had to catch hold of her before momentum sent her crashing to the floor. Further along the corridor, the sailors tried to reach Bullman, their movements impeded by what amounted to a carpet of writhing bodies that filled twenty feet of corridor. These were the unfortunate folk that Bullman had toppled.

"Holmes," I shouted again. "Take my knife. Stab the monster in the heart!"

Holmes, panting with the exertion of combat, shook his head. "Thank you, Watson ... however, as there isn't enough ... space down here I will decline your kind offer ... as I'm likely to injure the passengers."

Bullman charged at Holmes again, forcing him to retreat backward, past where I was standing. Bullman paid no heed to the other passengers now, or to me. Evidently, his target was Holmes, and only Holmes. For some reason the monster craved to snuff out my friend's life.

Holmes called out, as he moved back along the corridor: "Watson! I'm going to lure him out on deck. Once there, he will no longer be a danger to the others!"

"No, Holmes. The storm is raging out there. You'll be swept overboard!"

However, Sherlock Holmes will never shirk from what he sees as his sacred duty, even though his own life might be in danger. He moved with the speed of an athlete, bounding along the corridor, and out through a door into the shrieking hurricane. Bullman put his head down and charged after him, a seven-foot colossus of bone, sinew and muscle. A monstrous beast, hell-bent on killing my friend.

I followed the pair out onto the ship's deck. If being inside the ship during this nightmare storm was an ordeal, then being outdoors was truly hell. The deck slanted this way and that. Sometimes the prow rose so much that the deck seemed to instantly turn into a vertical cliff. Then I found myself sliding downward over sopping deck timbers.

Lightning illuminated the scene in front of me. Holmes dodged this way and that around the deck with the Bullman in pursuit. Holmes used cables, ventilation housings, and pillars that supported the superstructure, to prevent Bullman from rushing directly at him. This was the most violent pursuit I have ever witnessed. As clouds above me discharged electricity in blue-white flashes, Bullman swung fierce punches at Holmes. Each time, Holmes managed to avoid the blow. He even managed to return a couple of jabbing punches—yet he might as well have tried to smash a brick wall with his fists. Bullman's face was impervious to blows.

Waves broke over the decks, forcing both Holmes and me to grasp at rails or cables to prevent ourselves from being swept into the ocean. Bullman, however, simply surged through the water as if that deluge was no more troublesome to him than a shallow puddle.

Above us, the funnel threw out smoke and orange sparks into the night sky. Spray blasted me in a quantity and with a speed that simultaneously hurt my face and blurred my vision. Even so, I could make out that my friend was tiring. Sherlock Holmes possesses incredible agility and stamina. He can draw on nervous energy to power his limbs when his companions are exhausted to the point of sluggishness. Yet, this night, Holmes had begun to tire. The storm and relentless pursuit by the giant had taken their toll. Holmes began to slow down. More than once he suffered a glancing blow from one of those hammer fists. My friend's battle would certainly end in his defeat if one of the brute's massive fists should solidly and squarely strike Holmes on the head—such a blow would knock the wits, if not the life, clean out of him.

Thunder from the sky, and thunder made by the crashing waves, drowned out my shouts for Holmes to move faster. To evade those killer blows.

At last, Bullman drove Holmes back to the guardrail at the edge of the deck. With a blaze of savage fire in his eyes, a fire that seemed to even outshine the lightning storm, those massive feet crashed against the deck as he charged toward Holmes.

That was the moment when Holmes' intellect was put to its ultimate test—that is, to save his own life. Holmes had studied unarmed contact from an oriental master of that art. Ju-jitsu didn't require the exponent to use great strength, instead ju-jitsu turns the aggressor's own strength against themselves. With great dexterity Holmes did this now. With a dip of his knee, he seized hold of Bullman and simply made a slight adjustment to the trajectory of the thug's headlong rush before side-stepping him.

Bullman's ferocious charge was so powerful, so overwhelmingly fierce, that he, himself, could not stop in time. The giant struck the guardrail with his stomach before toppling over the rail.

I immediately rushed to stand beside Holmes where we both stared down into the boiling white mass that was the ocean. Briefly, a bald head surfaced. A globe riding through frothing spume. Then a wave of immense size rose up and over that head, set with burning eyes that stared up at us in silent rage. The wave came down. The head vanished. And even though we stood there, side by side, for a full ten minutes we never did see Bullman rise back to the surface again.

Chapter 3

The next morning, I went out on deck to watch our approach to New London. The sun shone down from a cloudless sky. The storm had vanished from our lives as quickly as the rampaging brute last night. If it weren't for grazes and bruises from our encounter with both storm and giant, I would have begun to wonder if the two incidents had been nightmares. Now, in the bright light of a brand-new tropical day, the turbulent events of the previous night seemed remote.

I must confess, also, that memories of Bullman's rampage were pushed aside by the excitement of seeing what would be our new home for a while.

The steamship glided slowly past a small island that featured a fortress of pale, sun-bleached stone, above which flew the British flag. Presently, our vessel chugged into a wide estuary. Almost instantly, the swell of the blue ocean gave way to a brown river. At the same moment, the temperature changed dramatically. During the sea voyage, lively breezes had kept us cool. Now the air around me, which rolled out from the land, felt so hot and humid it was like being immersed in a bathtub of hot water. I have travelled through the tropics before so have experienced

I stood there at the guardrail watching New London emerge from the heat ...

extreme heat, coupled with high humidity, that leaves one gasping for breath until the body acclimatizes. This was no exception. With the heat came the pungent odor of river water mixed with herb scents from plants growing on the banks.

Ahead of us lay the wharves of the port. And rising above the port on a hillside were hundreds and hundreds of buildings, home to eighty thousand people—though should I specify that most of those people were inmates? Shielding my eyes against the sun's pitiless glare, I gazed at the river as it flowed from jungle-covered hills to the Atlantic Ocean. To my right, stood New London, the administrative capital of the island, known by its closest neighbors on the African mainland as Yagomba. Above the buildings, I glimpsed pointed church spires that echoed the old stone churches of England, while smoke rose from thousands of chimneys that were either for domestic or industrial use.

My years of training as a doctor has endowed me with the ability to retain facts pertaining to medicines, symptoms, and the intricate structure of the human body. This ability to absorb facts has become something of a habit. So, as I stood there at the guardrail watching New London emerge from the heat haze, I mentally revisited what I'd gleaned about Yagomba from reading newspaper articles in the past.

Yagomba, an island of just over nine thousand square miles, lies off Africa's Gold Coast. There is no indigenous population of Yagomba, and after Britain claimed sovereignty over it, this curious island became something of a test laboratory for various experiments sanctioned by the British government. Its fertile soil has been planted with trees and plants from around the world, and a cousin of Sir Charles Darwin has introduced a variety of animals, from Asian tigers to South American monkeys, in an attempt to prove various aspects of Darwin's theories, especially that notion of the "the survival of the fittest."

29

Most extraordinary of all, an influential group of people, campaigning for prison reform, lobbied Parliament to allow for prisoners serving terms of more than five years to be granted the right to settle on Yagomba, where they would live in what is—essentially—a jail without walls. This prison colony would largely be self-sustaining and would be administered by a small number of civil servants and a prison governor. This semi-independent nation of convicts, both male and female, had existed for thirty years, and is considered as a model for how nations around the world can deal with the seemingly never-ending dilemma of overcrowded jails. Admittedly, a brave experiment, though not without problems of its own. One being that quite large numbers of prisoners, not wishing to live under rules imposed by the prison governor, decamped from New London and live as 'outlaws' in the jungle.

Facts stream from my pen onto this paper as smoothly as the ink. Holmes would approve. He prefers hard fact to picturesque descriptions of places, regardless of how exotic they are. His own profession as a detective always drives him toward the shining, indestructible kernel of truth at the center of every event. Of course, my pen glides across this paper to inform the reader of the mysteries we encounter and the crimes that Holmes solves. My task is to set such cases as my friend, Sherlock Holmes, investigates in a manner that will entertain as much as they inform. Therefore, from here on in I will be sparing of facts relating to the geography, economy, and somewhat bloody history of Yagomba, as there is a far more interesting story to tell of our visit there.

So, please allow me to paint a picture in words that illustrates what I saw as I stood on deck, on the morning of our arrival. There, the muddy river. Floating upon its brown waters, dozens of tree branches drifting downstream from the jungle-shrouded interior of the country. Over yonder, magnificent government buildings rising high above neighboring shops and houses. And ever clearer, as the ship nudged toward the shore, views of the docks where hundreds of men and women labored, either carrying baskets on their heads, or hauling ropes attached to boats, or bundling sticks into bales—kindling for fires, I supposed, that would cook the population's food and so on. The men and women, inmates of this curious island that was a massive jail, wore pale blue jackets: on the back of each was emblazoned a red emblem in the form of a large X. This was the prison uniform, to distinguish them from sailors, government officials and visitors to the island.

More people joined me on deck. These were my fellow passengers—happily, they were largely unharmed after the berserk fellow ran amok last night—although some ladies, now clad in fresh muslin, did support sprained arms in slings of gauze that were a dazzling white in the fierce glare of the sun. The previous night, I had spent a considerable amount of time examining the injuries caused when Bullman trampled over passengers in the corridor. I treated minor physical wounds, including stitching the cut on the head of Garner, the ship's officer who had been attacked by Bullman. Fortunately, I had been able to reassure the man that the laceration would heal, leaving but only a small scar as a reminder of the night's dramas.

The passengers themselves had treated their ruffled nerves with gin and tonic at breakfast. Indeed, the potent spirit made everyone appear quite cheerful as they watched our approach to the docks. Several of the women would be joining husbands who worked in the municipal administration here.

I repeatedly glanced back at the doorway, expecting Holmes to step out to enjoy this striking view. However, he seemed to be devoting an inordinate length of time to examining the lion cage that Bullman had broken out of last night. Holmes himself, I should add, exhibited a few bruises from the violent encounter. Happily, they would be of no lasting harm—and Holmes, as was his custom when it came to personal injury, barely noticed them.

31

At that moment, the steward, who had spoken to us in the saloon the previous evening, joined me at the guardrail to gaze at the city adorning the hillside before him.

He shook his head while murmuring, "Tut-tut-tut."

I glanced at the man, wondering what had prompted his disapproval of the place in the form of tutting and shaking that grey head of his.

"Good morning," I said.

"Good morning, Doctor Watson." He continued to shake his head as perhaps a surgeon might shake their own head over a hopeless medical case.

I decided to ask the man to elaborate on what had troubled him about our destination. "Last night," I said, "you told me that the crew have their own name for New London. You say they call it Damnation."

"Damnation it is, sir. Damned from its highest roof to its deepest cellar."

"Why?"

"The place oozes insanity as a swamp oozes mud."

"Insanity? How can a city ooze, as you so colorfully put it, with insanity?"

"I wouldn't stay there longer than a month, sir," declared the steward with an expression of unease. "They say that a quarter of all new arrivals who stay here for more than six months lose their wits."

"The heat?"

The steward shook his head. "Something called the Lucifer Vine. It grows rampant throughout the city, sir. Oh, it looks a pretty plant. Climbing up the walls of houses and telegraph poles, all green with big heart-shaped leaves, and sprouting pink flowers as delicate as can be ... but, as the name suggests, the Lucifer Vine is the devil's own plant. Look over there. You'll see convicts chopping the plant off the warehouse walls. If teams of men didn't constantly remove the vines from buildings, the city would be drowned to death by the Lucifer Vine within the year."

I frowned, assuming that stories associated with the piquantly named Lucifer Vine were pure fantasy. "A plant growing nearby can't drive men insane, surely?"

"That's what local folk insist is the truth, sir." The steward appeared annoyed that I'd doubted his tale of madness-inducing creepers. "If you sleep in a room with the vine growing outside, strange thoughts soon invade your brain."

As the ship moved alongside the wharf, its propeller made the river foam white. Steam gusted in a loud whoosh from the funnel. Straightaway, I noticed a vine growing up a steel frame that formed part of a crane. The vine had such intensely green leaves that they seemed to glow, while amid the fronds, little pink flowers peeped out like so many watchful eyes.

"Is that the Lucifer Vine?" I asked the steward.

"It is that, sir. I implore you with all my heart to avoid the pestilent thing. Whatever you do, do not touch it. And always check your meal if you are given salad. There are bad people here who try to slip a leaf or two of that devil plant amongst the lettuce. Turns you topsy-turvy in the head, it does."

The steward's eyes had watered as he made that impassioned speech to me. I could see that he genuinely feared for my safety.

"Thank you," I said. "I will take care."

"The soil here is so fertile that the ground could be stripped of all vegetation down to the very dirt, yet within forty-eight hours greenery would be springing upward." Then he added darkly, "As likely as not, that greenery will include Lucifer Vine. Its creepers cling to buildings like the tentacles of an octopus can cling to a swimmer's face." The man was in full flow now. "And beware at all times. The city might look modern, with its roads, fancy buildings and big churches, but there are venomous snakes everywhere. Big spitting cobras that can kill you by squirting their poison into your eyes. Insects come out at night to bite every speck of exposed skin. And there are monkeys by the thousand. The little beggars are everywhere. You can be sitting there in a restaurant, eating your dinner, and a hairy hand will dart out from under the table to steal a potato off your plate."

Suddenly, he did stop talking. His Adam's apple bobbed in his throat. He despised the town in front of him so much he could barely speak.

I thanked him for his services as a steward on the voyage, then added, "Will you be going ashore?"

"No, Doctor Watson. I will not." He spoke very firmly. His knuckles whitened as he gripped the deck rail hard, as if afraid a wind might spring up and blow him into the city he hated so much. "I will remain in my cabin until we set sail for England tomorrow."

"Have a safe journey home," I said. "Good day."

Before I could leave, the steward abruptly gripped me by the arm. His eyes bulged as he stared at me, clearly wanting to share some secret that troubled him. "That madman last night, who caused so much uproar and distress ..." He gulped. "I do believe I've seen the fellow before. Not close up, mind, but far off. Last year it was. Of course, a man that's fully seven feet tall is someone you remember—isn't that the case? Well ... he was down there by the customs office. He wasn't a raving madman then, sir. No. He was dressed like a gentleman in a suit of pure white linen; shoes all polished to a princely shine. And there he stood, down by that very wall I'm pointing at now." The steward's eyes shone with horror. "And I distinctly saw him reach out his hand and pluck one of the pink blooms from the Lucifer Vine—and then he put the flower to his nose and inhaled its perfume. That is true, sir. I swear on my life."

Chapter 4

Sherlock Holmes stepped off the gangplank onto the dockside to be greeted by a young man, clad in the typically glum clothes of a civil servant, yet wearing a yellow straw hat with the broadest rim I've ever seen.

"Mr. Holmes, Mr. Holmes," the man in the straw hat sang out in an excited voice. "Welcome to New London. My name is Nolan. I've been sent by the governor to meet you from the ship."

Holmes greeted the man with a handshake, just as the steamer we arrived on gave three smart blasts of her whistle. Clearly this was a signal to the dockworkers, because they rushed aboard, using a separate walkway, in order to carry the passengers' luggage from the ship to the wharf.

I stepped off the gangplank onto the solid ground of Yagomba. This rather pleased me. Having immobile *terra firma* beneath my feet came as a relief after a week enduring the constant and, occasionally, nausea-inducing motion of the ship.

After politely greeting me, Nolan led the way. We, as special guests of the penal colony, were spared the tedium of paperwork at the arrivals' office, which the other passengers had to undertake. Already the English menfolk had begun to perspire in the sultry heat, while the ladies in their white muslin dresses produced fans, which they used to cool their already very warm faces. Indeed, my own shirt collar began to prickle my neck as the heat became more uncomfortable by the second. Holmes remained as poised as ever—but then I've always maintained that he is a cold-blood creature of pure logic. Intense heat never appears to trouble him.

We moved briskly along the wharf until we reached a line of offices at the dock gates.

Nolan beckoned us into the shade of an awning. "Gentlemen, please wait here for a few moments, while I bring a carriage."

"Are we to be taken to a hotel?" I enquired.

The young man in the straw hat grinned. "No, Doctor Watson. I thought you would prefer a suite of rooms in Baker Street."

He's mad—quite mad, I told myself in astonishment, for London's famous Baker Street lay many thousands of miles away to the north.

Nolan laughed as if pleased with a joke he'd made. "To honor our own dear capital of the old country, New London has named several thoroughfares after ones you will be very familiar with. Here in New London, you will find Oxford Street, Fleet Street, and, of course, Baker Street."

"I see," Holmes said. "Also, you have what appears to be a replica of Nelson's column over yonder." He nodded at a tall stone pillar on which stood a statue of a man in military uniform.

"Ah, we deviate somewhat," admitted Nolan. "That is Waterloo Square, where we display our statue of General Wellington, the Englishman who defeated Napoleon's French army at the battle of Waterloo."

What Nolan had just said struck me as a trifle odd. It was as if we were visitors from a far-flung village in China and had no knowledge of British history. The steward's claim that New London's residents often became insane suddenly had an unsettling ring of truth.

Nolan, honoring us with a courtly bow as if we were both royal princes, removed his straw hat to reveal a head of curly red hair. "Mr. Holmes, Doctor Watson. I am delighted that you are here. I absolutely intend to be at your lecture, Mr. Holmes. Even though I am but a humble civil servant, I find your abilities to solve crimes of the most complex nature fascinating."

Holmes smiled. "Thank you, Mr. Nolan. I look forward to seeing you in the audience. Though, it will be quite a novelty explaining my methods of detection to what I suppose will be an audience consisting largely of convicted criminals. Then, nobody should be beyond reform and redemption, if they choose to become law-abiding citizens."

"Absolutely, Mr. Holmes. Though most of the population was shipped here from British jails, many Yagombans were born here of convict parents, and there is a new generation on this island that has never committed any crime whatsoever. This is a glorious new nation in the making." With that eager statement, Nolan, hurried away to find the carriage. The broadness of the hat brim resulted in him walking in his very own pool of shadow. Now I realized that the man had not chosen that straw headgear due to some unusual taste in bizarre hats. Clearly, the ability to shield oneself from the burning sun was a necessity in this searing climate.

I loosened my shirt collar a little in the hope of admitting cooler air. Then I gave Holmes a sideways glance. "Baker Street, Holmes? Here? In the tropics?"

"Without doubt, New London is a remarkable place. It's certainly prosperous. Mycroft informed me that there are high hopes that New London will be to Africa what New York is to America. An economic nexus of immense power."

Holmes' attention was caught by a green plant that grew across a fence near the gate.

"The soil is abundantly fertile here," he said. "I almost believe one could grow an entire city from seed." He smiled. "If you will permit such an absurd flight of fancy." He reached out, clearly intending to touch the heart-shaped leaves that were such an extraordinarily brilliant green.

"Holmes!" I gripped his wrist to prevent him touching the plant. "I shouldn't do that. That's Lucifer Vine. The ship's steward warned me about its decidedly unpleasant qualities."

"And why, pray, should one avoid touching the vine? After all, it has such dainty, little flowers."

Rather than disgorge what I took to be a fanciful tale about the plant inducing madness, I merely said, "The Lucifer Vine harbors poison of some sort or other. Touching the plant can result in ill effects."

Holmes, instead of retreating from the plant, studied its leaves and flowers more closely—thankfully, without touching them with his fingers. Nevertheless, I decided to distract him, lest he be tempted to take a sample of the Lucifer Vine for one of his laboratory experiments.

"Holmes. That was quite tussle you had last night with the monster."

"Hmm. Bullman. The sailors gave him a very accurate nickname. Bull-like by physique ... and temperament." Holmes turned away from the plant, much to my relief. "Ultimately, he was defeated by his own strength. He ran at me so furiously that it only required a slight nudge to send him over the ship's rail and into the waves before he could stop himself."

"I dare say the world is a safer place, with him now residing in Davy Jones' locker."

Holmes became thoughtful. "I would much rather have had the opportunity to study him instead of sending him to his death. The man's aggression, coupled with such an extreme mental state, created a formidable opponent."

"That and sheer brute force. Did your examination of the cage yield much information?"

"Only that the steel bars of that particular cage could

not contain such a formidable creature as he. The man bent solid steel as easily as if it had been woven from lambs' wool. Although there was one clue I found in the cage that might interest you."

"Oh, and what was that?"

"Bullman had found a carpenter's nail somewhere inside the cage and scratched fourteen letters on the steel floor."

"By Jove. What did they spell?"

"Oh, Watson, surely you can guess?"

At that moment, a muscular man appeared, wearing a blue jacket with the tell-tale red cross, and hauling a cart piled with luggage. "Mr. Sherlock Holmes?" he sang out to passengers gathering next to the gate. "Bags and boxes for Mr. Sherlock Holmes?"

The handcart contained luggage belonging to Holmes—his name was written on cardboard labels attached to the handles of steamer trunks and the like. Then I understood what my friend had been hinting at.

"Ah," I breathed. "Fourteen letters ... *Sherlock Holmes.*" Despite the heat, my blood ran cold. "Good grief—so that monster scratched your name on the floor?"

Holmes tilted his head, a thoughtful expression on his face. "Which gifts us a deliciously baffling mystery. How did Bullman, a man found adrift on a derelict schooner, know that I was on board the steamship that rescued him?"

Chapter 5

True to his word, Nolan arrived in a horse-drawn carriage, just moments after he left us. The driver wore an impeccably crisp white shirt beneath his prison-issue jacket. Nolan spoke to another man in a second cart who began loading our steamer trunks into the back. Evidently, the luggage would follow us to our lodgings.

Soon I occupied a seat beside Holmes in the carriage, shielded from the unforgiving equatorial sun by a red-and-white striped awning. Nolan sat on the seat facing us, straw hat resting on his lap. The instant the driver cracked his whip, the horse trotted off, pulling the carriage away from the docks, across Waterloo Square beneath the statue of Wellington, and into a broad avenue lined with large, stone buildings.

"This is Fleet Street," Nolan told us. "It will take no more than ten minutes to reach Baker Street."

Holmes gazed at the teeming people. "Mr. Nolan. New London lives up to its name. Your workforce has done remarkable work clearing jungle in order to recreate what is a very accurate copy of old London's thoroughfares and buildings. Even the cast-iron gas lamps are near-perfect facsimiles of the originals."

Nolan smiled, flattered by Holmes' praise of the city. "Our mission, Mr. Holmes, is to carve civilization out of a wilderness and what was once immutable jungle." Then, almost as an afterthought, he added, "Oh, and to create opportunities for convicted criminals to continue reforming their lives and to become individuals of worth and probity."

I noticed a dozen men with white handkerchiefs tied across their mouths and noses. In addition, they wore protective goggles as well as thick leather gloves. They were busily cutting Lucifer Vine from where it had overgrown the window of a draper's store.

I felt compelled to comment on what I saw. "However, Mr. Nolan, it must be pointed out that the jungle is fighting back by endeavoring to secure a foothold again in the city."

Nolan shrugged. "Weeds, Doctor Watson. That's all. Merely weeds, like those you'd find in any town in Britain."

"Hardly ordinary weeds," Holmes corrected. "They must pose a danger to those workmen; otherwise, they wouldn't be wearing goggles, masks and gloves to protect themselves from the plant."

Again, Nolan shrugged as if the Lucifer Vine posed no threat to human life. "Oh, their sap can irritate the skin, which is distinctly uncomfortable, and there are local legends that the scent of the vine can inspire strange dreams. And care must be taken at night to sleep inside mosquito nets draped over one's bed. Also, animals do wander into these streets when the sun has set." He languidly waved a pale, freckled hand at the thoroughfare through which our carriage rumbled behind a line of hansom cabs. "One must take care at night because it's not unusual for leopards to prowl the alleyways. And monkeys can be bothersome pests."

"Stealing food from people's plates," I added with a smile. "Holmes and I have travelled to the likes of India and Africa."

Holmes nodded. "Indeed, we've witnessed examples of such thievery aplenty from our hairy cousins."

I followed the line of his sharp eyes as they fixed on a point at the top of a three-story-building that bore a large sign, which read *NEW LONDON TIMES NEWSPAPERS.* Sitting on the roof high above us were several olive baboons, one of the most common primates on the African continent. The creatures appeared to be watching the flow of human beings in the crowded avenue with great interest.

"Such observant animals," Holmes murmured. "I wonder what those monkeys make of us, scurrying down here in the depths of the city?" He smiled. "Perhaps they consider us overly busy creatures, rushing from one inscrutable activity to another, never having the time, unlike baboons, to sit in the pleasant sunshine with sociable companions."

I recalled the deranged brute that had run amok last night and wondered if baboons had a predilection to murderously attack members of their own species, too. However, the baboons on the building's roof were serenely at peace with other members of their troupe and, seemingly, with the world in general. Some of the creatures yawned lazily, exposing sharp teeth in their dog-like jaws. Other baboons groomed one another—an activity demonstrating affection for their neighbors.

For the rest of the journey, Nolan proudly pointed out fine restaurants where he promised we would dine like kings. He also indicated New London's theatres that staged modern plays, and his chest puffed out with yet more pride as we passed the city's railway station, gloriously adorned with tall stone pillars: a faithful copy of the Parthenon in Greece. Although Nolan did concede that there was much work to be done with regard to the railroad itself, which extended three hundred miles or thereabouts into the interior of Yagomba. Eventually, the line would, he assured us, reach all areas of the island, thus enabling goods and passengers to be efficiently transported to and from this burgeoning city.

Our carriage delivered us (according to a plaque on a wall) to Baker Street. Upon climbing down from the carriage, I stood gazing up, open mouthed, totally astonished, indeed breathless with amazement. There, in front of me, a row of connected four-story buildings, with doors that opened directly onto the street. At ground level, those buildings consisted of shops that specialized in all manner of goods from hunting rifles, to clothing, to fine wine.

"Extraordinary," I breathed. "Why, Holmes, this is an exact copy of the building that contains your apartment. This is London but not London. This is Baker Street but not Baker Street. Amazing!"

Holmes smiled. "Hardly an exact copy, Watson. A fair approximation, I'll grant you that. Our very own Baker Street in England, I must declare, never felt the touch of a sun as powerful as this." He held out his hand, palm up, feeling the heat of the blazing sunlight.

Nolan still spoke with pride. "New London is destined to become a great city—prosperous, beautiful, shining with modernity."

Holmes' smile tightened the way it did when he made a point politely, yet one that some might find painfully close to an unpalatable truth. "And yet, Mr. Nolan, I must echo Doctor Watson's earlier observation: Mother Nature, herself, battles to reclaim this wonderful city of yours." He pointed at small green tendrils snaking from a gap between paving slabs near his right foot. "More Lucifer Vine intruding into your metropolitan marvel. Yet more baboons peer down at us from that church tower over yonder. And that paw-print in a little patch of mud, in your otherwise clean gutter, is, I venture, the paw-print of a hyena."

He nodded, satisfied with his appraisal of the town. "My dear Nolan, the jungle is not going to surrender this portion of land to your people without a bitter fight. And if you should lose that fight, New London will become the dominion of the Lucifer Vine, the hyena, the baboon, and all the vicious predators the wilderness out there harbors."

This comment left Nolan subdued. He stood there, clutching his straw hat, as he stared at the paw-print left by one of nature's most savage creatures, certainly one that could endanger human life—that print forcefully casting doubt upon his proud boast about the bright future of city he clearly loved.

Nevertheless, Mr. Nolan did not forget his manners— with a courteous gesture toward the door of 221B Baker Street, he said, "Please step this way, gentleman. Your rooms are ready. I'm sure you will be most comfortable. You will find modern gas lighting, hot and cold water, and a telephone. Also, I think you will be pleasantly surprised by your accommodation's décor."

Our guide led the way through the front door into a small hallway where a flight of richly carpeted stairs ascended to the next floor.

I must admit to being greatly surprised by what I found there. "Goodness me, Holmes, New London has gone to great pains to recreate the interior of the Baker Street property."

After climbing the stairs to the next floor, with Holmes and myself following, Nolan opened a door. "Here are your rooms, gentlemen." My astonishment had helped restore his pride, for he smiled broadly as he gave a bow, flourishing that huge straw hat as he did so.

We entered rooms that were familiar yet ever so slightly strange. Everything here was new, unlike Holmes' eclectic mix of furniture that was very well worn, albeit comfortable. The sofa in the center of the room was identical to his. A purple dressing gown, just like his, hung on a peg behind the door. On the table by the window, laboratory apparatus: a Bunsen burner, retort and test tubes. Unlike Holmes' much-used equipment back in London, these items were pristine. And now, drifting into the room to pleasantly scent the air, the aroma of just-baked bread added to my sensation of delight for this homely apartment.

My speech became a torrent of "Ooh," "Aah" and "Goodness gracious" and "Oh! Upon my soul" as my swiftly roving gaze took in details of furnishings and decorations that must have been carefully replicated from newspaper accounts of my friend's home.

As Holmes coolly appraised his surroundings, I enthused, declaimed, applauded! "Holmes. There is a Persian slipper, stuffed with tobacco! And cigars in the coal scuttle, just where you keep yours. Oh, upon my soul! They've even fired pistol rounds into the wall to spell out *VR*—just as you have!"

"They are not bullet holes, Watson. The black pockmarks have been painted on the wallpaper." No doubt mindful not to appear impolite or unappreciative of the care devoted to creating accommodation that mirrored his own residence, he smiled at Nolan. "Thank you, Mr. Nolan. I do appreciate your considerable effort to make me feel comfortable here."

Nolan smiled with what seemed enormous relief. Perhaps he'd worried that New London's illustrious guest, the greatest detective in the world, would have been disdainful of the facsimile of his home.

Nolan immediately hurried to a plush rope hanging from the ceiling by the fireplace, saying as he did so: "Whenever you require the services of the maid, simply pull the bell-rope. And the maid—Miss Dembe is her name—will deliver whatever meals you require. Oh ... and you will find whisky, gin and brandy in the Tantalus on the sideboard over there. There is also a telephone fixed to the wall on the landing, just outside your sitting-room door. Your bedrooms are at the back of the apartment. You will, of course, note some differences from your London residence. At the rear of the building, there is a veranda where you can sit out and enjoy the fresh air. You will also find mosquito nets arranged over your beds. It is essential you ensure that these are properly closed at night to protect you from insect bites."

"Which might result in malaria," I added in a sober voice.

"A very slight risk," Nolan said, not wishing to portray his hometown as a dangerous venue for tropical diseases. "I recommend healthy doses of quinine in glasses of gin to stave off any illness."

I am a trained medical man and know full well that quinine does not cure all ills. Rather than quash the young man's pride again, however, I simply assured him we would carefully arrange the mosquito nets around our beds to keep all insects at bay.

Presently, a young maid arrived, presumably the aforementioned Miss Dembe. Dressed in traditional servant garb of a long black skirt, blouse and a white apron trimmed with lace, she carried a silver tray, upon on which stood a teapot and cups. Swiftly, and in absolute silence, her dark eyes turned down, not looking at us once, she placed the tray next to the rack of test tubes on the table and quickly withdrew.

Nolan clicked his tongue. "The girl should have poured the tea."

Holmes waved the problem away with a relaxed gesture. "Watson and I are quite capable of serving ourselves. Would you care for a cup, Mr. Nolan?"

"Yes, please. It would be an honor to take tea with gentlemen as famous as yourselves."

"Then please sit down." Holmes smiled as he poured the golden liquor into porcelain cups. "We are most grateful to you for delivering us to our splendid rooms."

"A veritable home from home," I added.

Nolan perched himself on a straight-backed chair at the table. "I am so delighted you like the place. Oh, by the way, Doctor Watson, I have been longing to tell you how much I enjoy your magazine articles about Mr. Holmes' cases. They are most thrilling."

"Thank you, sir."

"'The Adventure of the Speckled Band' set my hair on end. As I read about the case, I shivered from head to toe, even in this heat. As for—"

47

Nolan's breathless torrent of appreciation had abruptly been interrupted by a sharp knock on the door. As if we'd never left the rooms in Baker Street, I immediately followed the habits of old and opened the door to the landing to find a silver-haired man, dressed severely in black, standing there with a black top hat in his hands. He favored the very upright stance of the kind that men who exercise a modicum of power so often adopt. He even contrived to look down his nose at me, as if finding my presence unwholesome.

"I am here to speak with Mr. Holmes," he boomed in a voice that was unnecessarily loud.

Holmes gave a slight bow. "I am he. How may I help you?"

The visitor stared hard at Holmes, with grey eyes that were as severe as they were cold. "My name is Wentworth. Sir Nigel Wentworth."

Nolan immediately jumped to his feet, a respectful expression filling his face. "Sir," he began in a nervous voice, "I had no idea you would be visiting Mr. Holmes and Doctor Watson."

Wentworth didn't so much as glance in Nolan's direction. "You have conveyed our guests to their accommodation, for which I thank you, Nolan. You may leave us now."

"Yes, Sir Nigel." Picking up that marvelous straw hat of his, the young man dipped his head in a bow. "Good day, gentlemen. It has been an honor to serve you, and if—"

"Thank you, Nolan." Wentworth's booming voice became even louder.

Nolan all but fled the room.

When he heard Nolan's footsteps receding down the stairs Wentworth moved confidently, even arrogantly, into the center of the room, attempting to dominate us with his presence. "Good morning, gentlemen." His loud voice even made the window rattle. "I am the deputy prison governor of Yagomba."

"We are delighted to meet you," Holmes said.

"And we are very impressed by your city," I added. "Such marvelously imposing buildings. Some even outshine those of Europe's finest capitals."

"Indeed. New London is a remarkable achievement." Holmes spoke politely, though I suspected he was disdainful of this arrogant, strutting man with his lordly air. "I am very much looking forward to giving my lecture to your police officers."

Sir Nigel Wentworth didn't respond, other than to glare at Holmes in what, at the time, seemed to be an expression of cold fury. He clenched one of his fists until the knuckles turned white.

Then he abruptly flung himself down into an armchair, put his head in his two hands, before crying out, "Mr. Holmes, for pity's sake, tell me you will help me."

I stared at the man in astonishment. He'd been transformed from an imperious, cocksure fellow into what appeared to be an emotionally broken man in nothing more than a moment. His shoulders heaved. He covered his eyes with one hand. I confess I stared in astonishment as tears rolled down his cheek.

"Good heavens, man," I exclaimed. "Please pull yourself together."

Holmes evidently considered a better course of action was to ask questions. "Sir Nigel. Something has happened. What exactly?"

"The prison governor, Mr. Holmes." Wentworth's voice dropped to a horrified whisper. "He has vanished."

"When?"

"Exactly one week ago."

"Where was he when seen last?"

"In his bedroom. The door was locked from the inside. When his butler managed to enter the room, he found that Lord Delaney had disappeared with just the clothes he stood up in."

"His footwear."

"I beg your pardon?"

Holmes' shrewd eyes fixed on Wentworth's face that was a picture of utter woe. "Footwear. What shoes was he wearing when he disappeared?"

"Well ... that's the oddness of it, Mr. Holmes. He hadn't left home wearing shoes or boots. Lord Delaney must have walked out into the street in his bedroom slippers."

"Hmm, intriguing." Holmes went to the window to gaze down at horse-drawn hansom cabs briskly trundling along the street. "Is there any indication where Lord Delaney may have gone?"

"None, sir."

"I take it," Holmes said, "that you are here to ask for my help in tracing the governor?"

"Oh no, Mr. Holmes. That is only of secondary importance."

Rarely do I witness my friend being taken aback by a surprising comment. He did so now, swiftly turning to stare at Wentworth. "Then what on Earth would you like me to do?"

Wentworth's eyes were nothing less than beseeching when he made this extraordinary request: "No, I don't ask you to investigate the disappearance of the governor. I am here to ask you—no, beg you!—to take charge."

"Take charge of what, exactly?"

"New London. Yagomba. The entire prison island. Everything."

Holmes frowned as if not sure he was correctly hearing what had been said to him. "Sir. Are you asking me to become governor of this place?"

"Yes."

"That is such a bizarre request. I must refuse your offer."

"Don't say that, Mr. Holmes." Wentworth trembled. The man was clearly scared out of his wits. "It is vital that you become the new governor. Now. With immediate effect."

I couldn't remain silent. "But why do you beg my friend here to become governor?"

"Gentlemen. I have kept the disappearance of Lord Delaney a secret. Apart from myself, the head of police, and two of my closest advisors, nobody else knows that the man has gone missing."

"And the butler," I pointed out.

"True," Wentworth admitted. "I had him locked in his room. His meals are served by a deaf mute. No one will hear from him that Lord Delaney is missing."

"Why the secrecy?" Holmes asked.

"The population here is very superstitious. Perhaps it's the heat that does strange things to one's mind. Alas, even the most skeptical of Englishmen, who arrive here on the island, often become—dare I say—gullible, when it comes to tales of juju and magic. I fear that many would immediately suspect that witchcraft had spirited Lord Delaney away as a prelude to the town being invaded by demons. In turn, that would lead to panic." He pressed the palms of his hands together as if in prayer. "Listen to me, gentlemen. New London would descend into chaos overnight. There would be massacres. We, ourselves, would not escape with our lives."

I found myself utterly bewildered. "But, dash it all man, why do you ask Mr. Holmes to become the new governor? How will his acceptance of the role avert the disaster you believe will befall this place?"

"Mr. Sherlock Holmes is legendary. The population know of his powers and his unfailing ability to solve every problem."

"Hardly every problem," Holmes remarked.

"Sir. That is how the people of Yagomba see you. Even the most barbaric of convicts, who cannot read, hear those marvelous stories about you. Often at night, in the taverns by the docks, those who have an education will read Watson's accounts of your cases to men and women as they sup their ale—and those readings are listened to with great interest—many sincerely believe that you possess magical powers, enabling you to look into the human mind, and that you are able to identify criminals with a single glance."

"On the contrary, my methods are purely scientific."

"Mr. Holmes, the people of this prison island would trust you as leader. They would respect your role as governor. I can't say plainly enough that without you civilization here will instantly collapse into terrible savagery. Without your intervention, the blood of men, women and children will soon be running in the gutters."

Holmes sat down in an armchair, his long legs stretching out before him. "Sir Nigel, I must be granted a few hours to consider what is a highly unusual request. After all, I am a detective, not a prison governor." With that, Holmes closed his eyes, and said nothing more.

Wentworth turned his beseeching gaze to me, hoping, no doubt, that I would persuade my friend to accept the role of governor. I knew Sherlock Holmes' ways, however.

"Sir Nigel," I said. "Mr. Holmes will give you his decision soon. He now prefers to be alone with his thoughts."

Chapter 6

After Sir Nigel Wentworth left our rooms, which had so cleverly been made to resemble Holmes' apartment in the old Baker Street, we largely kept to ourselves for the rest of the day: I, recording an account of recent events in my journal, and penning letters to my wife and various acquaintances back in England. My companion remained in monkish isolation in his room, devoting himself to silent introspection. Admittedly, Holmes and I did meet up again in the sitting-room for meals; however, he did not refer to Sir Nigel's visit, and I knew better than to interrogate Holmes while he was still considering the matter. Then, later that same evening, we retired to our respective rooms at the back of the building. I heard Holmes pacing back and forth in his room, no doubt still deep in thought, and pondering the extraordinary plea that he accept the role of prison governor in order to avert the island's descent into bloody anarchy.

I unpacked my trunk, placing my clothes on shelves in cupboards within the room. I then drew mosquito nets around the bed. These hung down from a wooden frame affixed to the ceiling, in effect creating a room within a room, so that when I lay in bed, I would be entirely enclosed by fine mesh nets, which would hold mosquitos at bay.

I lit the gas mantle on the wall as dusk fell—for the sun sets very quickly near the equator. I knew from past experience that darkness comes so abruptly one can be left groping sightlessly in a room, searching for matches to light one's way. In fact, by the time I'd lit the gas and adjusted the flame the sky outside had turned black. Wishing to allow some fresher air into the stuffy room, I went to the window. A crescent moon painted enough light onto the landscape to reveal that the ground behind Baker Street had yet more rows of buildings lying higher than ours on the slope. And, as young Nolan had pointed out, unlike the original Baker Street houses, back in "old" London, this copy boasted an external balcony that could be accessed from a door in my bedroom.

I lit a cigar in the hope that tobacco smoke would deter biting insects from venturing too close. After that, I leaned against the frame of the open window to catch the somewhat cooler air drifting inland from the sea. There was, unfortunately, precious little in the way of that hoped-for breeze. In fact, what little breeze there was soon vanished entirely, and a mist rose from the earth to lie between the buildings like a milky-white canal. A most eerie, ghostly effect.

At the end of the day, I often find that memory begins to flow in a meandering, haphazard fashion. I recalled our arrival on the steam ship. Those first glimpses of New London's enormous buildings, rising above the brown river. Creeping up and over the face of many of the buildings was the green blush of the Lucifer Vine. A plant that, according to the ship's steward, had the power to induce madness. Then, a little later, came the carriage ride through those replicas of London's streets. Yes, this metropolis faithfully copied my dear old London Town. Yet there were anomalies. Troops of monkeys occupied the rooftops: no doubt enjoying the high vantage point, which allowed them to spy down on humans, walking along streets below. Perhaps the monkeys busily plotted the best way they could steal from their near-hairless *Homo sapiens* cousins.

My gaze strayed upward, to the roof tops fifty yards or so from my bedroom window. Indeed, there were monkeys atop those buildings. They were clear enough in the moonlight. A group of large males, together with the smaller females, some holding babies to their breasts. For some reason, they were agitated, moving swiftly along the ridge tiles, while glancing back over their shoulders. I wondered if they were being chased by a rival group of monkeys.

My eyes followed the roofline—an apex topped with ridge tiles. Instead of seeing a raiding party of baboons or some-such creatures, my gaze locked onto a figure standing there on the roof. An astonishing sight. In fact, so astonishing my heart lurched painfully with shock. For there, in silhouette, with the crescent moon shining behind it was the figure of a tall man. I could discern no features, only the shape of a man standing on the ridge tiles: as motionless as a statue, his head as round as a skull. A giant. A sinister behemoth.

The first word that flew from my lips with a startled gasp was: "Bullman."

Dear God, the figure resembled the monstrous brute that had run amok on board the ship last night.

"How can it be?" I whispered. "Holmes pitched the devil into the sea. Bullman drowned. He must have done."

For no man could survive in such mountainous, storm-torn waters as that.

No mortal man, that is.

Despite the heat, I shivered as if pieces of ice had been tipped down my back.

The figure remained absolutely still, standing with legs slightly apart, feet planted firmly on the roof tiles.

One inescapable fact struck me with the force of a clenched fist. Bullman, if that was he, appeared to be staring at the building that Holmes and I occupied.

... a man standing on the ridge tiles: as motionless as a statue ...

I remembered only too vividly how Bullman had spied Holmes in the ship's corridor. He'd then trampled over the passengers in his searing desire to reach Sherlock Holmes and to attack him.

Maybe the heat robbed me of all caution, because I darted to a chest of drawers, opened the top drawer and pulled out my revolver. I was dressed and still wore my shoes, so I knew I could rush over to the nearby building within seconds.

And if the watcher on the roof is Bullman? Well, I had my revolver. The man would then either be my captive or be decorated with a fine array of bullet holes.

Exiting my bedroom onto the veranda, I found a staircase that led to the ground.

Once again, I admit to allowing the fever of the hunt getting the better of my common sense. There I was, venturing out into a city that I didn't know. I had been warned that hyenas and leopards crept out of nearby forests to pad through the streets by night. Hyenas are massive, dog-like creatures that wise humans avoid. Leopards are even more dangerous. They can run at speeds close to forty miles per hour—clearly much faster than a fleeing human. Despite leopards being smaller and lighter than a lion, they are notorious man-eaters. When a leopard kills its prey, it is strong enough to haul even large animals up into a tree where it can devour its prize. That includes full-grown men, such as I.

I placed my trust in my pistol. That would save me if faced with danger. What's more, my blood was up now. All I could think of was racing to that figure, cornering him, and satisfying myself that the man was indeed Bullman.

Even though I now rushed across the deserted street at ground-level, I could still make out the figure on the roof. However, seconds later, he turned and walked down the roof at the other side. Clearly, he'd seen me and intended to make off. And by the time I'd run around the building, the giant had reached the ground, too.

He moved with a smooth grace along the street. Little moonlight penetrated this space between the houses, so he always remained a shadowy figure. The gloom and mist meant I didn't have a clear view of his face, although once I fancied I glimpsed a pair of blue eyes that burned with that same fury that had made Bullman's eyes so shocking.

The giant ahead of me must have been seven feet tall, enormously powerful, and uncannily quick. I followed him along an alleyway that led downhill to the river. Once there he ran along lines of large storage huts on the riverbank. There were no people about. Perhaps they heeded warnings that to venture out at night wasn't safe, bearing in mind that predators roamed during the hours of darkness. The river glinted—an expanse transformed from muddy brown to glittering, liquid silver in the moonlight.

The man-creature I pursued repeatedly vanished into shadow before briefly reappearing again in moonlight. He also seemed to have the ability to move in absolute silence. There were other sounds, however: the croak of frogs in the river, and chirrup of cricket-like insects in the trees. From somewhere in the distance came the blood-chilling roar of a big cat—a deep, vibrant rumble that shimmered so uncannily on the night air. I knew from past experience that the roar of a lion can travel for miles; therefore, I hoped the particular animal that had just given voice to its ferocious strength occupied some region of the forest a long distance from me—certainly far enough away not to pose a threat.

The figure I pursued cut through a gap between two huts. The river flowed just thirty paces away to my right. Rowing boats were moored to jetties, roughly constructed from planks of wood.

Just ahead, movement. More figures. Allies of the giant? I ducked behind the decaying remains of a large boat that lay above the high-water mark.

There, in the moonlight, I made out men carrying bundles of some sort or other to a ship with masts—this was one of the old-style sailing clippers of the kind that could swiftly carry tea from India and China to Europe. At the same time, and even using the same jetty, more men, these armed with rifles, chivvied a line of figures toward the shore from river boats. I noticed these figures wore iron collars around their necks. From each collar two yards of chain connected the next fellow's collar. In that way, eight men were linked together to form a human train.

The gunmen urged their captives to walk toward dry land—their heads down, their eyes dull, as if either drugged or beaten into submission.

From my vantage point, I could see this activity clearly enough. Occasionally, one of the gunmen would murmur to another, or prompt the human procession to move faster, either with a grunted word or a jab from a rifle.

By entering a hole in the side of the rotting vessel, fortuitously high and dry on the shore, I could pick my way through the debris and darkness within to reach another yawning hole in the woodwork at the other side. I was a good deal closer here, my view much improved.

Of course, being in a position where I understood that it would be unwise, even dangerous, to reveal myself to the gunmen, I also understood only too well that the giant fellow I had pursued would escape easily now that I could not follow. Instead, I decided that I should observe the activity here, then report what I saw to the assistant governor. At that moment, I was quite baffled by these strange goings-on. Admittedly, this island was a gigantic prison, so I should not have been surprised to see convicts chained together. Were these prisoners that had escaped, then been recaptured? Or did I witness the return of a chain gang that had been laboring somewhere upriver?

Just then, I spied a man who carried a bale of objects contained in some sort of fabric mesh or net. Instead of heading toward the main jetty, some thirty paces away, he now approached another jetty just five paces from the beached vessel that was my hiding place. I guessed that a quota of bundles, whatever they contained, would be placed in a rowing boat tied to a mooring post nearby. At that moment, the man's boot slipped on a patch of wet mud. He cursed in English as the bale fell from his shoulder. When it struck the ground the netting burst, scattering the bundle's contents across the dirt in the direction of the derelict vessel where I had concealed myself.

I could clearly see dozens of dark brown objects, which had formed the bundle, come tumbling to within three or four paces of me.

Leaves, I told myself; large, dried leaves. Are they transporting tobacco—but why load the ship at night? Why the secrecy?

Then I studied the items on the ground more closely, remembering Holmes' advice: '*Carefully examine that which is the object of your scrutiny—merely glancing at a mass of objects in their entirety will not suffice.*'

The man who had carried the bale began gathering its spilt contents. He crouched five paces away, with his back to me, so I was able to dart one hand out from the hole in the side of the vessel and grab one of the bundle's items. My movements were as silent as they were swift, and the man didn't see me, concealed as I was within the decaying hulk. Nor did the other men notice me, either. Meanwhile, one of the fellows chained to his companions fainted, causing the other men linked to him to tumble into the dirt. The thugs who guarded the prisoners berated the fallen men. They jabbed them with the muzzles of their rifles to encourage them to rise back to their feet.

A cloud passed in front of the moon. All became instantly gloomy again. This lack of light meant that I could not see the object I had picked up just seconds ago. The item felt dry to the touch. However, rather than being a leaf it felt more like dry leather. Its edges were crisp. The tips of my fingers told me that the inner part of that flat object was smooth, even a little oily. There were holes in the material, too.

Then the moon emerged from the cloud. Light fell through the gap in the timber flank of the vessel. That's when I saw the horror in my hand.

Lying there, just a little larger than my open hand, was a human face.

To be more precise, the skin from the upper half of a man' face. I made out the smooth expanse of the forehead. Beneath that, two pairs of almond-shaped holes: clearly where the eyes had been. Several eyelashes remained on a single eyelid that had survived whatever process had been used to reduce this segment of a man's face to something that is known as 'biltong' in parts of Africa, and 'jerky' in America.

I glanced at the pieces of dried meat and skin the man gathered back into a bale. As a medical student I had studied human anatomy. So, even by moonlight, I could identify those pieces of flesh on the ground—skin from hands, feet, legs, stomach, back, neck. A gruesome list could be made of the fleshy parts of the human body that must, in the most hideous of kitchens, been cut from the bone, then cured, just as meat from a pig is turned into ham or bacon.

Many years ago, I was an army surgeon in Afghanistan, and, since then, I have for a long while followed a civilian career as a doctor. I have witnessed the effects of bullets, explosions, and all manner of mutilations of the human body, as well as the ravages of disease and extreme age— but this? *This?* What I saw scattered in the dirt threatened to send the contents of my own stomach rushing up through my throat.

This sight was sickening. Truly sickening. I am not a naïve man. I knew exactly what I witnessed here. Men were loading bales of processed human meat and skin onto the ocean-going clipper (the bale destined for the small dinghy nearby must be for local consumption). Without a shadow of doubt, cannibalism drove this activity on the riverbank. The sailing ship's hold was being filled with a cargo of human flesh. This would undoubtedly be carried overseas, where all manner of Hellfire Clubs and debauched gentlemen who lusted after the most hideous of experiences and immoral gratification would pay a great deal of money in order to eat the skin, flesh, kidneys, hearts and so on, of other men. I had read about this practice. Many people, even so-called civilized gentlemen, insist that to eat the flesh of another human produces wonderful results. Modern day cannibals testify that to swallow the skin of another human being, or chew tender morsels of fried belly fat, is not only delicious but benefits one's own body and mind, too. What's more, they will tell you, such a diet increases intellect, banishes guilt and stimulates virility.

Poppycock! All of it damned poppycock! I gently laid that fragment of human face down. Then I pulled back the hammer of my revolver, for I had a burning urge to aim my pistol at the thug's head just feet away from me and blast him into eternity.

However ... however! There were a dozen men out there armed with rifles. The man who had dropped the bail of human misery finished gathering up the pieces and moved away along the jetty toward the smaller boat.

The line of prisoners was being led, sometimes encouraged by kicks from the gunmen, to one of the large sheds where sparks rose from a chimney. When a door opened to reveal a brightly lit interior, I felt decidedly queasy: for there were piles of blood-red meat on tables. Men in butcher's aprons moved about inside the building. One chopped at what looked like beefsteaks with a cleaver. Another man sharpened a knife on a stone.

"Ye gods," I hissed as the chained men were led toward the hut. "Lambs to the slaughter."

Just then, a commotion, the moonlight revealing what happened next. A boy of perhaps thirteen tried to scramble from one of the river boats and flee the jetty. He didn't get far. One of the gunmen grabbed hold of his arm, then began pulling him roughly toward what was tantamount to a slaughterhouse. This little lad must have understood what fate awaited him. He yelled, struggled, tried to hold onto a mooring post to prevent himself from being dragged to the violent ending of his life. However, his strength wasn't great enough. His captor merely pulled harder; the child's bare feet slithered across the jetty's planks. Nothing he could do would prevent him joining the other chained men.

All too clearly, I understood the process. Captured individuals, possibly those leading a vagrant life, and so, unlikely to be missed by neighbors, were brought downriver by boat. They were then taken into the sheds where they were killed: the meat stripped from their bones, then the flesh would be dried in ovens to render it into biltong. The meat, preserved in this way, could be despatched on a journey northward for several days without it deteriorating. In a month or so, smug gentlemen in the vilest of clubs, would sip their port wine while chewing strips of that fragrant delicacy—meat that they believed would turn them into supermen. *Shame on them. Shame on them!*

And shame on me.

My face burned with embarrassment as I thought: *Am I going to hide here while the boy is dragged to a butchery table? Am I going to cover my ears with my hands, so I don't hear his agonized screams as the sharp knife begins to slice?*

No. A thousand times no!

The boy was perhaps twenty paces from the shed. The thug that held him cruelly twisted his arm to subdue him.

I leapt from the opening in the side of the derelict boat. At the same moment, the man who had dropped the bale had already returned to the riverbank after placing his burden in the rowing boat.

"Hey!" he shouted as he saw me, and immediately tried to block my way.

With a savage swipe of my arm, I struck him with the butt of the pistol. Oh, the satisfaction—the full-blooded *gratification*—when I heard the clunk of my pistol against his dense skull. He fell with a loud grunt. Although the man I struck did not rise to his feet and appeared to be out cold, that grunt alerted the other men on the riverbank. They immediately whirled around, seeing me in an instant. The men called warnings to one another. Those holding rifles cocked them. The thug gripping the boy pulled a pistol from his belt.

This was it. I'd committed myself to a line of action. No going back. No surrender. When a surgeon wields the scalpel, they must do so in a decisive manner. They unflinchingly cut flesh in order to heal the patient. I had to be just as decisive. Raising the pistol above my head, I fired off a single shot upward into the air—that warning shot had the desired effect of making the men stand absolutely still. Thank heaven. The precious element of surprise was mine.

I moved forward in powerful, bustling way, hoping to dominate that group of scoundrels.

"You there," I shouted in as strong a voice as I could muster. "Remain absolutely still, or I will fire."

I levelled the pistol, aiming at each man in turn. The men, however, quickly recovered from their surprise—they glanced at each other as if to convey a silent message. That message, I knew, plainly stated: *Look, there is only one of him. He is no match for us.*

Moving forward briskly, I pointed my revolver at the wretch holding the struggling child. "Let the boy go," I demanded. "Everyone, put down your guns. You are under arrest."

For the first time, the men smiled in amusement. That's when my blood, which had, hitherto, been pounding hotly through my veins, turned as cold as snow. They outnumbered me. There were five bullets left in my pistol. Even firing with perfect accuracy, I could only despatch five men. There were ten. Even those that didn't have firearms were now drawing long-bladed knives form their sheaths.

For my reckless attempt to rescue those poor souls

destined for the oven, my reward would be death. Possibly, my flesh would be carved from my bones, too, to be cured for the delectation of others. The men stepped forward, grinning, levelling their rifles at me.

The one holding the boy barked out at me in a gruff voice: "You've been a proper fool, haven't you, pal? Throw down your pistol, or you're a dead man."

"I'll do nothing of the sort," I replied.

"All right, men," he said with an odious smile. "On my count of five, shoot the fool down. One ... two ..."

The men tucked the stocks of their rifles against their shoulders. Their eyes glittered at me as they aimed.

"Three." He twisted the child's arm who cried out in pain.

I pointed my pistol directly at the bully's face. On his count of five I would despatch him from this life. A small victory at least, even though it would be my last action in this world.

"Four."

A voice cut through the night air. "What goes on here?"

Once again, the men were startled enough to stop their planned cold-blooded murder. They spun round to see a young man with red hair stride out of the shadows. Behind him were three men in uniform—the local police, I surmised, though their pale brown uniforms were unfamiliar to me.

Just then, moonlight fell on the redhaired man's face—a familiar face at that.

"Nolan?" I gasped in surprise. This was the young man who had met Holmes and I at the dockside before delivering us to our rooms earlier that day.

"Doctor Watson." His face was tight with anxiety. "Please come across here to me. I'll take you back to your apartment."

I, however, did not budge, for the young captive's anguish was shockingly apparent. The lad's cheeks were wet with tears, the whites of his eyes sorely-pink—they all but shouted to the world the boy's suffering.

"Nolan, arrest these men," I told him. "They are slaughtering people for the meat on their bones. They are supplying cannibals with human flesh."

"I understand." Nolan's expression told me he was extremely troubled. Yet instead of disarming the men, he beckoned them to him. They stood in a huddle, talking in such low voices I could not make out their words. I saw heads shaking. Occasionally, Nolan would glance back at me, suggesting all too plainly that I was the topic of conversation. On other occasions the thugs would glance at me with expressions of hatred. Those glances reminded me of the phrase *If looks could kill.*

The man who held the boy stood a little apart, though he turned his face to the group of men, listening to the conversation. At last, the men began to nod. Words were spoken, but in whispers that weren't intended for my ears.

Nolan moved toward me with one of the police officers by his side.

Nolan awarded me a grim smile. "You are unhurt, Doctor Watson?"

"I am perfectly well. How the dickens did you know that I'd be here?"

"For your and Mr. Holmes' safety I instructed two police officers to guard your apartment, albeit at a discreet distance, so you wouldn't feel like prisoners. When they saw you hurrying out of doors, carrying a pistol, one alerted me while the other followed you here."

This wasn't the moment to say so, but that explanation didn't ring true. After all, how did the policeman that followed me communicate my whereabouts to Nolan? Evidently, however, Nolan, along with other policemen, had been secretly observing the rooms occupied by Holmes and I. To protect us? To prevent us from leaving New London? Such questions, however, had to wait because other matters were more pressing. Quickly, I explained how I'd seen these ruffians carrying bales of human remains onto the sailing clipper, and how I'd witnessed them bring chained victims from the smaller boats.

"Nolan." I spoke in a heartfelt way. "You'll find captive men in the shed. That's where they will be butchered."

Nolan appeared unsure how to respond to my statement, and it wasn't until after a prolonged moment of indecision, where he clearly struggled to decide his best course of action, he said, "Doctor Watson. My men will attend to matters here, while I escort you back to your lodgings."

"No, sir. Not until you arrest these brigands."

"Please, Doctor Watson. It isn't conducive to one's health to remain by the riverbank. The mosquitos are more prevalent here. Moreover, crocodiles often emerge from the water at night."

I stared at him in shock. "You intend to do nothing about this vile business here. That is so, isn't it?"

His face became stony. "Doctor Watson. Please come with me now. I insist."

"Good heavens, man." My voice grew hoarse with anger. "You are corrupt. These men are bribing you to look the other way. That's the truth, isn't it?"

"Life is different here in Yagomba to that of your homeland."

"I disagree. English law applies just the same in this country."

"There must be allowances regarding local customs."

"Customs!" I spluttered. "Cannibalism isn't a custom. It's a crime."

"Doctor—"

The child screamed as the man began dragging him to the shed.

I shouted at the thug. "Let go of him."

"Go to hell," he replied.

"Let him go."

The thug ignored me as he dragged the lad toward that hell's kitchen. I could stomach no more of this cruel business, so I fired my pistol, its bullet kicking up a spurt of soil just inches from the man's foot. He flinched in surprise at my audacious shot. In fact, the nearness of the bullet startled him so much he relaxed his grip on his victim. Quick as a flash, the boy wriggled free of his clasp before sprinting away into the shadows. Seeing the young fellow escape into the safety of the darkness was a massive relief—and knowing that he would escape the butcher's knife filled me with such happiness that my heart surged in my chest.

The thugs muttered in anger at losing their prey—the meat of the child would be highly prized by the degenerates that consumed such food. Large sums would be paid for even small morsels of such tender young flesh.

The time had come to repeat myself in the strongest terms I could muster: "Nolan. The law demands you arrest these scoundrels, and that you save the lives of the poor wretches in that slaughterhouse."

At last, Nolan gathered up his resolve. He nodded to the policeman standing next to him. "Venables. You know what you must do."

Venables responded promptly with, "Yes, sir."

That's when the policeman raised the rifle, and then used its butt to strike me on the side of the head.

Of the rest of the night, I know nothing more.

Chapter 7

The dream became a nightmare.

As I lay there, I saw myself entangled in Lucifer Vines. Green tendrils, resembling the bodies of long green snakes, wormed outward from the earth, slimy and wet. They entangled me, held me down. I could not move. Then I saw the man-monster Bullman staring at me. He grinned at my plight, the vines wrapping themselves around my neck, tighter and tighter until I could not breathe.

Bullman's stare locked onto mine, his eyes blazing with murderous fire. He reached down, placed a massive hand on my forehead and pushed until my head began to sink back through the Lucifer Vine, and deep into the earth, until the plant's roots wormed their way into my ears, then into my nostrils and mouth.

I reached up to fend off the massive hand.

"Watson ... try to relax. It is I, old friend."

My heart pounded. I was quite breathless. Yet I immediately experienced a wave of relief on seeing Holmes gazing down at me with concern shining in his grey eyes.

I pulled myself into a sitting position, my head aching abominably. Yet my senses were thankfully intact. I realized I'd been asleep on the sitting-room couch.

"Holmes?" I said, "What on Earth is going on?"

"Don't be in a hurry to get up, Watson."

Gently he pressed his hand down upon my shoulder to discourage me from leaping to my feet. I allowed my head to sink back onto the cushion. It was then that I felt a band of tightness across my forehead. When I tried to touch the skin there, I found fabric. "A bandage? Ah ..." Memory came rushing back. "Last night, Holmes. A policeman clubbed me with a rifle. I'd followed that abominable creature from the ship down to the river, and ..." I grunted as a stabbing pain shot through my skull.

"Try and rest," murmured Holmes soothingly. "You are not badly hurt."

"Men were led to a slaughterhouse. Butchered for meat. I swear."

"Nolan told me what happened. That was admirably brave of you to tackle so many armed men single-handed."

"But Nolan sided with them."

"So it might seem, Watson, but the situation here in New London is somewhat complicated."

"Dash it all.... One of Nolan's men knocked me unconscious."

Holmes pulled up a chair so he could sit close to me as I lay there on the couch.

"Watson," he began in soft tones, no doubt mindful that a louder voice would inflict yet more pain upon my poor head. "Nolan explained everything. How your actions allowed the vagrant boy to escape. He also told me that to avoid a gun battle with a local criminal gang he had one of his men knock you down with the rifle."

"Confound him! The fellow might have killed me."

Holmes gave a sympathetic smile. "There is surely no such thing as inflicting a gentle blow with a rifle butt. However, Nolan assures me that the police officer struck you in as a restrained way as he possibly could."

"Holmes, I'm not concerned about the assault. As you well know, I have a hard skull and have suffered much worse. What is far more important is that vile thugs are kidnapping people and bringing them to New London where their flesh is processed."

Holmes lightly rested his hand on my chest as I lay there. "Dear chap, what you have discovered is wrong. Murder coupled with cannibalism is as repugnant as it is profoundly wicked. Moreover, it proves to me that New London is a dangerous city."

"You will see to it that the villains are arrested?"

"We must tread carefully."

"But Holmes-"

"I'm sorry, old chap, but there it is. Society here exists on a knife-edge. Last night, after the policemen wheeled you back here in a handcart, I questioned Nolan. The young man was far more candid than yesterday when he was strenuously puffing-up the more agreeable aspects of his hometown. Indeed, last night he revealed that many people here, corrupt government officials as well as prisoners, earn enormous sums of money from illegal practices. That includes supplying human flesh to those in Europe who wish to indulge cannibalistic fantasies."

"Truly sickening, Holmes. The evil practice must be stopped."

"Yes, it must." He sat back, steepled his fingers together, and regarded me with those deep-set eyes of his that were so wise and so solemn. "For now, however, we must tread with great care if we are to avoid having a knife planted in our backs. This is a metropolis of eighty thousand people. Yes, most are law-abiding, yet there are wrongdoers here as well, who bribe officials to turn a blind eye to their criminal activities. And if you stir into that mix a great number of convicted prisoners, who have slipped back into their wayward habits of old, then this becomes a very dangerous place indeed."

"Surely the assistant governor, Wentworth, the man we met yesterday, hasn't been corrupted?"

"Nolan tells me that although Wentworth is an honest fellow, he lacks the qualities of leadership. That is why

Wentworth begged me to assume the role of governor to ensure that New London doesn't collapse into anarchy."

"Holmes, at the risk of overfeeding your ego, I am the first to declare that you are a remarkable detective. However, I would further declare that you are not—*absolutely not*—qualified to govern an overseas prison colony."

Holmes gave a grim smile, the skin of his thin face tightening. "Indeed, I doubt if I would make an effective ruler, nor do I wish to even try. What does haunt me, Watson, is recalling what happened to other societies when the rule of law broke down. Therefore ..."—my friend gave a troubled sigh—"... therefore, if I reject Wentworth's plea that I become governor, will that lead to riots and slaughter?"

Sherlock Holmes fell silent as he wrestled with a problem of huge importance. I daresay we could have boarded a ship for England, either that day or the day after, leaving New London behind. If Holmes did so, and with nobody in charge who had the stature to prevent the collapse of civilization here, then how long before looting began? How long until criminal gangs decided to seize power and rule the city for themselves? How long until New London's streets were red and wet with human blood?

A knock sounded on the door.

Holmes' clear voice rang out: "Come."

Miss Dembe, the maid, who had served us our tea yesterday, entered with the breakfast tray—sliced fresh fruit in bowls, scrambled eggs, sausages, grilled kidneys, toast and a dish containing a creamy scoop of butter. Once again, she wore the traditional maid's garments of skirts and blouse, over which she'd tied a crisp, white apron. I judged her age to be twenty years or so. Her dark skin had the healthy lustre of youth. Her large brown eyes were really quite striking. Almost spiritual, as if she was given to spending any moment she had free gazing serenely at the world, and perhaps divining those mysteries that 'lie behind the veil' of what we call reality.

"Good morning, gentlemen," she said in such a small voice I could hardly hear any actual words.

"Good morning, Miss Dembe. And thank you," Holmes said. "Please put the tray on the table."

She crossed the room with quick, silent steps. As she did so, I managed to ease myself up into a sitting position on the sofa, for lolling supine in the presence of a woman hardly strikes me as being gentlemanly. Even though my head still ached quite stridently, good manners should prevail over one's personal discomfort.

Holmes smiled. "As we already know your name, Miss Dembe, please allow me to introduce ourselves to you. I am Sherlock Holmes. This is Doctor John Watson. He had an unfortunate accident last night. Nevertheless, he will be fully recovered soon, I fancy."

Miss Dembe set the tray down upon the table. "I do hope so, sir."

"Have you lived in this city long?"

"For a little over five weeks."

"Miss Dembe. Is it a good place?"

"To me it is, sir."

"Peaceful? Well-governed?"

"In the words of the poet, sir, 'alas, I know not anything.'"

"Ah ... the wisdom of Tennyson."

"I do enjoy reading poetry."

"And writing it," Holmes added, "using your left hand."

"I do not deny writing verse, sir." She lifted her chin and straightened her back; a distinct change in posture that challenged us to criticise her interest in being the author of such things. "Some might tell me that a domestic servant should not dare to compose poetry."

Miss Dembe, a slightly built young woman with a powerful gaze, which suggested that her inner strength was considerable, began to tremble. Not with fear. Absolutely not with fear. This trembling was born, I would guess, from the anger of remembered insults, and

73

disparaging remarks made by so-called "betters" intended to belittle her. To make her feel small, powerless; merely tolerated in order for her to work long hours scrubbing floors or serving food on silver trays to rich men and women, who couldn't even bring themselves to offer her a word of thanks for her diligent service. Yes, I saw all that in those large brown eyes—the humiliation of verbal abuse so cruelly heaped upon her.

Holmes, too, clearly saw that was writ large in her powerful gaze. No doubt he saw a great deal more, too.

Still with her chin raised fearlessly, she asked quite directly, "Mr. Holmes. How did you know I engage in writing?"

He answered in understated, matter-of-fact tones, "Your left hand bears traces of ink. Your right hand does not. Therefore, I note you are left-handed. There is a slight crescent-shaped indentation in one of your front teeth. If the grove in that tooth was narrower, I'd believe it was caused by using your teeth to bite through thread when sewing. But no; the crescent shape of that dimension, though it is barely discernible to the lazy-minded observer, would accommodate the round stem of a pen. Such an effect on a material as hard as tooth enamel would occur only over a long period of time. So, I envisage you sitting at a table, paper in front of you, absently gripping the pen between your teeth as you search your mind for the perfect word for your verse. All of which points most powerfully to the conclusion that you labor hard over your art, Miss Dembe. In fact, you strive so hard to achieve excellence that you do not realize you grip the pen tightly in your teeth, hence the very slight wear to your front incisors."

Miss Dembe's body tensed as she heard these words, probably expecting Holmes to add some scornful comment that her pages of poetry must be fit only for the fireplace.

Holmes smiled. "Your literary ambitions are a credit to you, Miss. I admire your enterprise."

The woman's shoulders dropped a little as she

relaxed—her relief at being congratulated on her vocation was clearly visible.

"Thank you, sir." She smiled, too, though her eyes darted downward, as if she was so unaccustomed to compliments that she momentarily felt embarrassment.

Heartily, I said, "Miss Dembe! Good for you, and I wish you every success in your endeavors. Has any of your work been published?"

"No, sir. At least not yet. However, I have posted several of my poems to magazines in London and New York."

I chuckled. "I'm something of a writer myself and know the frustration of magazine editors rejecting one's work."

Miss Dembe allowed herself a smile of triumph. "Oh, but I received a letter just yesterday. It arrived on the ship that brought you here. The *New Society Magazine* in London has written a most pleasant communication to me, sir, informing me that they wish to buy three of my sonnets for publication."

"By Jove." This pleased me so much I completely forgot the ache in my head. "Well done. Congratulations."

"Congratulations, indeed," Holmes added. "I dare say that your success is the result of great self-sacrifice, not to mention hard work."

"Mr. Holmes," she began. "Your singular talent as a detective meant that you could deduce that I spend all my spare time working with pen and paper."

"A simple observation, that is all," he declared with rare modesty.

"Then may I share an observation of my own with you?" Miss Dembe's expression became grave.

"Of course."

"Believe me, sir, I have not eavesdropped. Yet I noticed the demeanor of the assistant governor when he left these rooms yesterday."

"Go on."

"From what I witnessed, there is only one conclusion I can draw." Her eyes fixed on his face. "That you have been asked to become Lord of Damnation."

"Lord of Damnation!" Despite her serious expression, I laughed. "That, Miss Dembe, is a rather lurid title."

She fixed me with that strong gaze, which seemed to penetrate my skull and look deeply into my own mind. "The Lord of Damnation—that is what local people call the governor of this island, sir."

Holmes went to the window where he gazed out into the street below, his hands clasped behind his back. "That, Miss, is a matter that I cannot comment upon."

"Very good, sir. If I may be excused?"

"Of course. It has been most pleasant speaking with you, Miss Dembe."

Before leaving the room, she declared with sudden boldness: "I like you, Mr. Holmes, and you, too, Dr Watson. You treat me with genuine respect. Therefore, I will repay your kindness." Her voice became stronger, insistent, and—dare I say it?—*forceful.* "Leave here, gentlemen. Rush to leave. Do nothing to delay your departure. Every Lord of Damnation has had a short tenure. What's more, they never leave Yagomba in the same state as they arrived."

Chapter 8

Holmes and I took a hansom cab to the Governor's House. Even in the midday heat, the streets teemed with people and horse-drawn vehicles. Shop windows, shaded by brightly colored canvas awnings in all the colors of the rainbow, offered displays of fashionable clothes for the affluent citizens of New London. Pavement cafés, modeled on those found in Paris rather than "Old London" back in England, bustled with smartly clad waiters serving their urbane clientele with plates full of food. Although at least one such "open-air" café received the unwanted attention of a vulture, which swept in on vast wings to alight on a recently vacated table, scattering cutlery and crockery alike onto the ground, before dipping its curving beak into what appeared to be a part-empty bowl of soup. A remarkable sight indeed.

Holmes observed, "Rarely have I seen such a city with inhabitants who are busy all the time. This is positively an ants' nest of activity."

"In this heat, too," I commented, wiping my perspiring forehead. "I shall never complain about snow again."

"You must have experienced hotter temperatures than this?"

"Yes, as a younger man, Holmes."

He smiled. "Nonsense, Watson. You're as healthy as any twenty-year-old. You merely need time to acclimatize."

A vendor on a street corner sold newspapers to the crowds rushing by, deftly handing over the folded paper while pocketing coins handed to him. As these swift transactions took place, the vendor called out the latest news. "Preacher's son taken by leopard! Preacher's son taken by leopard!" The front page of the newspaper had been tacked to a board, which stood on a frame beside the man. The newspaper carried both a photograph of a leopard's head and the image of a young man of around twenty-five years of age. The headline: *MANEATER STRIKES AGAIN. VICTIM PLUCKED FROM CITY GARDEN.*

Holmes murmured, "Watson, we are in the midst of the wonders of civilization, but wild jungle has, I am bound to say, laid siege to this city."

I followed the direction of his gaze to where green hills rose up around New London. Those millions of trees were nothing less than armies that encircled the city. In those jungles lurked all manner of savage animals that bided their time until they could sneak into town, under cover of darkness, to hunt human prey. At that moment, I sensed the relentless pressure of the jungle on the outer margins of this great metropolis. If the jungle had a mind, I knew that its single, burning desire would be to invade the city—for its trees to burst apart pavements, and to engulf houses and churches in rampant greenery. With a shiver, I had an uncanny premonition of gazing upon New London a dozen years from now: when vines shrouded its ruined buildings, when animals, not humans, scurried along broad avenues, and when ants by the million picked flesh from human bodies until all that remained were shining white skeletons lying in the dirt.

The jungle-clad hills utterly captured my attention. There, purple blossoms gleamed in the brilliant tropical sun. Millions of trees would whisper in a menacing fashion as the hot breeze ghosted through branches. Nature had become humanity's enemy here. Nature desired to annihilate this fine city. Nature wanted us dead.

"Watson? I say, old chap, are you feeling ill?"

"Hmm?"

"Maybe the blow on your head is troubling you?"

"Sorry, Holmes. That jungle over yonder—it has a way of intruding upon one's thoughts."

His grey eyes fixed on me with concern. "Are you sure you're well enough to accompany me today?"

"Don't concern yourself. I'm in perfect health."

As I firmly reassured him about my well-being, the cab came to a stop, for in the road a group of South American black howler monkeys were engaged in a confrontation with African olive baboons. The howlers had shaggy pelts, coal black eyes—their jaws were open, revealing pink gums embedded with sharp teeth, and they uttered loud, throbbing howls—the kind of howl that evidently gave the creature its name. Meanwhile, the dog-faced baboons, with pale brown fur, made a series of aggressive sounds that were a cross between a cough and a bark. The street had been a fast stream of carts and cabs. Now the traffic came to a halt, as our hairy cousins appeared to be trying to out-shout one another over a territorial dispute or some such grievance. There were perhaps twenty animals in each group of opposing primate battalions. They didn't attempt to bite one another. Instead, they preferred noisy debate.

I grinned. "Reminds one of the House of Commons. I've heard our members of Parliament make more noise than that when in the midst of an argument about corn laws or raising income tax or some such issue."

Holmes smiled back. "Indeed so, Watson, but this experiment, involving the introduction of species from different continents to what, for them, is alien terrain, and creating opportunities for creatures that would never meet each other in natural circumstances is a rather apt metaphor for a situation that could tear this society apart."

"What do you mean, Holmes?"

Holmes nodded in the direction of a building, fronted by a large yard in which children played. "Look at that school. What do you see?"

"Children playing with hoops and balls and the like."

"A little more detail, if you please, Watson. We require data."

Holmes detested allowing his mind to remain idle, so he'd clearly fixed his attention on some conundrum or other. As requested, I fixed my attention on the schoolyard where children, aged, I judged, between six years and eleven years of age, played. I gave Holmes the gist of my appraisal, adding, "The children wear school uniforms—white jackets, black trousers for boys. White jackets, black skirts and straw boater hats for girls. I venture, they appear to be the offspring of wealthy families. The argument between the two groups of monkeys must be a common occurrence, because the children aren't distracted from their games in the slightest. Oh, and there are four schoolteachers in attendance, keeping an eye on the children."

As a howler monkey climbed a lamppost to bellow its fury at a large male baboon, which sat on top of a mailbox, Holmes frowned. "My good fellow, what do you really see?"

I shook my head, puzzled. "Clearly, I do not see what you see. Is there a mystery here? Is there something amiss with those children?"

Holmes did appear a trifle uneasy as he said, "Notice the jackets of their school uniform."

"White."

"No, not all of them are white. Some are the palest blue. Moreover, they have the faintest of red lines that intersect on the back."

"Then they are prison uniforms," I said. "We have seen them before—the blue jacket with the red cross on the back."

"Hmmm." Holmes appeared thoughtful. "So, there are children as young as six years of age wearing a subtle version of the uniform worn by convicted criminals here on Yagomba. But not all are wearing the pale blue jackets, some are wearing pure white garments, with no cross on the back."

"Surely, the children aren't convicted felons that have been shipped to the island?"

"No, I suspect they are the sons and daughters of convicts, yet for some reason wear a stylized version of the prison uniform—whether by parental choice or governor decree, is a question well worth answering."

"Holmes," I said, "you told me, just a moment ago, that the conflict between the South American monkeys and the African baboons is a metaphor for what might trouble human society here. How so?"

"Consider this, Watson: thousands of convicted criminals have been shipped to this island over the last thirty years. Men and women who might have committed the foulest of crimes, yet, for some reason, were spared the hangman's noose. Thousands of those prisoners considered their arrival as a fresh start and became law-abiding citizens. Equally, there will be thousands of prisoners who simply decided to continue their career in crime. And some of those will be the most brutal thugs imaginable. And also arriving here, there will have been thousands of men and women, who have committed no crimes whatsoever and were deployed here by the government as civil servants, administrators, and municipal engineers and the like."

"Ah." I began to understand. "Therefore, there is a potentially problematic mix of law-abiding citizens living cheek-by-jowl with thousands of brutish men and women, hell-bent on breaking the law."

"Exactly. And you can also add to that volatile cocktail the children of criminals who have been born here over the last three decades and the children of government employees."

I pointed out: "However, you see the children of prisoners and government employees playing together quite happily."

"And yet, subtle differences in their uniform set them apart." He allowed himself a tight-lipped smile. "Don't misunderstand me, old chap. I do hope that there is a future of peace and prosperity here for those children. Nevertheless, I do fear that the seeds of conflict might already being sown, due to the fact that the children of prisoners bear the stigmata of their parents' ill deeds upon the backs of their jackets."

I nodded. "Then this experiment in penal reform might result in the inadvertent construction of a huge powder keg that might explode at any moment?"

"Indeed so, Watson. Let us hope that I am mistaken, and that the future for those children will be a happy one. Otherwise, the consequences are too dreadful to contemplate."

At that moment, a bell rang from the direction of the school building, and the children obediently filed in through its doorway. Coincidentally, that was the moment, when the two groups of monkeys decided that their noisy disagreement with each other had reached a mutually satisfactory conclusion, and the baboons climbed up the trellis, fixed to a church, where they sat on the roof, scratching themselves, or yawning, as if the time had come to relax. The howler monkeys, tails held high, ambled into a side street where they grouped themselves around a horse trough full of clear water and began to drink, no doubt cooling what must have been many hot throats after all that furious howling.

Now the traffic could flow freely again. Within minutes of recommencing our journey, the cab pulled over to the side of the road.

The driver called back, "Destination reached, gentlemen."

After Holmes had stepped out, I followed, finding myself standing before a towering mansion built in the style of a French château. Once again, this not only reflected the municipal planners' eclectic and cosmopolitan tastes, but it also further demonstrated the governor's exalted status as a man of power. I recalled the maidservant's alternative name for the governor of Yagomba as being the Lord of Damnation. Once more, a shiver ran down my spine.

Holmes approached a pair of grand entrance doors; yet before he could ring the bell both doors swung open to reveal the assistant governor, Sir Nigel Wentworth, once again dressed severely in black. The man's face appeared as grey as his side-whiskers.

"Good day, Mr. Holmes, good day, Doctor Watson." He spoke quickly, a sign of his anxiety. "Please step this way."

Holmes commented drily, "Thank you for opening the doors to us in person. A somewhat unusual occupation for the assistant governor."

The man's expression was grim. "All domestic staff are confined to their quarters until I hear your answer."

"My answer being whether I say yea or nay to accepting the post of governor."

Wentworth gave a sharp nod. "That's why you are here, is it not?"

"Firstly, I would very much like to commence my investigation into the disappearance of the man whom you wish me to replace as governor."

Wentworth glared at Holmes. I rather suspect he would have preferred to strike Holmes in the face rather than speak to him civilly, because I sensed that this arrogant and tyrannical individual expected Holmes to promptly agree to become the new "Lord of Damnation." Wentworth, admittedly, did attempt a polite smile. The action resembled a foul-tempered dog baring its teeth.

"Very well, Mr. Holmes, as you wish. Please follow me." He walked swiftly toward a broad staircase. Before climbing the steps, he glanced coldly at me—by this time I'd removed my hat, consequently he would have seen my bandaged head; however, he feigned not to notice. "Doctor Watson. Perhaps you would care to wait in the morning room?"

Holmes addressed the man somewhat sharply: "Doctor Watson accompanies me when I investigate a case. His interpretation of clues is always ..." Holmes paused, choosing the most telling word. "Interesting."

"Moreover, I write accounts of Mr. Holmes' cases," I told Wentworth.

Wentworth looked down his nose at me. "Then may I ask you to refrain from writing about this one for your little magazines? The governor is a high-ranking official of His Majesty's Government, and whatever tragedy has befallen him should not be described in print to entertain the rabble. Now, please follow me."

Wentworth led us up the staircase. Everywhere there were fine adornments, from huge, glittering chandeliers overhead to framed oil paintings of lions, to antique gilt furniture.

Wentworth pointed to a door with a brass handle. In that annoyingly pompous way of his, he declared, "Beyond that door you will find Lord Delaney's bedroom."

My companion's sharp eyes examined the door. "Has the room been cleaned since his Lordship vanished?"

"No. I locked it myself after his disappearance. Nobody has entered since." Pulling a bunch of keys from his pocket, he unlocked the door before turning to look Sherlock Holmes in the eye. "Sir, when will you give me your answer regarding my offer of governorship?"

"All in good time, Sir Nigel."

Wentworth scowled. "Time is in short supply Remember, if the public discover that this country's governor has vanished, there will be a rapid and utter collapse of law and order. Massacres will soon follow. I have—"

"Sir Nigel," Holmes interrupted. "You will have my answer in due course. Firstly, however, I wish to examine the room from which Lord Delaney vanished, while the clues are still relatively fresh."

"Of course." Once again, the man seemed to struggle to contain his anger. After clenching his fists at his side, he mastered his emotion and pushed open the door.

Holmes entered the bedroom first, followed by myself,

then Wentworth.

As Wentworth opened his mouth to speak, Holmes quickly held a finger to his own lips, demanding silence. Holmes then closed his eyes before inhaling deeply through his nostrils. After that, he opened his eyes again as he slowly began to turn around on the same spot, his gaze devouring every detail of the room—four poster bed, furniture of monumental size, and paintings of what I suspected were Lord Delaney's ancestors on the walls. These were, in the main, stern-faced aristocrats in white powdered wigs and wearing dark cloaks—a somewhat puritanical clan, it seemed to me. And certainly not the kind of faces that I would wish to see gazing down at me from their portraits when I opened my eyes at the first light of day.

Holmes then began to move around the room, paying particular attention to the back of the bedroom door, and then to male clothing hanging in a small antechamber that led off from the bedroom. When he was satisfied with his inspection of the clothes, he went to the large window that overlooked formal parkland, stretching down to the river. Holmes opened the window before leaning out in order to gaze down onto a veranda that lay between the house and a lawn.

Holmes closed the window. "Sir Nigel. You told me the butler discovered that Lord Delaney was missing."

"Yes."

"May I speak with the butler?"

"Alas, the strain has been too much for him. The fellow's quite lost his wits."

"Therefore, you believe I'll obtain no useful information from him?"

"Precisely."

"Was Lord Delaney alone in the bedroom prior to his disappearance?"

"He is a widower. He always locks the door from the inside before retiring to bed."

"Yet you did not have to break down the door?"

"No. The butler was able to use a pencil to work the key loose from the other side of the door and push it from the keyhole."

"Whereupon the key dropped onto a newspaper that the resourceful butler had already slid under the door beforehand, so it would catch the falling key, thus allowing him to withdraw both paper and key and then unlock the door."

"That is correct, Mr. Holmes."

"Just to recap, his Lordship vanished seven nights ago, wearing night attire and bedroom slippers."

"Yes."

"I take it," said Holmes, "nobody heard a commotion, saw anything unusual, or noticed any sign of a break in?"

"Nothing, Mr. Holmes. It was as if the governor vanished into thin air."

"Had the bed been slept in?"

"Yes, blankets and so on were lying crumpled at the bottom of the bed. "

Holmes crossed the room to the bed in order to examine the linen. "The pillowcases and sheets haven't been changed?"

"No. The butler merely tidied the bedding as you see now."

At that moment, a rapid knock sounded on the bedroom door. Once again, we were awarded with the sight of Sir Nigel Wentworth's ill-tempered scowl. Rushing to the door, he flung it open to reveal Nolan standing there, the red-haired young man who had saved my life the night before.

Nolan clutched that straw hat he always seemed to favor in trembling hands.

Wentworth barked, "I gave strict instructions that we weren't to be disturbed."

"I beg your pardon, sir," began Nolan. "There is a large crowd gathering at the gallows. They are getting impatient."

"Then get it over and done with. Hang the devils!"

86

Holmes stepped forward. "There is to be an execution?"

Wentworth gave a curt nod. "Five prisoners. They were discovered throwing Lucifer Vine into tanks that supply fresh drinking water to the city."

"They were to be hanged at noon," Nolan explained. "However, I require Sir Nigel to sign the death warrant first."

Holmes said, "They have been convicted in a court of law? Their guilt is beyond all reasonable doubt?"

"They are prisoners, sir, under the absolute jurisdiction of the governor." Wentworth spoke with cold dignity. "They do not stand trial like other men."

Holmes' expression turned to one of fury. "How dare you? They are subjects of His Majesty the King. As such, they are protected by law, even if they are ultimately punished by the law."

"They are prisoners—as such, they stand outside the law, and are not protected by the usual legal framework."

"I disagree. All men and women, if they are charged with a crime, must be granted the same rights with regard to justice."

"Mr. Holmes." Wentworth's face flushed red—a bright red—his anger threatened to overwhelm him. "Those men will pay for their crime. Nolan, I will come down and sign the warrant. Once I've done that, see to it that they are hanged at once."

"Nolan." Holmes' voice rang with authority. "You will do no such thing. The men must receive a fair trial. Besides, throwing weeds into a water tank should not invoke the death penalty."

Nolan anxiously clutched the hat in his hands. "Mr. Holmes, you evidently do not know the devastating effects of the Lucifer Vine."

"That can be discussed at the trial. Cancel the execution."

Wentworth shuddered. "The crowd is angry. If the men are not hanged in front of the townspeople, there will be riots."

Holmes said: "Sir Nigel. Take me to the gallows. I will attend to this problem myself."

"Be it on your own head, man. But very well!" Sir Nigel threw his hands up in despair. "First, I will assemble a police guard for you. The streets are dangerous when the townspeople are in a mood as vengeful as this. Please wait here!"

After yelling at Nolan to follow him, the pair rushed away along the landing in the direction of the stairs.

I turned to Holmes. "Are you sure about this? According to Nolan there is already a danger of civil unrest."

"I will order a stay of execution. The accused men will be given a fair trial in accordance with English law." He shot me a grim look. "This little pocket of civilization does indeed precariously exist on a knife-edge. One suspects that people here need not be pressed hard before they descend into violent anarchy."

I glanced back at the room. "Maybe this isn't the time for such a discussion, but did you learn anything here about the governor's disappearance?"

"I can say with some conviction that the man did not vanish from this room after arising from that bed. The bedding is still fresh and has not been slept in since being laundered. Either the butler lied, or it's Sir Nigel who isn't telling the truth."

We did not have a long wait before Nolan bounded up the steps, calling, "Mr. Holmes, Doctor Watson. Please come quickly. I'll take you to the execution yard. It's just five minutes' walk from here."

Chapter 9

The spectacle that greeted our eyes had the power to knock the air from my lungs. A seething mass of people filled the street. They shouted the vilest of curses through a ten-foot iron fence that formed a barrier between the road and a large, rectangular shaped yard.

A group of police officers had accompanied us from the governor's residence to ensure our safety. Nolan constantly urged us to move faster. Holmes and I were side-by-side so saw, at the same time, the focus of the crowd's attention. Five men stood on a raised platform, their hands tied behind their bare backs, while hanging beside them at the height of their elbows were five nooses—these were formed from stout ropes that were attached to a long section of timber set into a framework above the heads of the condemned. The gallows platform stood eight feet above the ground. The five men were motionless, dazed perhaps by the knowledge that soon they would be, as the more vulgar newspapers put it, "dancing on air."

The crowd roared for the men's destruction. They shook their fists in rage at the condemned wretches.

"Let us through," demanded the police at every step. "Let us through."

The crowd, seeing the police officers, must have believed that they were here to deliver the death warrant; therefore, that sea of people obediently parted to let us through.

Nolan hissed to us, "See what the people are like? If the men are not hanged there will be a riot. Dozens will be killed: ourselves included."

Holmes spoke forcefully: "I will not allow a mob to overthrow the rule of law. Those men still may hang. Not, however, until they have been tried before judge and jury."

Nolan groaned with a helpless kind of frustration, as if already in his mind's eye he saw riots turning the street red with blood, and that there was nothing he could do to prevent it.

The gates swung open for us. More police were in the yard, thereby preventing the mob rushing in to kill the prisoners themselves. Within moments, we were through that crush of angry townsfolk and into the comparative safety of the yard, the scaffold in its center, together with the grim array of nooses that were designed to snap the necks of wrongdoers.

As if to mirror stormy events below on Earth, the sky had turned ominously dark. Heavy layers of black cloud swept overhead to block out the sun. Although no rain fell, a loud rumble of thunder echoed over the town.

The hangman, a burly fellow in a leather apron, descended the steps of the scaffold whereupon he hurried across to Nolan to speak to him in rough tones: "Just in time, Mr. Nolan. The crowd wouldn't have remained patient for one more minute. Will you confirm you carry the death warrant?"

"Mr. Barton, there will be no hanging."

Barton actually recoiled in shock as if slapped. "You what? No hanging?"

"No."

"On whose orders?"

Holmes quickly answered: "Mine."

"Just who are you to demand that those damn rats don't hang?"

90

"Sherlock Holmes. That's who demands it."

The hangman appeared baffled. "You don't have the authority to cancel the execution. You're just that detective feller who's visiting here."

"On the contrary." Holmes straightened his back, standing taller, adopting a commanding presence. "I am the new governor."

Thunder rumbled even louder.

Barton shot an imploring glance at Nolan. "Tell Mr. Holmes that if I don't pull the damn lever on those men we'll be torn apart by the crowd. See how angry they are!"

Holmes said, "I will speak to them."

Barton's eyes bulged with fear. "You might be the new master here, sir. That don't make you God Almighty, because He's the only one that can calm that lot out there."

The crowd surged forward against the fence—a mass of sweltering, vengeful, enraged humanity. Some even climbed the iron railings to sit on the cross bars at the top. They were here to see men hang by the neck. Men that they hated with all their hearts. At that moment, a breathless calm suddenly spread through the crowd. There were no shouted insults, no gesturing, or shaking of fists—for they had no reason to suspect that the hanging wouldn't go ahead. Silently, they waited for a noose to be slipped over each man's head. They anticipated keenly, even greedily, the clunk of the lever as the hangman opened the hatches, which would swing down on hinges beneath the prisoners' feet, allowing them to drop until the rope pulled tight, despatching five human beings into the hereafter.

When the time came for my friend Sherlock Holmes to announce that the executions would not occur, I could not help but fear what the crowd's reaction would be.

Holmes climbed the steps and went to stand halfway along the timber platform, where he faced the crowd as if that grim structure was a theatre stage. The townsfolk fell silent, expecting the reading of the death warrant.

Naturally, I accompanied my friend, determined to loyally be at his side, come what may, do or die.

Holmes whispered to me, "Thank you, Watson. I appreciate your support."

"I would not let you face this alone," I whispered back. "Though, do you still believe it wise to cancel the executions? See that crowd? They will turn into a furious rabble in a heartbeat."

"I don't disagree, old friend—nevertheless, I refuse to permit what amounts to be a lynching."

"Then we are in your hands ... perhaps even in God's hands."

Holmes gave a regretful shake of his head. "Generally, I pride myself on being the engine that drives events. Today, I am forced to admit that events have now become the engine that drives me. For if I don't decisively react to this situation now, and law and order collapses in the city, I fear great bloodshed."

"I pray that you succeed, Holmes. Whatever happens, I will remain with you."

Sherlock Holmes stepped forward, to the edge of the platform as if this really was a stage from which he would address his audience massing beyond the iron railings. Many people were growing impatient now. Heads turned as they talked to the fellow next to them. *What's the delay? Why aren't the prisoners dead yet?* Oh, yes indeed, I could imagine them asking those questions.

Thunder rumbled. Clouds darkened until the sky turned purple and black. Even the approaching storm threatened violence.

The line of prisoners behind me shuddered with terror. Their eyes bulged from their faces at Holmes. To a man, they believed he intended to announce their imminent execution. Every prisoner had been cruelly beaten—lips cut, noses bloodied. Stripes of raw flesh across their backs told me they had been flogged. Without a shadow of doubt, confessions had been extracted from them.

Holmes waited for a wave of thunder to roll by. Then,

taking a deep breath, he spoke to the crowd—his presence magisterial, his voice loud enough to carry to the ears of every man and woman there.

"Ladies and gentlemen. There will be no execution today." His voice echoed back from distant buildings. "These men have the right to be tried in a court of law."

The crowd erupted. Fists pounded the iron railings, sending up a tremendous clanging. A thousand angry eyes fixed on Holmes. Instantly, he'd become the focus of hatred.

A man sitting on top of the railings yelled, "Who are you to stop the hanging?"

Holmes' voice rang out with astonishing clarity and power. "My name is Sherlock Holmes. I am the new governor of Yagomba." The mob became silent in an instant. They stared in amazement at that tall, thin man. "I represent his Majesty the King and his government."

Holmes did not explain the circumstances why he had replaced the previous governor, Lord Delany. Nor did anyone in the crowd shout out, demanding to know why the most famous detective in the world was now 'Lord of Damnation', as our maidservant had termed the role. Such was Holmes' charisma that they accepted his statement without question.

Holmes called down to the policemen, "Take the prisoners back to their cells. I will order a trial in due course." Then he added in a lower voice that only I could hear: "See that these poor devils are visited by a doctor to treat their wounds."

I heaved a sigh of relief before whispering, "Well done, Holmes. You have the crowd in the palm of your hand.

Holmes flashed me a glance of gratitude. Then, taking a deep breath again, his voice filled the air with nothing less than an electrifying power. "Ladies and gentlemen. Return to your homes. Tomorrow I will tour the city. After that, I will receive visitors who wish to speak to me about any concerns they might have about life here in New London." He called down to the redheaded man.

"Nolan. Have the newspapers publish special editions announcing that I am the new governor and have entered office with immediate effect. The headline should fill the front page in block capitals—have it read: *SHERLOCK HOLMES TAKES CHARGE.*"

"Yes, sir."

"Also, arrange a tour of the city for me in an open-top carriage. Visibility! That is the key. As many people as possible must see me. It's important for them to know that law and order here is as solid as granite. They must not fear riots. They must be reassured that they are safe."

"Yes, Mr. Holmes."

"Then make haste to the newspaper office, Mr. Nolan. A new era of true civilization begins this day in Yagomba."

Nolan grinned. Holmes' air of authority both reassured him and energised him. With an excited, "Yes, sir!" he ran away across the square. Meanwhile, police officers led the prisoners back to the jail.

Slowly, the crowd began to disperse. Their smiling expressions told me that they were overjoyed that Sherlock Holmes would now be their leader. They clearly knew of my friend's triumphant career, solving cases and saving lives. Many would have read my accounts of Holmes' exploits in magazines and newspapers. For them, this would be the bright dawn of a wonderful new epoch in New London's history.

Yet that day was just about to become one of the darkest, and most horrific days of my life. Thunder growled with utter menace. The storm was coming.

Chapter 10

Just five minutes after Sherlock Holmes descended from the gallows' platform, the storm broke.

Thunder crashed so loudly my poor head, already bruised from being struck by a rifle butt the previous night, hurt so much I had to press my hands to my temples. Lightning flashes seared my eyes. And still the rain hadn't come. Then I saw a sight that was as marvelous as it was strange. Winds, for surely it must be a surge of air, I reasoned, stirred the trees in the jungle beyond the city. For all the world, it seemed to me that a huge, yet invisible beast passed through the jungle, sending a wave of movement through the ocean of greenery. That wave of air, disturbing the huge trees, rushed toward the city as if some unseen beast of monstrous size, and the evilest of intentions, charged toward New London.

Several police officers, who had been guarding the closed gates set in the tall iron fence, moved back toward the building that served as both jail and police headquarters.

The hangman, Barton, meanwhile, vigorously cursed the storm as he quickly began to untie the ropes that terminated in those grim nooses.

Holmes called across to Barton, "Leave them, man. Take shelter."

"Not yet, sir," Barton shouted as thunder rumbled again. "Thieves will steal the ropes. I'll have to pay for new out of my own damn pocket."

Holmes beckoned to me to hurry in the direction of the building. Blues flashes of lightning dazzled my eyes. I glanced back at the iron fence that separated the yard from the road. Three men still sat atop the railing, staring at Holmes in fascination. They wanted to watch the detective—fame has that peculiar magnetic quality for some.

Just at the moment, lightning struck the fence. The sheer power of that electrical discharge exploded the three men perched on the top rail. 'Exploded' is not too strong a word. One second the men sat there gawking at my friend, the next, the force of the lightning's electricity, running through the ironwork, superheated the men's blood in their veins to the point it vaporized, causing their torsos to violently erupt, flinging internal organs and chunks of flesh high into the air, in gusts of steam.

"We must take cover from the storm!" I bellowed these words to both Holmes and the four policemen who had guarded the gate. "There is a very real danger the lightning will strike us, too."

As we hurried to the building, the day grew dark as night. Lightning burst in flashes of blue that were so bright they made my eyes water. That and the thunder! *And what thunder!* Louder than any artillery barrage. Ye gods, my head ... alas, my poor head! My skull hurt from crown to neck.

Then the surge of air from the forest arrived. Dust swirled in the yard. Grit prickled my eyes. Airborne dirt dried my throat in an instant. Holmes, the police officers, and I, began a violent fit of coughing.

How did I know that the winds were from the forest? My answer to that is there was a singular quality about that vortex of air spiralling round and around in the yard.

The air smelt of strange forest blooms—exotic scents that reminded me of cinnamon, myrrh and sandalwood, yet intensified to an inordinate degree. Mingled with those exotic scents, the stench of dead things, which rotted in the jungle. And running through it all, a sense of dread— for one spine-chilling moment, it seemed as if an evil spirit of the forest had breathed upon us. In that breath, a host of shocking images: of torn bodies, of faces ripped from skulls, of sticky rivers of blood flowing from a thousand murdered men. Admittedly, I saw none of those images with my eyes, but the smell alone flooding my nostrils, generated shocking portraits of death and mutilation within my brain.

Green leaves, heart-shaped, fluttered around me by the hundred.

I gazed at Holmes' sharp profile. My goodness ... how pleasant it would be to fire my pistol into that gaunt face. How satisfying to see a bullet, travelling at three hundred miles per hour, smashing through his skull to rupture the genius' brain—*pop!* As if it was a child's balloon.

More and more leaves sped into my face. They looked like green shooting stars. And for some reason I could not stop laughter erupting from my lips at the sight of that emerald shower.

A police officer grabbed my arm. "Sir! Cover your mouth and nose! Those leaves are from the Lucifer Vine!"

The plant that induces madness! I pulled a handkerchief from my pocket before pressing it tight over my lips and nostrils. Holmes and the other men did the same. More than once, a Lucifer Vine leaf hit my face, stuck there. Stuck tight. I felt the cool wetness of its sap, tingling on my bare skin and shuddered, wondering if its power to wreck the human mind would be visited upon me.

Meanwhile, struggling through the hurricane to the building became nothing less than an ordeal. Three steps forward, then two rearward, as the wind punched me this way and that across the yard.

... two figures approached through the swirl of yellow dust ...

And now two figures approached through the swirl of yellow dust and flash of green leaves.

One I recognised. "Bullman!" I shouted through the wad of cotton pressed to my face. Thankfully, the murderous thoughts that had taken possession of my brain just a moment ago had receded. I felt sanity returning.

The giant moved toward us. His blue eyes blazed with homicidal insanity. Next to him, a woman dressed in the spotted pelts of leopards—she fixed her bright, intelligent eyes on us.

"Miss Dembe!" I shouted in amazement. "Holmes, look! It's our maidservant!"

The woman, smiling, amused by my astonishment, raised her left arm. I saw that she held a spear tipped with a long, tapering point.

"Miss Dembe!" I reached into my pocket for my revolver. "Why are you here?"

Holmes shielded his eyes against the whirl of blinding dust. "Watson! That woman isn't Miss Dembe."

"Nonsense, Holmes. She looks exactly like her!"

"See her teeth?" He took away the handkerchief that he'd used to cover his mouth and nose. "Do you recall the crescent-shaped wear in Miss Dembe's incisors? That indentation isn't present in this lady's teeth."

One of the police officers began to panic and tried to rush by the woman. She drove the spear into his belly, whereupon he fell to the ground, writhing, bleeding ... dying. Bullman used those mighty fists of his to knock two more policemen to the ground. Despite the thunder I heard the neck vertebrae of one unfortunate fellow snap like a dry stick.

"Holmes," I cried. "Remember what Bullman did on the ship! It was you he wanted!"

I raised my pistol, aiming at Bullman's heart.

As fast as those flashes of lightning, the woman lashed at my hand with the spear. Fortunately, the spearhead struck the barrel of the pistol, not my flesh. If it had, I would have surely lost fingers. Even so, the stroke was delivered with so much force that sparks shot from the metal-on-metal blow. The resulting impact sent the pistol tumbling from my grasp.

Bullman lunged toward Holmes, hands outstretched, eager to complete the mission he'd begun on the ship— to kill my friend. I flung myself at Bullman, punching that massive face. Agony flashed up my arm from the force of the strike. Even so, Bullman never even appeared to notice. He caught hold of my shoulders, whirled me around so my back was to him, then thick fingers gripped my throat, choking me. Although I struggled mightily, I could not free myself from the monster's grasp.

Held like that, I was forced to see what happened next. The woman dressed in leopard skins glided toward Holmes, the spear held out in front of her. Then she raised the spear, moved her arm back, ready to send it flying into his chest.

At that instant, a figure hurtled out of the raging storm. Within a moment, that figure stood between Holmes and the warrior. Though my eyes had begun to blur due to the lack of oxygen in my body, as Bullman slowly asphyxiated me, I recognized the figure as our young maidservant.

In a queenly manner, with a straight back, and eyes locked on the warrior's face, Miss Dembe held up her hand. "Stop!" she demanded. "I forbid this."

The woman with the spear hissed, "Stand aside. He is our enemy."

"I will not." Miss Dembe took a step toward the warrior. Both women locked eyes with each other, a veritable battle of wills.

Gradually, the storm began to die away. Bullman's grip on my throat weakened, whereupon I was able to pull free. The giant stood there, a puzzled expression on his face, like a man who'd woken from a deep sleep. Meanwhile, the thunder grew softer. At the same time, the wind dropped, dust began to settle, restoring clarity to the air again. Leaves that had been stripped from Lucifer Vines by the storm quickly drifted to earth to form a green rug in the yard.

This lessening of the storm appeared to have a detrimental effect on the warrior, for she gave a cry of frustration. Her once-fierce expression turned into one of dismay and, lowering the spear, she stepped back before raising her face to the sky to violently snarl a word in a language I didn't understand or recognise.

Then there was silence. The sun began to break through the clouds. Noticing that my pistol lay at my feet, I snatched it up before whirling around, determined to put an end to Bullman with a well-aimed shot to the head.

Bullman, however, had gone. As had that warrior figure, clad in leopard skin.

"Holmes," I muttered. "Where did they go? How could they move so fast?"

Holmes appeared unsteady on his feet for a moment. "I—I have insufficient data," he muttered. "I cannot draw a rational conclusion."

Miss Dembe's sharp eyes glanced at Holmes then at myself. She spoke calmly. "In my language, what you have just witnessed is called *juju*. In your tongue you would use this word: sorcery."

Chapter 11

Everyone, who had been in the gallows' yard at the time of the storm, moved in a daze toward the building that housed the city jail and police headquarters. Barton, the hangman, had lain on the platform in a stupor. Fortunately, he recovered his senses enough to stagger toward the building, too, dragging his grim ropes behind him, across the matt of fallen vine leaves.

We left the bodies—both those of the policemen, killed by Bullman and that extraordinary woman with the spear, and those of the men struck by lightning. They would be cleared away later.

By the time we entered the building, Holmes had recovered his composure. He immediately fixed those sharp eyes of his on Miss Dembe. The young woman was dressed in the long skirt and riding jacket of the type a modern English woman would wear. We stood in an entrance hall that was, for now, deserted apart from we three. Nevertheless, there was activity elsewhere in the building— the sound of hurried footsteps on upper floors, the echoing murmur of voices from unseen individuals: the police were, perhaps, discussing what should be done next, in view of the extraordinary events of just moments ago.

Miss Dembe gave a sad shake of her head. "I regret that I didn't arrive quickly enough, otherwise the two police officers, and the other men would still be alive."

"The other men," I pointed out, "were struck by lightning. You could have done nothing to save them."

"On the contrary, Doctor, the deaths of those unfortunates were still the work of the evil individual that controlled the storm."

Holmes said: "Now, setting aside, for now, the impossibility of a human being controlling the weather—do you know the identity of the woman and that giant of a man?"

Miss Dembe shook her head. "Clearly, the giant was a servant of the woman. As for the woman, what I would say is that there are rumors that a band of prisoners live in a secret refuge in the jungle where they have studied the spells and rituals of sorcerers that live in my country on the mainland. Moreover, it is this band of prisoners' intention to sow the seeds of anarchy here on Yagomba before toppling the government so they can take control of the island."

I couldn't help but point out that Miss Dembe was remarkably well informed.

"I rather think," said Holmes, "that Miss Dembe isn't what she seems." He turned to her. "Isn't that so?"

"That is true, Mr. Holmes. You have been very fair to me, and to reciprocate that fairness, I should tell you the truth about myself."

"Ah," said he, "I did suspect that there was much more to you than met the eye."

Miss Dembe took a deep breath, then began speaking in that clear, confident voice of hers: "My name really is Dembe. I am the daughter of a successful merchant from the mainland. Rather than lead a life of well-heeled indolence in my father's mansion, I am ambitious to learn about the world, and to pass on my knowledge to my own people, who have too long been denied the opportunity of a full education."

I said, "That is most laudable, Miss Dembe. However, it begs the question why you used the pretense of being a maidservant? Which you did so convincingly, adopting such a meek demeanor, which is clearly contrary to your real character that radiates nothing less than a powerful aura of self-confidence."

Her intelligent eyes flashed with steely determination as she said, "Doctor Watson. Look at yourself, sir. You spend much of your time in the company of the great Mr. Sherlock Holmes—aren't you the recipient of an education that is second to none while in the presence of this man?"

Holmes smiled. "Ah, that is very kind of you. Now, I take it that you sought the position of maidservant in order to observe my scientific methods and hone your own skills in logic and in rational deduction, yet you accept that magic is a fact of life, and that sorcerers can cause thunderstorms. Surely there is an insurmountable conflict between magic and science?"

Quickly, she came back with, "Might a ghost be a perfectly natural phenomenon that hasn't been explained by science yet? Might the art of the sorcerer one day become a new branch of science?"

"What?" I chuckled. "Such as transmuting lead into gold? The irrational poppycock of the alchemist has been proved to be nothing but conjuring tricks."

Now her eyes flashed with a degree of anger. "Doctor Watson. Consider the work of the Italian scientist Luigi Galvani, now immortalized in the word 'galvanise'. Before anyone understood what electricity was, he and Lucia, his wife, took the first steps to investigate that exotic power— they caused the legs of dead frogs to convulse when they applied an electric current to the muscle. Back then, in the eighteenth century, his work, apparently causing dead creatures to imitate the living again, appeared to be sorcery. However, we now take electricity for granted. There are electric motors. Telegraph messages are carried by pulses of electricity along thousands of miles of wire. Therefore, do not tell me, Doctor Watson, that we should consider magic to be nothing more than superstitious twaddle for the gullible."

Holmes scratched his jaw, clearly thinking about what she had just said. "Therefore, as men of science, Watson, we should not dismiss magic without first considering the evidence. After all, we had a demonstration of powerful elemental forces today. And there is the decidedly mysterious appearance of Bullman and the wielder of the spear."

Miss Dembe nodded her appreciation at Holmes' comment, then said, "Gentlemen, I have pressing personal matters to attend to, so please excuse me."

As she spoke, footsteps sounded on the steps. Police officers were descending from the upper floors to attend to the carnage in the yard. Perhaps the delay had been a result of them mustering their courage.

Holmes held out his hand to Miss Dembe. "You have given us much to think about. And once again, thank you. I do believe that your intervention today saved our lives."

Miss Dembe shook his hand. "My presence in the yard may well have resulted in an imbalance of the occult forces that governed the storm, causing it to lose its strength. However, I might not be so fortunate next time." She glanced at each of us in turn. "If you wish to save the city from destruction, you must find whoever the sorcerer is. Then you must destroy them."

"Really," I protested. "Cold-blooded murder is too much."

"That individual used the Lucifer Vine against you, gentlemen. When you felt its touch on your bare faces, did not your minds fill with strange ideas and fancies?"

I remembered the irrational urge to fire my pistol at Holmes and shuddered.

Miss Dembe walked toward the door. On reaching it, she paused. "Remember, gentleman, you don't have the luxury of treating sorcery as fanciful nonsense. Today, that elemental power, known, as magic, killed men and put you in great danger of death. You face mysterious weaponry that is much stronger than yours."

Later, as we rode in the carriage, back toward Baker Street, Holmes, who had been silent for most of the journey suddenly slapped the palms of both hands onto his knees and declared loudly: "Miss Dembe! What a remarkable woman she is. In fact, she is one of the most remarkable human beings I have ever met."

After that singular outburst of admiration for the woman, Holmes fell silent again. His eyelids drooped as the extraordinary engine that was his brain considered what he had experienced today.

And, despite the heat, I felt a flush of ice-cold chills through my body, because I didn't require a soothsayer to warn me that the days ahead would, for us, be very dangerous indeed.

Chapter 12

"**S**o, Watson! I am Lord of Damnation!"

"A remarkable situation in which to find yourself," I said to Holmes. "You are now ruler of an entire prison island. Your word is law. You wield the power of life and death."

Holmes had flung himself into an armchair in the sitting-room, which was such a close copy of his own lair back in what would be a chilly London at this time of year. He stretched out his long legs, his hands resting, palm down, on the padded leather arms of the chair and gazed up at the ceiling. His expression told me he mentally appraised this extraordinary turn of events.

"Let me recap ..." he murmured. "I arrive with the intention of giving instructional speeches to Yagomba's police force and legal functionaries. Now I find myself lord of all I survey." Despite the decidedly traumatic morning saving tortured men from the scaffold, the storm, and encountering Bullman and that formidable warrior, Holmes gave a surprisingly wide grin. "Imagine the story you will pen about this, Watson."

"I daresay it isn't over yet, Holmes. You heard what Miss Dembe said. There are sinister individuals on the island who are hell-bent on taking control of New London while, no doubt, intent on slaughtering all the government officials and their families here. We have our work cut out for us. Sherry?"

Holmes waved my offer of drink away with a languid gesture of the hand. "I must keep my wits sharp. There is much to consider."

"As you wish."

"Do help yourself to a glass of sherry or something stronger. You've had quite a time of it, old friend. Bullman attempting to strangle you must have shaken your nerves somewhat."

"I suffered no ill effects." Nevertheless, I poured myself a large sherry, feeling the need for a little fortification. "Strange how that monster of a man became almost human again when Miss Dembe appeared. It was as if her presence there temporarily broke some malign influence over him."

"Watson, surely you don't accept that the woman with the spear is a sorceress capable of supernaturally controlling storms and that creature Bullman?"

Taking my seat on the sofa, I murmured, "I saw what I saw, Holmes."

"Though Bullman swimming across all those miles of ocean to reach land after he fell from the ship does more than hint at occult forces." He smiled. "Yet my mind is not so undisciplined to accept that there is witchcraft at work here. No, Watson. What is at work here are those ancient human emotions of greed and the hunger for power over others."

"Then you suspect that a criminal gang of some sorts, probably prisoners who have formed their own community in the jungle, desire to overthrow the government here and claim the territory for themselves?"

"Precisely."

"With no sorcery at their disposal?"

"I don't have sufficient data, so will not speculate, despite Miss Dembe's assertion that witchcraft is present on the island."

"Yet we are dealing with evil." I sipped my sherry. "The woman didn't hesitate in murdering the police officer with her spear. And Bullman snapped the neck of another poor unfortunate fellow."

"We have brought murderers to justice before, Watson. We shall do so here."

"Miss Dembe claims that the sorcerer poses an extreme danger to everyone in the city."

"Nevertheless, I will not destroy the so-called sorcerer, as Miss Dembe has demanded. I will bring all wrong-doers to a court of law, where they will have a lawyer to defend them, and the right to explain their actions."

At that moment, I heard the cry of a newspaper vendor in the street below. Climbing to my feet, I went to the window where I opened it.

A boy, carrying an armful of newspapers, was busily selling them to passers-by. As he did so, he repeatedly cried out the latest news: "*Mr. Sherlock Holmes in charge! Famous detective is the new governor! Mr. Sherlock Holmes in charge ...*"

"Nolan moved quickly." I closed the window. "The press has produced a special edition of the newspaper in less than three hours."

"Then word will quickly spread that the island is under my authority. If all goes to plan, that will help reassure the population."

For a while, we sat in silence. The fortified wine relaxed me to the point I could make a confession to my friend. "Holmes, earlier in the gallows' yard, when the storm struck, I felt the urge to ... well ..."

"Go on."

"I wanted to fire a bullet into your brain."

"Really?"

"Such an awful thing to admit, I know. It was as if my mind had been captured by an alien influence. Terrible thoughts gripped me."

"The Lucifer Vine?"

"Indeed, leaves carried by storm winds struck me. I felt the wetness of the vine's sap upon my face."

"Clearly, the plant contains a naturally occurring narcotic."

"A powerful one, too. I am sorry for harboring such violent thoughts against you."

Holmes smiled in a friendly way. "Watson. There is no need to be apologetic. Quite simply, the chemical within the plant distorted your mental process, that is all."

"I should have fought against its influence."

Holmes sprang to his feet, to pace back and forth in front of the fireplace. "You are a doctor. You know what effect the extracts of certain plants can have on the human mind. Tea and coffee stimulate the nervous system. Consume the peyote cactus and you will experience hallucinations. Cocaine from the coca leaf accelerates the mind a hundred-fold. Secretions of the opium poppy render the imbiber comatose. The Lucifer Vine can, I venture, be added to a long list of vegetation that transforms the way one thinks, and therefore acts."

"But, Holmes ... I wanted to kill you."

"And you did not! Therefore, I trust in your resilience against narcotic influence. You are much stronger than you yourself think." He clapped his hands together in the way he so often does when he judges that a topic has been dealt with and that there is nothing more to add. Instead, that powerful mind of his leapt upon another speeding train of thought. "Now, as for Lord Delaney ... leaving the previous governor's disappearance a mystery will be unforgivably untidy of me."

"You have reached a conclusion about what befell the man?"

Holmes, still pacing the room, spoke with such zeal his eyes blazed: "Imagine, Watson, that you are Lord Delaney. You rule Yagomba. This is a penal colony of astonishing wealth, and ambition. One has to only see the opulent buildings of New London to appreciate the scope of that ambition. The problem facing you now, is that your authority is being eroded by criminal gangs, formed from prisoners who have become outlaws, and no doubt live in secret communities out there in the wilderness. These outlaws cause all kinds of mischief, so undermining your authority—and bit by bit you are losing control of the land that you once ruled absolutely. So, faced with such a situation, where you are considered to be a failure, a busted flush, a veritable weakling, what action would you take?"

"I would resign immediately."

"Would you, Watson? After all, put yourself in his Lordship's place. He knows that if New London descends into lawlessness, then possibly thousands would die. You would have their blood on your hands. Also, remember that Lord Delaney is of that class of English aristocrats that cannot bear the indignity of failing in their duty."

"By Jove ... I begin to see what may have happened. Has Lord Delaney faked his own kidnap?"

"Yes, exactly that, Watson. He did so, knowing that I'd be arriving here shortly after he vanished. Equally, he knew that I would not shirk my duty and allow thousands of civilians, even if they are convicted criminals, to be placed in danger, and that I would feel obliged to accept the role of governor in his absence."

"The man's a manipulative cad."

"My dear fellow, let us not judge too harshly. Lord Delaney was a desperate man, with no choice left, other than to put me in a position where I must become governor of Yagomba."

"Your reputation precedes you, Holmes." I drained the glass of its sherry. "The crowd at the gallows yard obeyed you today. You are, indeed, the Lord of Damnation."

"An entirely temporary occupation, I trust."

I rose to my feet. "I take it you have a plan?"

"I do, Watson."

"Then what next?"

"What *you* do next, my friend, is go to your room and take a nap."

"But Holmes-"

"Last night you were clubbed. Today, half strangled. I insist."

"Very well."

"Besides." He smiled warmly at me. "With you tucked up in bed for a while, it will give me some time to myself to consider a number of problems." He plucked the tobacco-filled Persian slipper from the coal scuttle by the fireplace and began to fill his pipe.

I said: "The people who designed the décor of this apartment were very thorough in copying your own room back in London."

"Indeed, they were." After lighting the pipe, he blew out a cloud of smoke with great satisfaction.

"But, Holmes, I can't help but ask myself what they thought of your eccentric habit of keeping tobacco in an old leather slipper in a coal scuttle."

He laughed, and when he spoke again there was a mischievous twinkle in his eye. "Doctor John Watson, you have been my friend for many, many years. You know by now that although I am quite adept at solving mysteries, I, too, am a veritable compendium of mysteries that will never be unravelled. I am a living, breathing enigma. Therefore, shall we utter *Omnia Exeunt in Mysterium* and leave it at that?"

He sat down in the armchair, chuckling to himself, while blowing smoke rings at the ceiling.

And there I left him to his thoughts. Mister Sherlock Holmes: the man who solved mysteries. Yet undoubtedly the biggest mystery of all was—indeed—the man himself. And could anyone on Earth ever unravel the Gordian knot that was his mind?

114

Chapter 13

Before retiring to bed that afternoon, I'd closed the curtain to block out the sunlight—brilliant once more after the storm earlier. The thick material of those velvet drapes meant that total darkness filled the room.

But then, on suddenly waking, how did I see those figures? What enabled me to make out details of their bodies as they strode toward where I lay on the bed? I witnessed men reaching out toward me. The fronts of their heads had been stripped of skin and muscle, so I saw the hard bone of skulls that were wet with blood. They moved closer.

"Doctor, heal me," one of those terrible figures whispered. "Heal me, Doctor Watson. They have cut away my face for other men to eat."

More figures poured into the room: men and women butchered with the sharpest of knives. Some lacked stomachs: others had suffered their arms being hacked away. A young man, with a yawning void in his chest where his heart and lungs had been, jumped up onto the bed to stand over me. "Doctor Watson. Heal us. They harvest us for our flesh."

I leapt out of bed and dragged open the curtains, hoping to dispel the nightmare—for surely I'd been asleep and dreamt all this horror, hadn't I?

Opening the curtains revealed trees passing by. Steam drifted out into the jungle. The sound of wheels on a track reached me. Distinctly, I made out the *huff* of a steam locomotive that drew the carriage I now appeared to be riding in. Had I been drugged and carried onto a train that now sped along a jungle railroad?

The door swung open behind me. A tall, thin figure rushed in.

"Holmes," I shouted. "Thank God! Wake me from this nightmare!"

Holmes lumbered forward. All the flesh above his top lip had been cut away, leaving the bloody front of the skull, exposing nasal passages. I recoiled from his staring eyes that possessed no eyelids. This horrific relic that was once my friend staggered toward me.

"I have failed, Watson!" He shouted the words from those lips that were all that remained of a once, proud and noble face. "They are now coming for you, Watson. I'm sorry, old friend. I have delivered you to your doom!"

Then, most ghastly of all, he wept. The eyes that he could never close, because they lacked eyelids, glittered with tears. Meanwhile, the men and women that had been robbed of their internal organs, flesh and most intimate of bodily parts crowded around me.

"Heal us, Doctor. Heal us!"

Holmes fell to his knees, sobbing—his brave spirit that once feared nothing on earth now broken. The man wept with sorrow.

"This is a nightmare. This is not real," I shouted. "I will wake up and you will be gone!"

The locomotive blew its whistle. The people in the room screamed their agony at the universe, knowing that they were as dead as flesh on a skewer. I clawed at the back of my hand, digging my nails into my skin, praying that the pain would wake me.

Another figure approached. The butchered men and women stood aside—a red sea of bloody flesh parting before the figure, which appeared in the form of a silhouette, revealing neither face nor their sex.

Once again, I shouted, "You are nothing but a dream!"

The figure in silhouette laughed. "Doctor Watson," they said in a clear voice that was neither male nor female, neither young nor old. "You are not dreaming. These people you see here, Mr. Holmes included, are not the product of a nightmare."

"They are!"

"No, Doctor Watson. I have allowed you to glimpse the future. What you see here is what will happen to you and your friend. And the future, like the past is immutable. What will be will be."

Chapter 14

I awoke to find myself on the bedroom floor. Just moments ago, the room had been full of men and women who had suffered the horror of having parts of their bodies cut away—some without faces, arms; others with ghastly, yawning holes in their stomachs and chests where internal organs and muscle had been removed. Huge wet wounds that had glistened most vilely. What's more, just moments ago, I'd flung back the curtains to reveal that, somehow, I rode a train that steamed through dense jungle. After that, a sinister figure had manifested itself in order to declare that what I'd seen was no dream—that I had witnessed future events.

As I lay there, gasping, heart pounding furiously, I realized I was alone again. The strangers had all gone. My room was no longer a railway carriage. This was my bedchamber. And this was a solidly built house of brick and slate. I rose to my feet, staggered to the door, where I blundered into the hallway, feeling dizzy and unable to catch my breath. The door next to mine flew open, then Holmes dashed out to support me as I began to lose my balance.

"Watson, my dear Watson! What on earth's the matter?"

"Holmes. Your face ... it was ..."

That striking face, with skin tightly covering high cheekbones, was just as it always was.

I gasped, "An uncanny figure ... in my room ... they showed me such horror. You were ..."

"There, Watson. Lean against the wall for support. I'll be right back."

He darted into my bedchamber. A moment later, he returned before taking hold of my arm, whereupon he led me to the sitting-room.

I muttered, "What did you find ... is the spectre still there? Your face, Holmes. Ruined. Destroyed ..."

My friend spoke soothingly: "There, Watson, don't worry. There was nobody in your room. Nothing is disturbed but your bedding."

"I did see people, Holmes. Cannibals had carved flesh from bodies. The spectre revealed what would happen to you ... a vision. A horrible vision."

Holmes guided me to a sofa where he sat me down. "Clearly, you believed you saw horrors that shocked you. Nevertheless, I can assure you there are no people in your room. Nor any sign you've had unwanted visitors."

"What I saw seemed so real. Victims displayed voids in their torsos—muscle had been cut away."

"Here; drink this, old chap."

Holmes held a glass to my lips, whereupon I swallowed a tepid liquid—immediately, the tingling heat of brandy brought me back to my senses somewhat.

I said, "Then those terrible visions were just that—a dream? Maybe that blow on the head? After all, it occurred just a few hours ago."

Holmes' wore an expression of compassion. "You are a doctor. Your expertise in concussion and head injury is much greater than mine. But ..."

"But what?" I recognized that look in his eye. "You've found something, haven't you?"

"Yes. I looked out of your window. A vine had crept up the wall as far the windowsill."

"The Lucifer Vine?"

He nodded.

My heart lurched again with shock. "It wasn't there earlier. I went out onto the veranda this morning. I would have noticed."

"My understanding," he began, "is that certain myths surround the Lucifer Vine. That merely being in its proximity can induce mental aberration in otherwise perfectly sane individuals. After all, you experienced its effects during the storm earlier when leaves struck your face."

"Yes, I felt the wetness of their sap. By Jove. The Lucifer Vine is aptly named. It's a wicked plant, all right."

Holmes went to a table where bottles of chemicals stood. The apartment's designers had even provided laboratory equipment to make my friend feel at home. He selected a blue bottle. "This should deal most effectively with that unwelcome creeper. First, however, you might wish to take another swallow of that brandy...." Holmes put his hand in his pocket.

"Oh?" I asked, feeling a shiver trickle down my spine.

"I found something else in your room. On your pillow was this."

He pulled an object from his pocket. It was a necklace made from the sharp teeth that might have come from the dangerous jaws of a leopard. The largest tooth was covered in shining gold leaf.

Chapter 15

That night Holmes insisted I sleep in his room, well away from the evil plant that had grown up the outer wall as far as my bedroom window. Holmes made up a billet for himself on the sofa in the sitting-room while I retired to bed at eight-thirty, whereupon I slept soundly until eight o'clock the following day. When I awoke, I discovered, to my relief, that my head had cleared of what I suspected were the narcotic effects of the Lucifer Vine.

Once again, the sun shone brilliantly on that replica of London, built on a riverside in the tropics. Hansom cabs, drawn by sleek horses, briskly traversed Baker Street. Several men and women hurried along pavements, carrying baskets of bread. Others appeared to be heading toward their offices, suitably equipped with briefcases and open umbrellas. I noted the umbrellas with some amusement, because those voluminous devices were used here to shield the heads of settlers from the hot sun, not rain. Many of those people in the thoroughfare below wore the blue jacket bearing the red X on the back, which identified them as convicted prisoners who'd been transported here from Britain. They struck me as people determined to lead honest and industrious lives as they hurried through what, after all, was a huge prison without walls. And I realized that many men and women who had committed crimes in the past would, if given the opportunity, endeavor to "turn their lives around," as the saying goes, and strive to become law-abiding citizens.

Holmes and I were served breakfast by a young gent of sixteen or so. He wore the cutaway jacket of a manservant, which bore the regulation cross on the back, stitched faintly in red. He proudly told us, "The honey is the best in the world, your highnesses. My pa has a hundred hives up there on the hill. My pa has sent jars of honey to the King of England."

Holmes smiled. "Thank you. I look forward to tasting what promises to be such a remarkable delicacy. Although you do not need to call us 'your highnesses': we are not royalty."

"I beg your pardon, my lord."

"May we know your name?"

"Augustus."

"Thank you for breakfast, Augustus."

I added, "And the tea was delicious. Strong and hot, just as it should be."

"My pleasure, sir," the boy said, respectfully lowering his head as he moved backward across the room, carrying our empty porridge bowls on a tray.

Before the boy left the room, Holmes asked, "Augustus. What has become of Miss Dembe, our usual maidservant?"

"Your excellency, she paid me six pence to cover her duties for her. Today I will bake a turtle for your supper."

Holmes grimaced slightly. "Thank you, but that won't be necessary. Much as I'm sure your baked turtle is a delight, Doctor Watson and I will be dining out this evening."

"Very good, your worship." With that, the boy left.

I smiled at Holmes across the table as he spread honey on a piece of bread. "I didn't know you'd acquired so many titles on your arrival. Your excellency? Your worship?"

"Quite an exponent of comedy, isn't he, our new servant?" Holmes said with good humour. "When he had his back turned to us, I happened to notice his reflection in the brass door plate. The lad grinned from ear-to-ear."

"He was enjoying a joke at our expense?"

"I rather think so ... then, it's always cheering to know that young people the world over are capable of humor. Even those who live in a penal colony. Jokes are what divide human beings from the animal kingdom. Moreover, humor, on so many occasions, has the power to unite us. Ah ... speaking of the animal kingdom ..."

Holmes pulled his plate sharply toward him as a baboon reached in through the open sitting-room window to snatch a pepper-pot from the table. The monkey then swung itself out of the window and up toward the roof. More baboon faces, with their dog-like muzzles and intelligent eyes, peered at us through another open window, no doubt intending more thievery. Holmes quickly closed the windows, so thwarting their nefarious plans.

I spooned honey onto a slice of bread. "Rascals, aren't they?"

"Indeed they are, Watson. Goodness knows what that monkey intends to do with our pepper-pot."

"If Darwin is correct, baboons will be wearing top hats and using pepper-pots of their own given another million years of evolution."

Holmes chuckled. "Well, setting aside speculation of the rise of baboon supremacy, we should consider today's business."

"I, for one, am going to make sure that vine outside my bedroom window is dealt with."

"Have no fear of it anymore, Watson. I cut through the stem myself. After that, I soaked the roots in sulfuric acid. What's left of the plant is wilting admirably."

"Thank you, Holmes."

"I do wonder what the effect would be on my faculties if I dried some Lucifer Vine leaves in order to smoke them in my pipe."

"Good heavens, Holmes, you'll do nothing of the sort! That vile specimen of a plant is likely to shatter your mind once and for all."

I fumed with heated outrage at such a notion of using Lucifer Vine as tobacco. That is, until I saw the mischievous twinkle in his eye.

"More tea, Watson?" He lifted the teapot.

"Holmes, you are incorrigible." I shook my head, smiling. "And if you've quite finished teasing me, perhaps you will reveal the business of the day?" I slid my cup toward him across the table.

"Ah ..." He poured the fragrant amber liquid into my cup. "The business of the day is to make myself as visible as possible to the public. The residents of New London—indeed, all Yagomba—must be confident that I really am the new governor.

"Also known as the Lord of Damnation. Despite all the finery of civilization hereabouts, this strikes me as a deeply sinister place. I still shudder when I think about that necklace of leopard teeth you found on my pillow."

"Delivered by a human hand, I'm sure, Watson, not from the reptilian claw of some demon."

"You did not find any sign of windows or outer doors being disturbed?"

"No, Watson, I did not."

"All the windows and doors were still fastened from the inside?"

"They were." He sipped tea from his cup. "An engaging mystery, though it must wait. It's time we made our rounds of the city."

What followed thereafter was a full day of riding through the streets in an open-topped carriage, so that the city's population could see the world-famous Mr. Sherlock Holmes for itself. Every so often, he asked our driver to stop in order to introduce himself to pedestrians, and shake their hands, or raise his hat to ladies in their long dresses of white muslin. Thereafter, we visited the offices of the *New London Times,* where Holmes invited a reporter to interview him, and then Holmes took great pains to speak fulsomely about the wonders of the city where he now resided. Holmes also stated how honored he was to be made governor of the island, adding that he would work tirelessly to ensure that law and order was maintained in an exemplary manner. When the interview was over Holmes posed for photographs, his expression radiating calm authority.

After that, Holmes and I paid a call to the court building to meet with judges and barristers. Then swiftly onward to the hospital, where we inspected the wards that were more than satisfactory to my medical eye, boasting modern equipment and exuding that reassuring aroma of carbolic soap, which told me that the nurses were correctly scrupulous about hygiene.

The most alarming aspect of the hospital was the fact that three secure wards were devoted to Lucifer Vine cases. The doctors escorted us through iron gates into wards where the lunatics were confined. These were people who, a doctor assured us, had the misfortune to spend too much time in close proximity to the Lucifer Vine. Chained to beds in the male ward were individuals of all different ages—yet with a singular trait in common. They had lost their minds. Some prayed loudly to some profane deity of their own deranged invention. Others ranted gibberish, their eyes rolling—lips glistening with an incontinent outpouring of spittle. One man lay flat on the bed, staring at the ceiling, while muttering over and over, "Heal me, doctor. Heal me."

I've been a doctor for many a year, treating both physical maladies and mental cases. Even so, sight of those tragic patients with ruined minds saddened me greatly. Holmes appeared troubled, too. For a man so renowned for hardly ever revealing emotion, his expression of worry was plain to see.

Early that afternoon, we left the hospital for what New Londoners referred to as City Hall. This, a large building of brownstone, stood on high ground, lending the structure a commanding presence that spoke volumes about its authority. City Hall was the seat of power in the penal colony. Earlier, Holmes had directed that an announcement be placed in the newspaper informing townsfolk that they were welcome to visit him here from three o'clock until six, to discuss any matters they thought fit to bring to the new governor. Accordingly, we entered a large office that housed the biggest desk I've ever seen. Constructed from black ebony, this magnificent piece of furniture stood on an elevated platform at the far end of the room. Again, this was a bold statement of the governor's power.

Just before three o'clock, Holmes took his place on a throne-like chair behind the desk—the office doors were opened, admitting what could be described as the "movers and shakers" of the island to speak to Holmes.

Many of the gentlemen simply wished to introduce themselves to Holmes, hand him their cards, to express their loyalty to him and the Crown, and to invite him to social gatherings. Holmes thanked each one politely as I wrote down the names and addresses of this stream of well-wishers. A number of men came with specific proposals, such as to build a high fence around New London to keep out troublesome wild animals. Others petitioned their new governor with requests for more workmen to be tasked with clearing away the ever-bothersome, and dangerous, Lucifer Vine from the town. A man in the garb of a priest beseeched Holmes to place a twenty-four-hour guard around tanks that stored fresh water for the city. The priest declared this initiative would prevent rogues from maliciously throwing Lucifer Vine into the aforementioned tanks in order to pollute the water supply. The priest wore the traditional garb of his calling, black robes and a white collar, and carried a small Bible in one hand. As he turned to leave, I noticed that he, too, wore the red cross on the back of his vestments—and so yet another man, convicted of a crime in a court of law, had very visibly renounced a life of illegality and now followed quite a different path.

Holmes spoke sincerely to each visitor, promising to consider every request put to him most carefully. At every opportunity, he reassured people that he, as governor, would ensure that the safety of everyone in Yagomba was his highest priority, and that the rule of law would be robustly enforced.

We did dine out that evening, at a hotel restaurant where we were served a very fine buffalo steak. With that substantial cut of meat came an assortment of fresh vegetables, together with glasses of a most agreeable Beaujolais wine.

We returned to our apartment just before midnight. I noted that our cab driver rested a shotgun on his lap, wary of marauding hyena packs and leopards. I'm pleased to say that we encountered none of these dangerous animals during our short journey home.

What we did encounter was a figure that flitted from the shadows as we climbed down from the carriage.

"Mr. Holmes, Doctor Watson."

The figure pulled back a hood to reveal a face.

"Miss Dembe?" I said in surprise.

"You have important information?" Holmes' shrewd eyes fixed on the young woman's face.

Miss Dembe said, "You have not heeded my warning to leave New London to save your lives. Therefore, the only way of doing so is finding the sorcerer that now plagues New London and destroying them."

"You know who this individual is?"

"No—other than they were shipped here as a prisoner."

"Ah," breathed Holmes, "then we will need to dig deeper for more information."

"However ..." she began. "I have discovered where they have hidden themselves upriver in remote jungle territory."

"Then I will go there and ..."—he gave a grim smile—"... introduce myself."

"You must understand, Mr. Holmes, it will be a dangerous journey." Then she added, "But a necessary one if you are to remain alive.

Chapter 16

Noon, the next day. Before the train departed from New London Station, two of the soldiers went mad. As simply as that. They were helping load ammunition for the artillery gun that had been mounted on a flat-backed truck at the rear of the train. One soldier fell to his knees on the platform and began praying in a bellowing voice, his bulging eyes fixed upward on the sky above him. The other soldier tore the lid off an ammunition box, and then twisted the nose cap fixed to one of the explosive shells to be fired by the artillery gun. The twisting of the nose cap armed the detonator, transforming the brass cylinder, which was the size of a wine bottle, into an extremely dangerous piece of ordnance.

The soldier raced along the platform to where Sherlock Holmes stood.

The madman raised the shell in readiness to hurl it to the ground, where the force of the impact would trigger a violent explosion. Already in my mind's eye, I saw the blast ripping Holmes and myself apart.

Just then, a shot rang out. I spun around to see Nolan there, holding a smoking pistol. The bullet had slammed through the deranged soldier's heart, killing him on his feet. As the man toppled, lifeless, Holmes had the presence of mind to dart forward, catching hold of the shell that was crammed full of high explosive.

"Quick thinking, Holmes!" I exclaimed, letting a *whoosh* of air from my lungs with sheer relief at our lives being saved.

Holmes nodded his acknowledgement of my praise as he twisted the nose cone of the shell, safely disarming the detonator once more. Then he called back to Nolan, who was placing his revolver back in its holster: "Good shooting, Mr. Nolan. That single shot of yours saved a dozen lives today."

Nolan stared at the man he'd killed, an expression of horror on his freckled face. My understanding was that Nolan served purely as a civil servant here in New London; therefore, I suspected that was the first bullet he'd ever fired at a living human being.

The bustle of loading the train continued only after the briefest hiatus while the dead soldier and his insanely babbling comrade were taken away.

Holmes had stayed up all night preparing for departure today into the interior of Yagomba. Our mission: to find the individual that Miss Dembe claimed was some kind of magician—though I suspected, in the cold light of day, that the so-called magician was purely a troublemaker who intended to sow consternation and panic amongst the population prior to launching a violent insurrection to oust the governor from office. I've known Holmes to go without sleep for two or three nights at a time when the situation demands. My friend can refresh himself with a nap of no more than twenty minutes before bounding back to work with the energy and sharpness of mind that would be the envy of a man of twenty years of age.

Consequently, as I'd slept last night, Holmes had made telephone calls, marshalled information, summoned the assistant governor, and then the head of the military, one Colonel Maltby, and had told them to prepare a steam locomotive and assortment of carriages that would carry ourselves, together with thirty soldiers, into the jungle. As the city's many church clocks struck twelve to signal noon, we found ourselves standing on the platform watching the troops in their light brown uniforms and pith helmets carrying food, casks of water, and ammunition onto the train, along with everything else we would require on this journey into what would be verdant wilderness.

Holmes watched with the alertness of a hawk—an apt comparison, considering that sharp beak of a nose he possessed as well as a pair of the most penetrating eyes I've ever seen.

"Holmes," I said, "won't your absence from New London result in social instability? After all, the assistant governor was adamant that if you weren't here at the helm, the city would descend into chaos."

"My absence will only be temporary. I intend to be back here within three days at the most. I'm sure the population can bump along without me for a while."

"I imagine you are correct, Holmes."

"Besides, I have no intention of remaining here for the rest of my days. The city will have to find a new governor who will earn the respect and confidence of the people."

"Speaking of confidence." I lowered my voice to a whisper so only Holmes could hear. "Dare we trust these soldiers? Two have gone mad before we've even left the station."

Holmes grimaced at this unpalatable truth. "I'm afraid we have no option but to trust these fellows retain their wits. We must make this journey, come what may."

Just at that moment, the engine driver put an end to our conversation by testing the steam pressure of the locomotive. Steam gushed noisily from beneath the engine to fill the station with a white fog. The smell of hot, well-oiled metal filled my nostrils, while my ears were swamped by yet another hiss of steam that gushed forth from valves. Meanwhile, the bustle continued with soldiers scrambling into one of the carriages that would house them during the journey. Some, however, opted to climb up onto the roof, where perhaps the air would be cooler.

Another huge blast of steam discharged from the locomotive, reducing visibility to no more than a dozen feet. And it was from this white cloud that a slightly built figure stepped with bright, shining eyes. The figure carried a small suitcase made from woven cane.

I stared at my friend in astonishment. "No, Holmes. Surely not. This expedition is far too dangerous."

Miss Dembe's eyes flashed—there was fire there, and the heat of sudden anger at my comment. "Do not ask Mr. Holmes to speak on my behalf, Doctor Watson. I insisted that I travel with you—isn't that so, Mr. Holmes?"

"The lady speaks the truth," he said.

"Miss Dembe gave you a map," I protested. "Surely, that is enough to guide us. Dash it all, what if—"

Miss Dembe interrupted: "I am better equipped for this journey than you, Doctor, even with your soldiers and all their weaponry."

I stood my ground. "Nevertheless. This journey will be a dangerous one. And we don't know what we will encounter out there in the jungle."

Holmes rested his hand on my shoulder—a gesture of reassurance and friendship. "Watson. Miss Dembe and I had quite a chat last night." He glanced at her. "As I suspected, she is a formidable human being. Also, dare I say it, when she removes a mask to reveal the person within, there is another mask there, concealing the real Miss Dembe. Am I right?"

"Indeed so, Mr. Holmes," she said. "Doctor Watson. When you first me in Baker Street, you believed me to be a maidservant. Then I revealed that I am the daughter of a prosperous trader on the mainland, and that I am deeply interested in science as well as poetry. However, I was also raised within my community to be a priestess—a holy woman in the service of my country's pantheon of deities. As such, I was instructed by witch doctors in the art of magic. Therefore, I know what the sorcerer you will confront is capable of. Doctor Watson, in effect, I will be your advisor on all matters pertaining to the magic, as practiced by the witch doctors of my people. Moreover, it is my belief a rogue witch doctor has instructed the individual that menaces New London in the arts of our magic, which is powerful *juju* indeed."

"I see," I said, though somewhat baffled. "Then you believe we will face occult forces during our expedition?"

"Yes, and I will attempt to shield you from harm, though it will not be easy. If our enemy has learnt well from the witch doctor, then you will face a powerful adversary, Doctor Watson. They will have the power to conjure a thousand different enemies to attack you—everything from a malarial mosquito to a rampaging elephant."

"There is no such thing as magic," I insisted stoutly.

Miss Dembe's gaze remained steady on my face. "Mr. Holmes told me that a spectral visitor to your room showed you a vision of the future, where Mr. Holmes had been horribly mutilated about the face."

"Yes ... well ... that is ..." I began in a somewhat flustered way. "A dream, that's all—a dream."

"And the necklace of leopard teeth? They were placed there in your bed as proof that your adversary can deliver a physical object into a location where you are most vulnerable—the place where you sleep. What if that object had been a scorpion? Or even a single leaf from the Lucifer Vine?"

"I ... I ..." Words failed me. Because I now saw how exposed we were to our enemy's machinations, despite being surrounded by the soldiers with their rifles.

Miss Dembe continued, "And you experienced another demonstration of occult power. During the storm in the gallows yard, you saw a woman with a spear who looked just like me. What if you were riding in a carriage with Mr. Holmes, here—however, it transpired that it wasn't Mr. Holmes after all? What then, Doctor? What then?"

Holmes' face tightened as he was gripped by an inner tension. Evidently, he saw the dangers all too clearly.

Briskly, he declared, "Then there is no time to lose. After you, Miss Dembe." He opened the door of the carriage.

"Thank you."

I offered to take her suitcase; however, she shook her head. "Thank you. I will keep it with me. You have your pistol, Doctor Watson, I am equipped with my own weapons. They will be needed to combat whoever awaits us." Before climbing into the carriage, she paused, glancing down at the soldier's blood that still formed a reddish, sticky smear on the platform.

"One of the men became deranged," I explained. "Regrettably he had to be killed in order for innocent lives to be spared."

Her eyes fixed on me. "Quite possibly one of our opponent's spies will have added a few shreds of Lucifer Vine to the poor man's food. Once they lose their minds, they can be controlled from afar. Yes, Doctor, magic. And you will see many more examples of the occult arts before we have completed our quest." She glanced at each of us in turn. "Take care of what you eat, gentlemen. Your enemies might be much closer than you think."

With that, she climbed into the carriage. Holmes and I entered after her. Miss Dembe swiftly continued along the corridor to her sleeper compartment, no doubt to unpack her belongings, as well as checking that the weapons she had brought with her (whatever they were) were safely stored.

Within moments, the locomotive whistle blew, the train lurched, juddered, and with blasts of steam and smoke, that wheeled behemoth lumbered out of the station— an engine that would carry us deep into the mysterious terrain of this island.

Holmes murmured, "We are at the start of what will, inevitably, be an extraordinary journey. Always keep your revolver close, and your wits sharp. There will be attempts to thwart us, Watson—for our foe clearly wants me dead."

Chapter 17

Themetransformation of the landscape, from the modern buildings of New London to the wilderness beyond the fringes of the city, was as remarkable as if we had passed from metropolitan order to a land of strange enchantment. To one side of the railway track flowed the Yagomba river, a mile-wide body of sluggish brown water. To the other side of the track lay tropical forest. To say that jungle was vast would be an understatement, for that ocean of green seemed a limitless universe of vegetation—tall trees, lush plants, flowers of every color. From the frothy green expanse of treetops, vultures watched our locomotive waddle along the uneven track, drawing carriages and the flat truck on which the artillery gun had been bolted. When the train wheezed around a bend, I caught a glimpse of the carriages attached to the train. A dozen men lay on the roof of one such carriage. They seemed to find the top of that particular conveyance much more comfortable than its interior. Those men were our porters, should we need to leave the train in order to strike out through the jungle on foot, although the prospect of endeavoring to penetrate that dense mass of vegetation was a daunting one. Walking through that

... vultures watched our locomotive waddle along the uneven track ...

sweltering wilderness would be immensely difficult, for there would be no roads to follow. Even footpaths would be a rarity. As for the heat? Ye gods, that humid air felt very much like a boiling hot towel pressed to one's face. What's more, the pungent smell of vegetation was nothing less than a living presence in its own right.

Holmes and I occupied a first-class carriage to ourselves. Unlike the regular layout of such a vehicle, with bench seats running crosswise, the cabin boasted an unconventional arrangement. Seating consisted of freestanding armchairs and sofas. A long table stood in the middle of the richly carpeted floor. This carriage would serve as Holmes' office as well as the place where we would dine during our travels. And it was here that Holmes sat to the table, writing notes in a book, as the carriage rattled and swayed. Our speed was quite slow, not much more than that of a trotting horse, due to the decidedly uneven nature of the track.

Holmes pulled a map from his pocket. "This," he told me, "has been drawn by Miss Dembe. She has marked on it the river, the railway line, certain villages and farms." He held up the map to show the precisely drawn features of the landscape we travelled through. "The darkly shaded area at the end of the railway line is the territory, according to Miss Dembe, occupied by a vicious company of outlaws, where we will find the individual who is a sorcerer, or poses as one in order to strike fear into the inhabitants of this island that believe in such devilry."

"Remarkable," I observed. "The map would be the envy of any cartographer. Such accuracy."

"And all to scale," remarked Holmes.

"So, that shaded area ... this is where we will find our prey?"

"In theory, yes. Although that apparently small area on the map translates into five hundred square miles of terrain that will be utterly hostile to human beings."

"Then we will have our work cut out to find them."

Holmes gave a grim smile. "I rather suspect we won't have to find our 'prey,' as you term it, Watson. Our prey will find us."

"Ah, and we may turn out to be the prey?"

"Precisely."

Those words were ominous enough to send my gaze darting in the direction of the window. Just feet beyond the glass towered enormous trees, strung together with vines. Behind any one of those towering trees, an assassin could conceal themselves with a gun. A sharpshooter of even moderate ability could kill Holmes where he sat at the table.

"Perhaps we should close the window blinds," I suggested. "You are too plainly in view there."

"If I am going to successfully coax our foe out of their lair, then their spies must plainly see that I'm riding on board this train."

"Good heavens, Holmes. You are using yourself as bait?"

"My dear fellow, I see no other option."

"That troubles me gravely," I said. "As does the fact that we have been unable to bring those vile men to justice that I encountered down by the river, herding those poor wretches into the butchery sheds, where they were cut up as if they were nothing more than farmyard beasts. I wish I'd put a bullet into at least one of those scoundrels."

Holmes noticed how angry I was and how my hands shook with fury.

"Your sense of outrage is one I share." Holmes settled back in the chair and gazed out at the greenery passing by, as the train clattered along the uneven track. "As I mentioned before, we are living through perilous days here, and if I ordered the arrest of corrupt soldiers who are dealing in human flesh, then there is a distinct possibility that the very criminal gang we seek will exploit news of the soldiers' detention and might well agitate other wrongdoers into a full-scale mutiny. Needless to say, that would be disastrous for the people of Yagomba.

140

Innocent blood would spill."

"Nolan refused to arrest those villains I encountered down by the river. Is he part of that den of corruption, too?"

Holmes shook his head. "I do believe Mr. Nolan to be an honest man. However, he knew full well that to arrest those people might well result in nothing less than civil war. Therefore, he instructed his companion to give you that tap on the head."

"Dash it all, Holmes. My blood boils at just the thought of that vile practice continuing—of human flesh being sold to satisfy the perverse appetites of so-called civilized gentlemen."

"Please don't upset yourself, old chap. I have taken steps."

"Oh?"

"New London detectives have, at my request, identified the corrupt military personnel in question. Subsequently, I asked their commanding officer, an honest fellow, I'm glad to say, to despatch all the troops connected with that evil butchery to a remote part of the island's coast to guard a rocky promontory against becoming a base for pirates." He smiled. "Of course, there are no pirates, and the rocky promontory has no strategic value. However, those butchers of men are now so far away they cannot continue their vile trade. For now, they will claim no more victims."

"But these scoundrels will be brought justice?"

"They will, Watson. And, I daresay, that many of them will hang for their crimes."

At that moment, a knock sounded on the carriage door. My hand went instinctively to the revolver in my jacket pocket.

Holmes beckoned to a pair of figures beyond the glass in the door. "Don't be troubled by our visitors, Watson. It's Mr. Nolan and the commander of the militia. Allow me to introduce him to you."

Nolan entered the carriage first, followed by a man of fifty years, or thereabouts, in the pale brown uniform of the penal colony's army. His uniform bore no army insignia that I recognized, though it was adorned with medals and what appeared to be a regimental badge made from gold in the form of a lion's head, its jaws open in a golden roar of fury. The man carried his cap in one hand, which revealed that his entire head had been cleanly shaved of every single hair, something that could not be accomplished easily, if using an open razor—his only slip was evidenced by a small nick in one cheek. His round face was flushed red with heat, and the only variation of that red flesh was the blackness of his small, precisely trimmed moustache, and his keen blue eyes that locked onto my face—no doubt this solider had the habit of getting the measure of a stranger on that first moment of meeting. I am certain that he didn't suffer fools gladly. Indeed, I'm sure he didn't relish the company of civilians, either.

Holmes introduced me to the man in uniform. "Doctor Watson. This is Colonel Maltby. We have him to thank for providing our bodyguard for this trip."

Holmes cordially invited Maltby and Nolan to sit at the table opposite him. Then, for the next twenty minutes, Holmes chaired a strategy meeting where he outlined his plans—these plans could be summed up as making all possible speed to the end of the track, some three hundred miles away from our present position, deep in the interior of the territory, where the band of outlaws would be traced, arrested and brought back to New London for interrogation, and if deemed to have broken the law, tried before a judge and jury.

Colonel Maltby had sniffed in contempt at this. "If you ask me, the damn wretches should be shot down like mad dogs."

Holmes calmly pointed out, "While I am ruler of this island, Colonel, I will scrupulously adhere to our laws. The gang will receive a fair trial."

"If you wish," Nolan said as he ran a fingertip along his moustache, as if wiping away something distasteful that had attached itself to its short black hairs.

Holmes then turned to Nolan who wore a troubled frown. Indeed, the expression "the man was miles away" could accurately be applied to him. Nolan even glanced back over his shoulder, as if hopeful that the train would abruptly reverse all the way back to New London. I sensed that Nolan did not like being away from the comforts, and the protection, of the city he loved.

Holmes spoke quite gently: "Mr. Nolan. You did us all a great service today by ... shall we say ... dealing with the unfortunate soldier who became deranged and intended to blow us all sky-high with the artillery shell."

"Thank you, Mr. Holmes." The young fellow's manner appeared distracted. He seemed to have difficulty in concentrating on the matters we were discussing.

"Mr. Nolan. Shooting down another human being is an utterly distressing experience for most. Would you care to retire to your sleeper cabin and rest?"

"Oh no, Mr. Holmes. Please excuse me if I've seemed somewhat at a distance. I won't let it happen again."

"Do you have the timetable for this journey?"

"Yes ... yes, of course." Nolan fumbled in the pockets of his jacket. "Um, please bear with me, while I ... um." He pulled out various slips of paper from his pocket, searching for the required item.

Holmes, rising to his feet, moved behind the men seated at the table, while glancing down in a compassionate way at the young man, who covered half the table with old railway tickets, and bits of paper of all sorts of shapes and sizes. Meanwhile, the train lumbered along a bridge, which crossed a number of streams that fed into the big river to our left. Colonel Maltby clicked his tongue impatiently as Nolan struggled to find the timetable amongst the clutter he'd placed on the table.

"Ah, I have it." Perspiring, Nolan held up a sheet of paper bearing a list of what appeared to be stopping times and places. "This journey isn't part of the scheduled service, of course. We have the train entirely to ourselves. However, I thought you might find it useful, Mr. Holmes, if you knew when we would be stopping for meals, and when and where we would spend the night before continuing tomorrow."

"Can we not eat as we travel?" asked Holmes. "Indeed, we should sleep on the train while it continues on its way—thereby completing our journey as swiftly as we can."

Nolan shook his head. "That's not possible, sir. There is no means of preparing cooked meals while the train is in motion. And it would be too hazardous to travel during the hours of darkness, as the driver cannot see ahead. Unlike your modern locomotives in other parts of the world, our machines are somewhat primitive in comparison."

"I see."

I added, "This stop-start business rather hinders our progress, doesn't it?"

"Even if we fixed lanterns to the front of the engine, it would be unsafe to travel by night, Doctor Watson."

Colonel Maltby added, "As you might imagine, there are some prisoners who refuse to abide by the laws and chose to cause all kinds of mischief—including taking up sections of railway track. If our driver cannot adequately see ahead in the dark, then we risk being derailed."

Nolan said, "There is also the question of Lucifer Vine."

"Lucifer Vine?" I echoed in surprise. "How can a fragile plant possibly endanger the train?"

"The plant grows across the track."

"The growth wouldn't be dense enough to hinder the train, though, surely?"

"You don't understand, Doctor. Wheels shred the plant, throwing sap into the air in such a fine state that airborne droplets would be inhaled by passengers on the train. With unfortunate results."

"You mean, we might all go mad?"

Colonel Maltby laughed. "Stories regarding the Lucifer Vine are rather exaggerated." He gave a regretful sigh. "Although my men tend to believe all too readily in plants

144

that crash one into lunacy. Come to that, they believe in all kinds of tales of witchcraft and ju-ju."

Holmes stood at the window, gazing out at water buffalo wallowing knee-deep in a pond. White birds perched on the beasts' massive backs, pecking insects from black fur. And above in the trees, Asian gibbons squabbled with African macaque monkeys. This island, I observed, had become a seething cauldron of flora, fauna from the four corners of the world, together with all types of humanity, flung carelessly into the same pot without regard for potentially dire consequences.

At that moment, the note of the locomotive's engine changed.

Holmes glanced back. "It very much sounds as if we're coming to a halt now."

Maltby said, "I gave orders to stop at a supply station, to take on more coal for the locomotive."

"We've only been travelling for two hours."

"That is so, but the next station is quite some distance away. We need to replenish fuel here, lest we run out in this godforsaken wilderness." Maltby shook his head. "That, gentlemen, has happened to me before, and it is far from pleasant being stranded on board a dead train in the middle of nowhere."

Gradually, the train rumbled to a stop, hissing—wheezing.

Maltby held up a finger as an idea occurred to him. "While we're waiting, Mr. Holmes, perhaps you will entertain us?"

"Entertain you?" Holmes said with surprise. "What on Earth do you wish me to do?"

"Why, sir. What you are world-famous for."

I spoke up, protesting on my friend's behalf. "Mr. Holmes doesn't give demonstrations of his powers of deduction for the purposes of mere amusement."

Maltby glanced sideways at Nolan, who sat beside him at the table. "Nolan. What do you say? Shall we test Mr. Holmes' skill as a detective?"

Nolan had begun gathering together the pieces of paper that he'd scattered across the table, no doubt intending to return them to his pockets. However, he paused this activity in order to reply to Maltby's question. "I'm sure Mr. Holmes prefers to rest. I gather he was up all-night making preparations for the expedition today."

Holmes appeared a little put out by Nolan's hint that he was not "up to the job," as the saying goes. "Mr. Nolan, rest assured: my mind is as clear as mountain air. Besides, you told me that you were keen to hear my lecture on detection."

"Yes, I am. I don't think there is a man in all the world who is as skilled as you."

"Yet you now praise me without a shred of sincerity." Holmes turned to glare at the man. "In fact, your praise of me is completely false."

Nolan turned in the chair so he could look back at Holmes in surprise, even with a touch of anger. "Why do you accuse me of that? You are a genius. I don't believe there is a single task you can turn your hand to which would end in failure."

"No?"

"No, Mr. Holmes."

Perhaps it was the heat, or even over tiredness, but I'd rarely seen Holmes so quick to take offence at what seemed gushing praise. Colonel Maltby, it must be pointed out, smiled. He was enjoying what appeared to be the beginnings of a fiery argument between the two men.

Holmes clasped his hands behind his back as he stood by the window. "Mr. Nolan, you have faith in me?"

"Yes."

"Liar."

"Sir, that is a false allegation. I do not lie when I say I have faith in you."

Holmes' sharp eyes bored into Nolan's face. I have seen that expression of my friend's before. The same look a hunting dog assumes when it sees its prey at its most vulnerable.

146

"Mr. Nolan. Here is a demonstration of my powers of observation. This morning you told your wife that you have no faith in my ability to govern this island. What's more, you fear that New London will descend into anarchy. You, sir, are afraid for your wife's safety. Not only did you tell her so, but you have also taken practical steps to help her protect herself if there is an outbreak of civil disorder. What I say is the truth, isn't it, Mr. Nolan?"

Nolan stared at Holmes in absolute shock, his mouth hanging open. "How ..." he stuttered. "How do you know what I told my wife in the privacy of our own home?"

Holmes nodded in triumph, pleased that he was right. "I shall tell you. You slept poorly last night because you were worried about your wife being left alone when you accompanied me on this journey." Holmes touched his eyes. "The signs are on your face for all to see. Redness here, dark rings beneath the eyes. You rose early, dressed in the dark, so as not to disturb your wife asleep in bed."

"How can you know all this?"

"Is it true?"

"Confound it, yes!"

"One of your shirt buttons is fastened in the wrong buttonhole. A common mistake when dressing quickly in the dark. You then left the house, rushed to the nearest gunsmith's, and bought two pistols. One, a large caliber weapon for yourself, which you used most skilfully earlier." Holmes' air of command grew as he spoke, his sheer presence dominating the carriage, discouraging anyone from moving so much as finger, let alone speaking. He continued in that swift, precise way of his. "You also bought a small caliber pistol that would be light enough for your wife to use if she felt threatened by would-be intruders, should law and order collapsed in your absence.

Nolan leapt to his feet, his face turning as red as a strawberry, as he shouted, "Yes, it's all true! How can you know this? You must have spies, or ... or recourse to witchcraft."

"Or recourse to my eyes, sir." Holmes spoke gently now. "When you pulled out that veritable snowstorm of papers from your pocket, I noticed the anxious way you stared at one slip of paper—that was a receipt from a gunsmith. I saw today's date. I also could make out that you bought two pistols. A .45 Webley, and a .22 Hunslett. You also purchased a dozen cartons of ammunition for the .22 revolver, which you gave to your wife before leaving today. Such a large amount of ammunition states plainly that you fear your wife will be forced to fight for her life, while you are away from her. Which brings me back to your belief that I cannot be trusted to be an effective governor, and that society will collapse into violent anarchy and rampant bloodletting."

Nolan sank back into the chair, his head in his hands. "I'm sorry, Mr. Holmes. I love my wife and I am frightened for her safety."

"Please trust me, my friend." Holmes spoke in that same gentle manner he had used just a moment ago. "I have left the police force with strict instructions that they must maintain law and order at all costs. Your wife will be safe."

Colonel Maltby showed his appreciation of the deduction by thunderously clapping. "Bravo, Mr. Holmes, bravo. Capital. It was as if Nolan's skull became as clear as glass and you could see right inside his head and read the chap's thoughts."

"I observe clues," Holmes remarked. "Even the smallest of clues can tell me such a detailed story that a thousand words would not compare to what I can glean from, say, a cut on a man's face."

Maltby flinched. His hand rose to scab clinging to the upper part of his cheek.

Holmes moved around the table, until he faced Maltby. "It's also an extremely interesting little mystery," murmured Holmes, "that a man I noticed to be right-handed when I met him last night, should be left-handed today."

Seconds ago, Maltby's pink face had been all smiles. Now his expression turned to one of fury.

Maltby growled, "You are making fun of me."

"You wanted to be entertained by my methods of observation and deduction."

"You see nothing in me, sir." Maltby sat at the table, his hands clenched into fists before him. His anger grew by the second. "I am a closed book to you."

Holmes sighed. "On the contrary. I see that you are a man of fifty years of age or thereabouts. You've been shaving for, I daresay, thirty-five years, yet you clumsily slice off a mole that's high on your cheek above your bristles—a mole that will have been there for decades. Even if you didn't have a mirror to hand when you wielded the razor, you would realize that the mole was still there. That fleshy nodule was part of your face after all."

"Right-handed," snarled Maltby. "You said I am right-handed. What makes you believe I have switched hands?"

"Right-handed men shave the right-hand side of the face more cleanly than the left. I see you've missed some stubble hairs on the right-hands side of your face, whereas the left portion of your face is smoothly shaved of all hair. Odd that, isn't it? That you should decide to use your left hand to hold the razor this morning."

"There is no law against using a different hand."

"No, Colonel, there is not. Although a right-handed man opting for the left does seem peculiar, for he will lose his usual dexterity."

Nolan frowned. "Mr. Holmes, I'm not at all sure what conclusion you draw from the cut mole and the Colonel using a different hand to grip the razor."

"Ah." Holmes fixed the Colonel with a penetrating gaze. "The inescapable conclusion I have reached is that Colonel Maltby here, is, in fact, no longer the Colonel Maltby I met at his home last night."

Maltby sprang to his feet, turning over the table as he did so in nothing less than an explosion of movement. He clenched his hands tightly into fists and held them above his head, but this was not so much a gesture of victory, like a sportsman signaling "Look at me. I have won!" No, this gesture was much stranger, almost a ritualistic sign of the kind a priest from some obscure religion might make. Then this! A most shocking sight—the man's expression changed to one of such gloating contempt: one that blatantly proclaimed his certainty that Holmes was a weakling that he could snap with his fingers, then cast aside the mangled remains as if they were nothing more than a filthy old rag that was loathsome to his touch.

The man hissed, "Mr. Sherlock Holmes. You bring your own trivial conjuring tricks to Yagomba, but here you will face real magic. You will be brought to your knees by forces you have never experienced before." He laughed, his eyes blazing with nothing less than the ecstasy of a someone who knows they wield absolute power. "Mr. Holmes, before I grant you the mercy of death, you will weep, and you will beg. That is before I take control of you and order you to kill Doctor Watson here with your own bare hands."

Nolan backed away from Maltby. "The Colonel's gone mad."

"No, he hasn't," Holmes said. "Seemingly, his mind has been beaten down so that another can replace it." He pointed at Maltby. "Isn't that right, whoever you are? Because I know you crave to see the government of this island toppled. Its officials slaughtered. But I, Sherlock Holmes, swear that will not happen."

Colonel Maltby opened his mouth to emit a vile, purring voice. "You are already too late. Why do you think I ordered the train to stop here? Gentlemen, this is where the journey ends for you." With that, Maltby picked up a chair before hurling it through the window, shattering the glass. After that act of destruction, the man raced to the broken window where he called out in a huge, booming voice. "NOW! DO IT NOW!"

Chapter 18

Colonel Maltby's full-blooded yell of "Now! Do it now!" was an order to attack the train. Men dressed in quasi-military uniforms of mottled green fabric appeared from the bush-covered slope to our right. They were armed with rifles, and they immediately began firing upon the train. Bullets struck wooden panels with a loud *clunk* while other bullets smashed windows in the carriage.

Holmes shouted, "The carriage walls are too flimsy to stop the bullets. Take cover behind the table!"

Maltby had upended the table just moments ago, so Holmes only had to turn that heavy piece of wooden furniture so that it formed a barrier between us and those murderous pieces of lead that punched through the carriage to strike chairs and cabinets.

Holmes, Nolan and I took refuge behind the table that now lay on its side.

Colonel Maltby, however, stood in full view of the attackers shouting encouragement: "My people! Kill them! Destroy every last one!"

Above the din of gunshots from the hillside, I cried out, "The man will be killed if he remains standing there in clear view of the snipers."

"I agree, Watson." Holmes rose to his feet. "And the man will only be of value to us if he remains alive."

"Holmes," I shouted. "You cannot reason with him!"

"I don't intend to."

As Holmes bounded toward the window, Maltby turned to face him, his eyes blazing with excitement. "Mr. Holmes. You only have moments left to live. Tell me how it feels."

Holmes answered by way of a swift uppercut to the man's ample jaw. Holmes is an adept boxer and the punch knocked Maltby cold, the soldier immediately collapsing to the floor with a huge thud, whereupon Holmes swiftly hauled the unconscious fellow behind the table where we crouched.

Nolan helped drag the man the last few inches, making sure he was protected by that stout barrier of oak that formed the tabletop.

"Mr. Holmes," panted Nolan, "you made the correct decision. The carriage timberwork can't stop the bullets; this table can."

Even as Nolan uttered these words, speeding rounds from our enemy's rifles tore through the thin panels of the carriage walls before thudding into the tabletop where they split the planks. But they did not pass through—if they had done so, we would have been killed for sure.

I drew my pistol now, firing back at the men who popped up above the green mass of bushes to discharge their weapons at us.

"My revolver is no match for rifles," I shouted.

"My opinion exactly," Holmes replied. "It's time we gave back as good as we are receiving."

Nolan ducked as a bullet splintered the edge of the table. "Why aren't our soldiers returning fire?"

"I suspect that our friend Maltby here, when he was no longer his rational self, gave strict instructions to his men not to retaliate, even when people were shooting at them." Holmes raised himself into a crouching position, still sheltering behind the table. "If Maltby wakes up, knock him on the jaw. It's better for all of us if the fellow sleeps through this."

"Holmes, where are you going?"

"I'm going to order our troops to take part in this merry little battle before we're over-run." With that, he sprinted along the carriage toward the rear of the train as bullets struck, shattering windows, exploding lamp fittings, and ricocheting off metalwork with a piercing scream.

Nolan raised his pistol. "Perhaps we can spoil those chaps' aim." With that comment, he fired the pistol through the window in the direction of the figures that wielded rifles with such devastating skill. Our adversaries definitely knew how to use their weapons to deadly effect. In the space of five seconds, two men fell dead from the carriage roof. These poor unfortunates were porters that Holmes had hired to carry our supplies, should we need to move through the forest on foot. Now they lay dead at the side of the track; their spilt blood, however, still dripped through holes in the roof that had been left by bullets. Both Nolan and I fired our revolvers at our attackers. To my profound disappointment, our handguns were ineffective at that distance. I doubted if I managed to hit a single one of those determined sharpshooters.

Then, thankfully—gloriously—our soldiers on the train began firing back. Volleys of powerful rifle shots sounded from the trucks and carriages adjoining ours.

The firepower was so devastating that most of our attackers fled, back under cover of the bushes. Not all were fast enough. Several men threw up their arms in agony before toppling into the dirt, bleeding, their chests heaving, as blood loss and the trauma of the ferocious effect of the bullet smashing through their bodies robbed them of their lives.

"By Jove!" I hollered at the top of my voice. "Holmes has done it! He's persuaded our men to open fire."

Then the big artillery gun joined our shooting party. This weapon spoke with a very loud voice indeed. The gunner, no doubt directed by my friend Sherlock Holmes, fired explosive shells into the bushes. Each time a shell struck solid ground, a fierce explosion blasted greenery aside to expose bare earth. When the smoke cleared, I saw dreadfully maimed enemy riflemen—they either writhed on the ground, or lay still, smashed to pieces by the detonation of shells filled with gunpowder.

The door to our carriage opened and Miss Dembe sped toward us. Bullets smashed through what remained of the window glass as snipers endeavored to target this new arrival. Her eyes flashed with determination as she sped toward us.

I yelled, "Get down behind the table."

Nolan reached up, grabbing her arm, and tugging her down to the relative safety of our makeshift fortress. More bullets punched through the flimsy carriage walls to embed themselves in the table. I could smell burning as the wood began to smoulder from all those hot metal rounds that had lodged themselves into the oak. Quickly, I fired my revolver back at men who had ventured from the bushes to fire off well-aimed rifle shots.

That was their last act as mortal men, for an artillery shell exploded directly in front of them—fragments of the shell's metal casing struck their faces, chests, throats, releasing a spray of blood that created a red mist around them. A second later, they all lay motionless upon the ground.

Colonel Maltby abruptly sat up. He smiled when he saw Miss Dembe. "Ah, I rather hoped my assassins would have despatched you before now."

Miss Dembe glared at the man. And I suspected she already understood that a hostile intruder resided behind the military man's pink face. "Whoever you are, I know that you have learned your magic from a rogue witch doctor of my people. I have my own weapons that will defeat you." Miss Dembe glared into Maltby's bloodshot eyes—yet once again, it seemed as if she did not speak to him ... no, she addressed another personality that had invaded his mind: "You would do well to surrender to Mr. Holmes immediately. He promises you will receive a fair trial."

"Ah, Mr. Sherlock Holmes." The voice that purred from Maltby's lips was one oozing with hate. "I am acquainted with that interfering meddler. It's a pity that my servant did not kill him on the ship. But then one's plans don't always work out as one hopes. However, in the meantime ..."

Maltby lunged at Miss Dembe, his hands grasping for her throat.

The clunk of my pistol striking the man's shaved head was a loud one. Instantly, Maltby flopped down, as limp as a discarded jacket.

Miss Dembe looked up at me. "There, Doctor Watson. You know the truth—a sorcerer imposed their will on the Colonel. He became their puppet."

I stared back at her, wanting to refute her assertion with scientific logic, yet before any words reached my lips the carriage gave a lurch.

Nolan immediately shouted with relief: "The train's moving! We shall leave those swine behind!"

My gaze remained on Miss Dembe's calm face. To disagree with what the woman had just told me wouldn't be easy.

The click of wheels on the iron track quickened as the train picked up speed. Presently, the rifle shots petered out before finally stopping. We were safe. For now, that is, because I could picture danger ahead of us: as if the threat we faced was a blood-red light that pulsed ominously in the jungle at the end of this journey—a journey that was already stained with the blood of so many violent deaths.

Chapter 19

The battle had been a tumultuous one. A hail of bullets left our carriage in quite a poor state—broken windows, holes in walls, shattered lamps, splintered chairs. Bullets had even raked white lines in the dark blue carpet that covered the carriage floor. Events after the battle were tumultuous as well. If Holmes expected a quieter time of things, for at least a little while, he would be utterly mistaken.

The train rattled along at thirty miles an hour or thereabouts, easily outrunning our enemy, who appeared to be on foot. Consequently, they stopped their shooting as soon as we had passed from their view. The hillside, covered with bushes, rose ever more steeply to our left. To our right, the muddy-brown river. Every so often, I glimpsed the monstrous form of a crocodile lazing on the riverbank. Sometimes the great head of a hippopotamus would break the water's surface as the beast rose up to gaze at the passing train. And, it must be said, monkeys are truly ubiquitous on Yagomba. They swung through the branches above the speeding train or moved in orderly troupes alongside the tracks. Constantly, baboons hooted their annoyance at the noisy locomotive that thundered through their green world.

Nolan and I attempted to tidy up the carriage, mainly by the expedient of throwing shards of glass through the broken windows. Miss Dembe had already set the fallen chairs upright. I did likewise with the table—the tabletop, itself, now boasting an interesting display of bullets of various caliber embedded in its woodwork.

Holmes bustled back into the carriage. "No one is hurt?" he asked.

We assured him we hadn't suffered so much as a scratch. "Maltby is sleeping soundly," I said. "Although I did have to tap him on the head after he woke up."

Miss Dembe was now busily rolling up the flapping window blinds, for the breeze gusting through broken panes caused the blinds to whip furiously. Upon noticing that Holmes had re-entered the carriage, she strode toward where we were standing. Once again, I was impressed by the sheer strength of her character.

Forcefully, she said, "So, you all now believe that Colonel Maltby has become possessed?"

Hesitant, lest I appear to be a believer of sorcery, I chose my words carefully: "Um. Well. The Colonel certainly gave the impression that his body had become the puppet of another individual's mind."

Miss Dembe glared at me. "Everyone here heard a stranger speak through the Colonel. It happened again when he recovered consciousness. Mr. Holmes, will you tell me that you believe that the mind of another individual took control of the Colonel?"

Holmes, placing the fingertips of both hands together, raised them until they lightly touched his chin as he considered Miss Dembe's extraordinary question. After a moment, he answered: "My experience of life runs to many decades now, and I have witnessed many remarkable sights; so, even though I consider myself an analytic reasoner of some renown, who am I to reject, out of hand, supernatural phenomena?"

Miss Dembe's expression softened as she nodded her gratitude at Holmes, pleased he hadn't dismissed her statement, and that he intimated quite clearly that he was not scornful of her beliefs.

Holmes continued in that brisk way he adopted when asking questions: "On that second occasion, after the Colonel awoke, what words did he use?"

Miss Dembe said: "Whoever it was, speaking through the Colonel, remarked that they hoped that their assassins would have killed me by now. Also, they knew about you, Mr. Holmes. In fact, they used the word 'acquainted.'"

I added, "And Maltby knew that Bullman attempted to kill you as we travelled to the island by steamer. However, he may have learned about that from other passengers, so ..." I allowed my voice to trail away, realizing that I did not need to finish the sentence.

Miss Dembe evidently divined from my expression a clear idea of what I was thinking because her voice rose in anger. "Oh! Doctor! You do not believe me that occult forces are work here!"

Holmes said, "It is important that I am fully acquainted with all the facts. Now ... on that second occasion, did Maltby adopt a voice distinctly different to his own?"

Nolan shook his head. "No. However, the way he delivered his words were different to how he would normally speak."

"Then the poor chap is probably unhinged," I said (my scientific instincts oh-so-powerfully resisted the outlandish notion that magic existed in the modern world). "After all, suggesting he is somehow controlled by another human being from possibly dozens of miles away is not possible."

Miss Dembe erupted. "Sir! I grew up in a community where magic is a regular occurrence. I have seen witch doctors control men's minds from afar. I have witnessed those witch doctors place a curse on a man, then I watched that man crawl into a hut to slowly die. Because you, yourself, have never witnessed such a thing, or read about it in one of your medical books, does not mean that it is impossible!"

"I have seen many strange things," I remarked. "They are always capable of rational explanation."

"You!" she thundered at me. "You, a man of medicine, of intellect, a man trained to identify symptom of illness. How dare you close your mind to the facts you have witnessed with your own eyes. Recall, sir, the storm on the day those men were supposed to hang. You saw a figure, diabolically moulded to resemble myself, appear before you. You saw the man they call Bullman. He even attempted to throttle you."

When I spoke it was with, I must confess, ice-cold stubbornness. "I have encountered mysterious occurrences, but I am a modern man of the twentieth century. I do not believe that human beings can conjure storms or invade the brains of others."

Her eyes glittered as she looked at each of us in turn. For the first time, I anticipated that emotion would get the better of this formidable woman. Yet when she spoke it was in tones that demonstrated her absolute iron grip upon her feelings: she was very clear; very calm. As the train rumbled along the track, the hot tropical air streaming in through the shattered windows, Miss Dembe spoke these words: "Mr. Holmes. Doctor Watson. Mr. Nolan. I have seen spirits rise from sacred lakes, I have seen demons emerge from forests to kill entire families ... no, Doctor Watson, let me speak. Magic, in my homeland, is as real as the rain that falls from the sky. Forest gods can be seen as clearly as one sees an antelope walking across a sunlit clearing. I grew up believing in the legends of our people. I believed in our ancient gods. And when I fell in love with a boy from a rival clan, when I was sixteen years old, I did something that you will find utterly vile, yet I did what was asked of me without question, because that was the way of our people. You see, my father found out about my love for the boy. My father killed him, and he brought his head home in a sack. My father cut flesh from the boy's face and told me to eat it. Because if I did that I would not be troubled by my lover's spirit. Naturally, I loved my father, too, and obeyed him, and did what must be done. Not long after that, I became a voracious reader of both poetry and scientific works. And I realized that I didn't have to live my life as my parents and ancestors had done for thousands of years. Gentlemen, I embraced science, logic, reason. Although I still believe in my ancestors' gods, I rejected the notion that they wield authority over me. And I believe in democracy. That is to say, we all have power over our lives, yet in order for civilization to function, we all willingly lend a portion of the power we have as individuals to a democratically elected representative, who will help govern a nation that benefits all of us, not just a royal elite."

She paused when the locomotive's whistle blew. Glancing out through the window, I realized that the driver had sounded the whistle in order to shoo wildebeest from the track in front of the train.

In firm, but understated tones, she continued, "I am prepared to carefully consider, and judge, all your beliefs; therefore, you should at least consider the validity of some of mine." With that, she sat down in an armchair that displayed holes from several bullets fired just moments ago in that dramatic battle.

I said: "Magic, sorcery, demons, forest gods; the ability to control men like this fellow here from afar?" I glanced down at the unconscious form of Colonel Maltby lying on the floor as I said this.

"Yes."

Again, my rational instincts protested this wholesale acceptance of occult shenanigans. "That is rather a lot to ask."

"You must," she said with a grave expression. "Because if you don't accept that the supernatural exists, then you will underestimate your enemy's power over you. They possess weapons that you cannot possibly begin to imagine. Moreover, if you do not believe that the threat of the occult is real, then the sorcerer will destroy you easily

161

because you will have not accepted that I bring with me defenses against curses and demons."

Clearing my throat, I raised a finger, ready once again to forcefully state that I did not give credence to such unearthly things, but Holmes interrupted before I could give voice to my disbelief.

"Miss Dembe." He spoke gently. "Forgive us. It is difficult to accept that wicked spirits and the like are real. However, I promise to keep my mind open. I appreciate that whether or not we return from this adventure alive might well depend on trusting what you say is the absolute truth." He nodded at her. "Therefore, from this moment on, I will not reject what you say. For the duration of this trip, just as I have armed myself with a revolver, I will arm myself with your rock-solid belief in the forces that are, so far, inexplicable to science."

"Thank you, Mr. Holmes. That is reassuring to hear. I hope Doctor Watson and Mr. Nolan will follow your lead." She looked at each of us in turn. "Because your lives will depend on my protection."

Chapter 20

olonel Maltby woke up with an extremely severe headache and having no recollection of the fierce battle waged just hours ago, or indeed anything which had happened since meeting Holmes last night. And although the man must have realized that he had taken a blow to the head (there was quite a bump on his bald cranium due to my rapping the butt of my pistol upon his skull none too gently), he did not ask any questions about what had happened to him. One suspects that, in the way which seems so peculiar to the English, he simply preferred not delve deeper into an occurrence that might suggest he was prone, as he might perceive it, to a "mental weaknesses" of some sort or other. The English, it must be said, are rather fond of the phrase "let sleeping dogs lie" and are quite happy to live according to the rule of that strange maxim.

So Maltby remained stoically silent as he sat there, holding his tender head with both hands.

What was clear to us was the fact that Colonel Maltby was Colonel Maltby again—and whatever, or whoever, had taken control of his mind had departed, for now anyway.

SIMON CLARK

The train, meanwhile, continued its clattering progress alongside the river. By this time, dusk wasn't that far away. Soon we would have to stop for the night before taking refuge under mosquito nets. For it is at night that those pernicious flying insects emerge from swampy places to bite living creatures. Humans are especially vulnerable to their bite. The itching spot they leave after feeding on our blood is nothing in comparison to the malaria that might then infect the unfortunate human being.

By the by, with regard to Colonel Maltby, I should add that earlier, Holmes and I, together with Nolan and Miss Dembe, had all agreed, while Maltby was still unconscious, that no mention would be made to the man of him being possessed. After all, to tell the man that his mind had fallen under the control of another wasn't likely help matters one jot; so, for now, we would keep him in the dark. Nevertheless, as a precaution against this piracy of his mind occurring again, and to ease the ache in his head, I dosed the man with morphine. I then instructed him to go to his sleeper cabin in the adjoining carriage, where he could take refuge beneath mosquito nets, secure in the knowledge that the drug would make him sleep soundly, and free of that monstrous headache, until morning.

Maltby's departure to his bunk left the three of us in the carriage that bumped along the uneven track. Holmes sat in an armchair beside one occupied by Miss Dembe. I took a seat at the table. The train's jerky progress made writing difficult. Even so, I did what I could to pen an account of the day's dramatic events.

Miss Dembe spoke calmly to Holmes. "You have not eaten human flesh?"

Holmes shook his head. "Never. Though I suspect the effect on one's emotions are much stronger than those on one's stomach."

"Indeed so. Often as a child, I was fed the flesh of our nation's enemies that were killed in battle. This was the custom observed by all members of our society. In

164

truth, human flesh has an addictive quality. Once you have eaten human flesh, you crave more."

"I hear that devourers of their fellow man claim that it gives them a great sense of well-being and strength."

"Indeed so—most cannibals believe they consume the essence of their victim's mind and soul, too."

Holmes absorbed this information. "Do you still eat human flesh?"

"I am now twenty-two and have not tasted it since I was seventeen." She paused, suddenly looking troubled as she sat in the armchair. "Though, I confess I still crave to eat human flesh. I think about doing so every day."

I said, "Then cannibalism is as addictive as opium?"

She glanced away, trembling with shame. "I ate flesh from the man I loved. My father told me that if I did consume the substance of my lover's body I would not be haunted by his spirit." A tear formed in her eye. "My father lied to me. Barely a night goes by when I don't see my lover in my dreams, and when I wake, I grieve all over again, and my soul burns with sorrow."

After a pause, Holmes spoke gently. "Miss Dembe. Knowledge is a formidable weapon in my armory."

"I'm sure that it is, Mr. Holmes. I have read Doctor Watson's narratives about your cases."

"Then you will appreciate that the more I know about my adversary the better equipped I will be to defeat them."

"You wish to question me about the magic practiced by my people?"

"That would be most useful to me."

"Please ask whatever you deem necessary."

"Thank you." As he sat in the armchair in that gently swaying carriage as it rattled and clunked along the iron track, he placed his fingertips together as he considered what questions to ask. "Does your family belong to a priestly class?"

"Yes."

"Both female and male family members are priests?"

"Only female."

"Your mother is a priestess?"

"Yes."

He nodded. "I see. And you were raised to be a priestess, too?"

"Indeed. But I rejected all sacred duties and privileges when I went to live in New London."

"I take it, Miss Dembe, that the role of priestess in your former community confers great authority."

"Absolutely. And that authority is derived from the use of witchcraft. Whoever is weaving magic here will have ordered those renegade prisoners to fire upon the train in the hope of killing everyone on it, including myself. And, believe me, that authority will have been absolute—the men would not have been able to refuse the order. Their minds would have been possessed by an evil power, just as we saw with the Colonel."

My blood ran cold. "Then we should expect more attacks?"

Miss Dembe nodded. "Oh, they will come, Doctor. And in extraordinary ways that you cannot possibly anticipate."

Holmes' expression became even more serious. "Therefore, I suspect that the assault on the train by men with guns was a crude show of strength—meant as an appetizer, as it were, before the main course of death and destruction was served."

"Evidently, our enemy is vicious, and will stop at nothing. Mr. Holmes, at the risk of repeating myself ad nauseam, you are the only man who can save the citizens of New London."

I said, "My friend here is a formidable man. I trust him with my life. However, what makes you believe he has the ability to thwart this anonymous despot's ambitions?"

"Mr. Holmes' intellect is second to none. If he cannot stop them, no one can."

Then Holmes spoke in that quick, clear way of his when making a vital observation, "Miss Dembe, you are testing me."

"Testing you? I have no idea what you mean."

"Ah, your eyes are full of youthful innocence. Yet you know exactly what you are doing."

"Mr. Holmes," she protested. "I am depending on you to save my life, too."

"Perhaps. Perhaps." He abruptly stood up in order to pace back and forth in the carriage, hot breeze flowing through broken windows. "The truth of the matter is that you intend to put science, logic and rational thought to the ultimate test. In short, you are pitting me, whom you perceive as the very essence of the rational man, against the individual you believe to be a sorcerer—an individual who is the very essence of ancient magic. Is that not so?" His sharp eyes locked onto her face. "This is your experiment, Miss Dembe. The sorcerer and I are your laboratory rats that you will test to destruction."

"You judge me harshly, sir."

"No, I do not condemn you. In fact, I admire your calculating mind as well as your machine-like ambition. It is you who has chosen this gladiatorial contest where science and magic will fight to the death."

Miss Dembe rose to her feet. Tall, graceful and with the posture of a queen, she gazed with cool eyes at Holmes. "Yes, you are correct." A ghost of a smile flitted over her face. "As you yourself might put it, Mr. Holmes: won't this be a delicious battle? You, a man of science, using his knowledge as a weapon to fight the ultimate duel with an opponent who is armed with the primeval arts of sorcery."

I stood up so sharply I nearly knocked the table over at which I'd been sitting. "Holmes? Miss Dembe?" Horror, nothing less than pure horror, chilled my skin all over, as if I'd been dipped into icy water. For the expressions on the faces of both my friend and the woman shocked me more than I could say, because when Holmes and Miss Dembe looked at each other an understanding passed between them. They were two people with a single shared thought. Excitement blazed in their eyes. They both loved the promise of the challenge to come: the duel between

167

Holmes and the evil magus. Science vs. Magic. The agent of logic pitted against the unpredictable maelstrom of occult forces.

At last, I managed to splutter these words: "Holmes. This is more dangerous than you can imagine. You will be entering unfamiliar territory, both literal and metaphorical. Your enemy will have all the advantages."

"On the contrary, my dear Watson." Eyes flashing with delight, he stabbed his right forefinger against the side of his head. "I have this! The most powerful weapon in the history of the world!"

My friend's ecstasy was terrible to see. At that moment, I understood that this was the battle he'd been born to fight. All his work as a detective, all the scientific disciplines he had instilled within himself—all that, together with his own sense of shining destiny, would be brought to bear in the greatest battle of his life.

Mr. Sherlock Holmes was going to war.

Chapter 21

After Sherlock Holmes' extraordinary conversation with Miss Dembe, I decided to get some air. The train had just moments ago stopped for the night, so it was a simple enough matter for me to open a carriage door before stepping down onto the stony earth that formed the foundation of the railroad track. Meanwhile, Holmes had gone to speak with the soldiers that accompanied us. He wanted to be certain that a sufficient number of men would stand guard at night—after all, although we had outrun those hostile outlaws who had attacked us earlier, there might be other members of their fraternity stationed along the track with the somewhat disagreeable intention of taking a potshot at us at the first opportunity.

By now, the sun had almost reached the horizon, sending a flood of blood-red light along the river. Already the green of the jungle that covered the valley's sides turned slowly black as those millions of trees became immersed in the gloom of approaching night.

The locomotive's fires were out, its steam expended from the boiler. The huge engine resembled a sleeping beast now. The only sounds I heard were the croak of frogs in the river mingled with the shrieking call of a monkey in a tree. Soon mosquitos would emerge from their lairs to sip the lifeblood of man and beast alike. I lit a cigar in the hope that tobacco smoke would discourage insects from dining on the red stuff that circulated throughout my own veins.

I strolled along the length of the train as the evening grew progressively gloomier. The distinctive stick-thin figure of Holmes was clearly visible as he stood on the truck that carried the artillery gun, which had had seen off our attackers earlier in the day. Holmes spoke to the soldiers, and although I was too far away to hear his words, I noted that the men listened to him with the utmost respect. They would obey him. Indeed, I firmly believed they'd willingly follow him into the jaws of death, if he so asked.

Meanwhile, the porters made up their own beds in one of the carriages, arranging mosquito nets about them to keep the pernicious insects at bay. These men wore the blue jackets, bearing the red X, that marked them out as prisoners. Like most of the other prisoners on Yagomba, transported here by the British government, they were well-behaved and had seemingly embraced the opportunity to lead honest lives, albeit on a tropical island, far away from the land where they were born. There is much to be praised about second chances. And those men in the carriage, smoking their cigarettes, reading their newspapers, chatting amongst themselves appeared, to me, to be quite content with their lot.

As I stood there, gazing out across the river, the daylight ebbing away, I could only marvel at my friend's unique personality. Earlier, when he realized that the time would soon come when he would pit his rational mind against the irrational forces of the supernatural, he had visibly demonstrated such a thrill of excitement. Then I knew only too well from past experience that he became easily bored if he had no mystery to solve, or no battle to fight against evil. Holmes was always disappointed if he found that his opponent was a feeble one. Holmes absolutely needed strong opponents to test his mettle. A powerful opponent was like a hard stone on which he could sharpen the blade of his intellect. On many occasions I've seen Holmes become so mired in boredom that he prefers to inject cocaine into his body—dangerous exhilaration for him is preferable to that of a safe life which most of us prefer.

Equally, I knew that the next few hours would become extremely hazardous. I hoped that Holmes' eagerness to do battle with such a formidable enemy wouldn't make him forget that he was as mortal as the next man—a bullet from a gun, or swipe of a dagger would still have a devastating effect on his body if they found their mark. Therefore, I resolved to stay close to my friend, my pistol always within easy reach.

By the time I'd finished my cigar, thousands, perhaps even millions, of insects were hovering above the river—so many insect wings flapping at once created the illusion that a pale mist hung suspended above the water. Soon those vicious little devils would go in search of blood to sup. Time to retreat beneath the mosquito nets, where we should be safe from the infuriating (and dangerous) little pests. To my relief, I saw Holmes walking in my direction.

Briskly, he said, "We've ample men to stand guard. Four will stand watch for an hour while the others sleep."

The whine of flying insects grew louder as they began to buzz around my ears. "I think it timely to bed down for the night under the nets. Our blood-thirsty little friends are arriving."

He slapped his bare wrist where a tiny bug had settled. "You're right, Watson. After you."

I climbed back into the railway carriage, Holmes following.

I said, "Miss Dembe has already retired to her cabin ... you know something, Holmes? She really is a remarkable woman."

Holmes nodded. "Switching from pagan priesthood to worshipping at the luminous altar of science. Quite a turnabout, eh, Watson?"

"And it is reassuring to know that she is our ally, but having said that, do be careful, Holmes. We are literally on a voyage into the unknown."

"I shall be as alert as a hawk." He smiled, though his eyes revealed that he was in a deeply serious frame of mind. "Truly, I know that you care about me, old friend. So, be reassured, I will tread carefully, because I suspect that we will experience much strangeness and horror in the days to come."

After bidding each other goodnight, I went to my sleeper cabin—a little room in a long line of such rooms that filled one carriage. Upon opening the door, which led off from the corridor, I discovered that the outer wall was picturesquely decorated with bullet holes. The hail of gunshot had been devastating earlier in the day. Already mosquitos were using these little round holes as doors to enter my sleeping quarters. After lighting a candle, I quickly swatted the airborne intruders with a rolled-up newspaper. After that, I tore strips from the same newspaper, scrunched them into little balls and, using a pencil, poked them into the bullet holes to effect a temporary repair. At least those little blighters could no longer employ those routes to enter the cabin in order to drill their needle-sharp probosces into my skin.

As soon I'd divested myself of my clothes, and changed into a nightshirt, I clambered onto my bunk where I carefully lowered the mosquito nets. That done, I checked my netted enclosure to make sure that no unwanted bedfellows had sneaked in. I'd left the candle burning in its holder on a shelf in the hope that even the subtle fumes of hot wax would discourage bugs from entering the carriage.

The day had been an exhausting one; therefore, I was relieved to lie down on my narrow bunk. Sleep, as maybe expected due to my profound weariness, came extremely swiftly.

When I awoke, the candle had burned itself out. Darkness filled my cabin, the warm air utterly stifling and my neck slick with perspiration. I eased the bedsheet down from my chin to halfway down my chest. Many people in the tropics reach for a cold gin and tonic when the heat is oppressive. This, however, often creates more problems than it solves, for alcohol is especially dehydrating in hot climates.

In that sultry hour of the night, wild dogs yelped in the distance. A bird screeched most unpleasantly, signaling powerfully that it suffered pain or injury. Time and again, I turned over, endeavoring to find a more comfortable position, as well as a cooler portion of pillow, that would allow sleep to blissfully steal me away for a few more hours until morning. Of course, when one wakes in the early hours, one is apt to be besieged by all kinds of thoughts and memories, as well as feeling the urge to make plans for either the near future or for more far-off times. I confess what troubled me as I lay perspiring on the bunk, listening to the calls of savage beasts in the jungle, was how Sherlock Holmes had declared quite firmly to both Miss Dembe and I that he would accept the existence of the supernatural. Now, let me say this isn't like Holmes at all. He is scornful of magic; he laughs with disbelief when someone tells him they have seen a ghost. He will have no truck with demons, sprites, vampires, banshees, hobgoblins. I do not believe in the supernatural, either, and ever since I witnessed Colonel Maltby's bizarre behavior earlier when he appeared (*appeared,* I repeat!) ... when Maltby *appeared* to be possessed by some external force, I assiduously listed rational explanations for such behavior in my mind: had Colonel Maltby been drugged with a hallucinogen? Were his bizarre ravings due to a bout of heatstroke? Or had some tropical disease inflamed his brain? In fact, there is a superabundance of medical conditions that might explain why he appeared to be in the grip of some outside influence. During my profession as a doctor, I have examined patients, suffering from some psychiatric disorder or other, who have claimed with great seriousness to be none other than Napoleon Bonaparte, or the King of Siam, or some other famous individual from history.

Out in the jungle, a monkey expressed its own primate thoughts by hooting loudly in the darkness. And the greater the effort I made to go back to sleep, the louder my own thoughts clamored within my skull. Again and again, I asked myself why Holmes behaved in a way that was alien to his usual manner. It troubled me deeply that my old friend had declared that he would not dismiss the occult, and that he had opened the door of his mind to the fact that magic might well exist.

"Holmes, my dear Holmes," I muttered to myself in that superheated darkness, "to say such a thing is so unlike you ... therefore, what could explain that profound transformation in your behavior?"

My thoughts became even more troubling. What if a man could indeed be controlled by another individual's mind? But what if that possessed man and his companions did not realize that this was so? Wouldn't it be a much more dangerous state of affairs when the parasite's decisions seemed to be the decisions of the host, and ideas were subtly whispered into the host's mind in such a way that they seemed to be the host's own ideas?

I sighed. No, I told myself, lying awake worrying about the possibility of parasite minds and what mischief could be wrought by taking control of another person's thoughts was not productive at this hour of the night. It was important that I should be properly rested before continuing the journey tomorrow, when I would need my wits about me.

"Come on," I whispered to myself. "Time to sleep."

And, of course, I remained steadfastly awake. The air became more stifling. Thoughts about opening a window were attractive ones. However, to do so, would allow a legion of mosquitos into the cabin.

Those minutes—those sleepless nocturnal minutes that seem so much longer than their daytime counterparts— crept by. And then (I cannot accurately say when I first noticed it) the scent of a flower reached my nose. Although subtle at first, that scent became relentlessly stronger.

"I wish I was at home. I wish I was with my wife." Suddenly, the image of her smiling face appeared inside my head with such clarity that I sat upright in my little tent of nets. "Now, here's an idea.... I could pull on my boots, run back along the track to the city, board a ship for home." Saying the words aloud caught me by surprise. "By Jove." I pressed my clenched fist to my lips to prevent myself from speaking out aloud again in such a peculiar manner. I sniffed the air. That perfume of blooms prickled my nose. Then ... a sound ...

A hiss ...

Slither. Slither.

The sound of an object furtively sliding across a dry surface.

"Snake, damn it." I spoke the words aloud to myself. "England. Cool rain. Green fields." Once again, I pushed my fist against my mouth, embarrassed that I'd said such odd words, as if some peculiar force compelled me to make strange utterances.

Slither. Click. Rustle ...

The scent of flowers became chokingly strong. My eyes watered. I sneezed—once, twice, three times!

"Doctor Watson. Do you not like your necklace of leopard teeth? They will protect you against Miss Dembe's wicked spell."

"Who said that? Who's there?"

I stared hard into the darkness, whereupon I received such a shock that my heart felt as if it lurched upward into my throat, because there, just two or three feet away from me, a human head manifested itself: barely visible, and yet ... and yet ...

... a powerful presence. Menacing. Frightening. Threatening.

I reached out to touch the material of the mosquito net hanging down. Fingers belonging to another pressed against the material from the other side meeting mine. With a yelp of dismay, I wrenched the drape aside. The darkness meant I could see nothing, other than indistinct, shadowy forms, and perhaps in my panic I only imagined those, for the cabin's interior was utterly without light. By touch alone, I located a box of matches on the table beside my bunk. The second I struck the head of the match, light flared brightly, indeed dazzlingly so.

"Dear God."

My cabin had been invaded.

"They're coming through the walls!"

I leaned out from the bed, holding the burning match high, filling the room with radiance, my eyes bulging at what I saw snaking into the cabin. Lucifer Vine—dozens of tendrils, sprouting leaves, ornamented with tiny pink flowers. They had pushed out the little pellets of newspaper that I'd used to plug the bullet holes. Now, through each hole, a green vine wormed its way through. Even as I watched, I saw a bullet hole extrude a tendril, which then flowed down the carriage wall, then across the floor toward my bed. What I'd initially identified as fingers pressing inward from the other side of the mosquito nets was more of the Lucifer Vine that had climbed, ivy-like, up the fabric, searching for a way into my small tent where, no doubt, it would weave a death mask of greenery across my sleeping face.

After lighting a candle, then using the barrel of my pistol to push aside vines that had crept into my boots, I pulled on my footwear, and rushed out into the corridor to raise the alarm. For I realized that the other cabin walls would be peppered with holes, too, punched through by those high-velocity rifle bullets. What I recalled only too clearly at that terrifying moment was that the Lucifer Vine has an evil reputation for causing madness. Even now, I might be too late to save my traveling companions.

I pounded on doors. "Wake up! Wake! We are in danger!"

176

Miss Dembe opened her door first. She wore a white gown that reached down to her ankles. Holmes' door opened with a bang. Already the man was explosively awake, ready to deal with any threat we faced. I also noted he was fully dressed; therefore, he must have decided to sleep in his clothes, no doubt anticipating that the train would be attacked again during the night.

Holmes' powerful gaze locked onto my face. "Watson, what's wrong?"

"The Lucifer Vine. It's in the train!"

Miss Dembe's eyes flashed. "I told you that our foe is cunning!"

Holmes pounded on a closed door. "Nolan! Wake up, man! You are in danger!"

When no answer reached Holmes, he shouldered open the door. I followed Holmes into the small compartment where Lucifer Vine covered the bed. Nolan lay there, wrapped in sinuous strands—an eerie mummy-like figure, encased head-to-foot in green death.

"Watson, help me!"

Holmes began stripping away the plant from Nolan's face. I immediately began to assist, too, working from the feet upward. Meanwhile, Miss Dembe dashed back to her cabin.

"He's still breathing," I remarked. "Although I shudder to think what effect the plant has had on his mind after being wrapped in the hellish stuff."

We tore the plant away from Nolan. Soon both Holmes and I had sap from torn leaves dripping from our hands; thorns punctured our fingertips. But worse—much worse—was still to come

I froze as I saw my wife glide through the wall. She smiled at me. "You do know that I'm dying, John? I kept the diagnosis secret. I didn't want you to worry ... not yet, anyway." Her smile became even sweeter, and she raised her arms in the way she did when she wanted me to embrace her. "John. There is only one person in the world who can save me." I blundered toward her,

Nolan lay there, wrapped in sinuous strands....

stumbling over vines that covered the floor, and I put my arms around her, this wonderful woman whom I love so much. And as I embraced her, she whispered into my ear: "Kill Sherlock Holmes. Then the person you seek will remove this disease from my lungs."

"Kill Holmes?" I whispered back to her. "No. Never."

"Please, John. This disease hurts. It hurts so much." My wife cried out in pain, her eyes growing ever wider with the shock of that agony—her staring eyes fixed on mine. My poor darling suffered, that much was clear. "Dear husband of mine. You must kill Sherlock Holmes."

At that moment, she slipped away from me; yet I was determined not to be parted from her, so I lunged forward, intending to hold her to me once more. However, I collided with the wall, through which those tendrils flowed like loathsome tentacles. Confused by the sudden disappearance of my wife and utterly disorientated, I tottered backward, my hand pressed against my forehead

Holmes grabbed hold of me. "Fight, Watson, fight! Don't let madness win."

"I saw her," I gasped, trembling from head-to-foot. "My wife is gravely ill."

"You were hallucinating." Holmes shuddered as he ran his long fingers through his hair; a gesture borne of nervous agitation. "I ... I have seen things, too—*dreadful* things. They're not real. The narcotic effect of the plant ..."

"How is Nolan?"

"I cannot wake him. We are too late."

Just then, a strong female voice cut through the stifling air. "Here. Drink this."

Miss Dembe handed a small glass bottle to Holmes, then another identical bottle to me.

"What is it?" Holmes asked.

"An antidote to the Lucifer Vine. The drug will work once; therefore, this is the only time you can use it."

Holmes muttered, "Drink, Watson, drink. It's our only chance."

I put the bottle to my lips, tipped it up, drinking that small amount of clear liquid in one. The tincture was so utterly sweet that my throat muscles clenched immediately upon swallowing. Miss Dembe, meanwhile, held Nolan in a sitting position as she poured the liquid into his mouth.

She said, "The drug should already be working."

"What is it made from?" I asked.

"Just water."

"Water?"

"Water left in a sacred place where the gods of my ancestors reside."

Holmes didn't comment on such a strange statement. Instead, he nodded. "Thank you, Miss Dembe."

How can I describe the effect of the drug—if it can be truly described as a drug? Recall the sensation of drawing a comb through your hair—the feel of the teeth passing through those strands of hair. Now imagine that you could pull a comb through your entire body from scalp to foot. That's how the drug felt. A most unusual sensation—and a powerful one. There was a strong impression that the Lucifer Vine's poison was literally being combed out of my body. My mind became clear again within seconds. I felt my muscles relax as nothing less than relief surged through me. I saw that Holmes had experienced the same effect.

Happily, Nolan opened his eyes, looked up at us in surprise and said, "Good heavens, what on Earth goes on here? And who dumped all these weeds onto my cabin floor?"

Chapter 22

After clearing the Lucifer Vine from the sleeper cabins, we returned to our diminutive tents, formed from mosquito nets, in order to catch a few hours' sleep. Holmes doubled the guard, and had the men equip themselves with lanterns. He then ordered them to walk back and forth along the full length of the train to make sure that pernicious vine did not return as we slept. By what means how, I don't know, but the plants must have grown literally inches by the second. When they had invaded my cabin, I'd seen them moving through holes left by the bullets as quickly as a snake can glide along the ground. Fortunately, the vines didn't return that night. Miss Dembe had said little more after providing us with the antidote to the madness-inducing venom of the plant. It was clear to me, though, that she suspected that the evil magic of our foe had conjured Lucifer Vine from the soil, making it grow so swiftly in order to invade the train.

Before retiring to my bunk, I had taken a moment to check on Colonel Maltby, whom I'd dosed with morphine some six or seven hours ago. The man slept like a baby. His cabin was the only one that hadn't been struck by bullets, therefore the deadly vine hadn't been able to find an entrance.

Luckily, none of us appeared to have suffered any ill effects physically, or indeed mentally, after that close contact with the plant. I daresay I suffered emotionally, however. That vision of my wife, declaring that she was dying of some dreadful illness, unsettled me. At the earliest opportunity, I decided to despatch a telegram to her to satisfy myself that she was still as healthy as the day I departed from our home in London.

The following morning, the sun rose into a clear, blue sky and, as it did so, the jungle quickly came alive with all manner of brightly colored birds that fluttered from branch to branch, whistling and calling to their avian brethren. As ever, the ubiquitous monkeys, sitting high in the greenery, chattered to one another in between mouthfuls of ripe fruit and berries, while down at a more earthly level, fawn-colored antelope of the most graceful kind, with long, slender legs and glistening coal-black eyes, came down to the river to drink.

After breakfast, Holmes insisted on climbing up onto the locomotive's footplate to stand with the driver. I checked that my revolver was in my pocket before joining him in that oily compartment just behind the engine's boiler. Already white vapor hissed from pipes, which ran between gauges that measured steam pressure and so on, while the morning sun gleamed upon steel levers that would govern the speed of that iron monster, which now grunted and hissed as the enormous force of something as simple as boiling water built up within the engine.

Nolan ran alongside the track to the locomotive, calling out, "Mr. Holmes. Everyone is on board."

"Thank you, Mr. Nolan," Holmes called back. "Are you travelling in the carriages, or up here on the footplate with Doctor Watson and myself?"

"I'd very much like to join you."

"Then step lively, sir. It's time we were leaving."

The young redheaded man climbed the steps onto the footplate.

"It's going to be a snug fit," I said. "There are five of us up here." I nodded in the direction of the driver, a white-haired man, with a sunburnt face from which a pair of pale blue eyes shone as innocently as those of a choirboy. Beside him stood a muscular fellow, sailor tattoos covering his bare arms; it was his job to shovel coal into the firebox. "We need to stand well back to allow these two gentlemen to do their work."

When Nolan had tucked himself into a corner of the footplate, where he wouldn't be in the way of the driver and stoker, Holmes reached forward to tap the driver on the shoulder—the man had been studying a pressure gauge. "Ready when you are, driver."

"Aye, sir," said the man, pulling back a lever, then turning a brass wheel, causing steam to whoosh from beneath the front wheels of the train. After that, he tugged at a chain loop above his head. This sounded the whistle. Birds, startled by the noise, flew up from the jungle that formed a green ocean of plant-life that surrounded us.

The train began to roll forward on its iron track, swiftly gathering speed until the point it attained such an exhilarating velocity, I had to remove my hat lest the gusting air blew it clean off my head. Holmes leaned sideways from the driver's cab, his piercingly sharp eyes studying the way ahead. The man suspected that danger might lay at every turn in the railroad line. Evidently, he wanted to be here on the footplate in case he needed to react instantly to attack.

I glanced at Nolan, who seemed none the worse for being engulfed in the Lucifer Vine the previous night. Moreover, rather than looking under the weather, as I would have expected after such a visceral experience, Nolan was bright-eyed, excited in demeanor—so much so, that I suspected he thrilled at the notion of embarking on this next stage of our adventure with none other than

Mr. Sherlock Holmes. In short, Nolan actually appeared to be enjoying himself!

Meanwhile, scents of smoke and the hot, oily workings of the steam engine filled my nostrils. The forceful breeze, caused by our rapid transit through the forest, couldn't be described as refreshing—however, that flow of air was preferable to the stifling hot fug that was permanently present beside the river. I noticed that animals loitering on the track ahead of us darted into the forest when they heard the clanking approach of what must have seemed a strange metal beast to them. Monkeys, antelope, jackals, warthogs, buffalo—they all moved aside as we approached.

By now, trees were a green blur as we hurtled along, which no doubt prompted our driver to turn to us, his blue eyes bright with alarm. "Hold on tight, sirs. We're going a fair old pace."

Holmes shouted over the clatter of steel wheels on the track. "You look concerned. Is everything all right?"

"It's the speed, sir. This locomotive has never moved as quickly as this."

"Is there a fault with the machine?"

"No, sir. Leastways not that I can tell." He tapped a gauge that resembled a clock face, yet it possessed just one trembling needle. "Steam pressure ain't excessive, yet we're accelerating as if we have maximum pressure in the boiler." The man's eyes gleamed with a mixture of fascination and horror. "It's like some force, other than steam, is drawing us along."

Holmes nodded. "Be vigilant, driver. If you see anything ahead that makes you suspicious, brake immediately"

Nolan said, "Mr. Holmes, do you believe that this is our enemy's doing?"

"In view of the lack of a rational explanation to the contrary I must say that is exactly what I believe."

I gripped onto an iron frame that supported the cab's roof. "They conjured Lucifer Vine out of the ground. I'd swear on my life that is what happened. The plants moved as quickly as serpents." Even as I spoke the words, I realized that I, too, had now finally embraced the notion that a sorcerer could wield an occult power over the natural world.

"You're right, Watson," said Holmes. "All of which means we are dealing with a formidable foe." The train vibrated as its speed increased. "Now I believe that our enemy is so eager to confront us in a final battle, they are drawing the train toward their lair faster than it could ever go in normal circumstances."

"Then that devil, whoever they are, has the advantage!" I had to shout above the locomotive's roar. "He or she intends to do battle with us at a time and a place of their own choosing!"

"I agree." Holmes once more fixed his eyes on the way ahead. "They will be mustering their forces and planning their ambush. We must be on our guard because they could strike at any moment ... and without warning."

Chapter 23

The train stopped briefly on one occasion to take on water from the river running alongside the track. Initially, the driver feared that his machine had run away from him and would not respond to the brake lever, bearing in mind its headlong speed. However, to his surprise, he succeeded in halting the engine. After that short stop we continued to move swiftly along the jungle-clad valley. If anything, the air became even hotter as we travelled deeper into the sweltering interior of Yagomba. We saw no people, only creatures of all different kinds—flamingos, cranes, hyenas, baboons, colobus monkeys, antelope, water buffalo, and many, many crocodiles basking on the riverbanks; those monstrous reptiles exuding such an air of menace. Vultures flew in circles, high above the railroad. Seemingly, those vultures, the devourers of carrion, had somehow foreseen that the occupants of the train below them might soon become their supper, and wished to keep us in view.

By this time, we had exchanged the engine's noisy footplate for the increased heat, yet greater comfort of our carriage. I confess, as I sat there with Holmes, Miss Dembe, Nolan and Colonel Maltby, I pondered upon those troubling visions I had seen in the last few days: I remembered my nightmare where Holmes wept for forgiveness in front of me, with part of his face cut away. Last night, I was sure I had witnessed my wife appear to me, as if she were a phantom, to reveal to me that a disease was slowly killing her. Despite the torrid atmosphere, I began to feel cold as I sat there in the swaying carriage.

Though I did experience a degree of emotional and physical discomfort, I did not neglect to cast a professional eye on Colonel Maltby. Just a few hours ago, the man had been possessed by a force of pure evil. He had been nothing more than a flesh-and-blood marionette, a puppet operated by a sinister individual that we still needed to identify. This morning, to my surprise and my relief, he had awoken with a clear head and in good spirits, and Nolan had confided in me that Maltby did appear to have returned to his normal self. Even so, I would keep a watchful eye on him, just in case he displayed signs of any ill effects from his experience, or, more alarmingly, if he showed any indication that his mind was being submerged beneath the will of our foe once more. At that moment, I realized that I had begun to accept the supernatural powers that had taken control of Maltby. Perhaps it was the heat, but my own skepticism with regard to the occult was evaporating. In the face of there being no scientific explanation of what had occurred, what option did I have? Other than believe in the impossible.

At that moment, Nolan stood leaning out of one of the windows that had been shattered by gunfire yesterday when our train had been ambushed. The man turned his head to look at us. "We're running into foul weather. There's a very dark cloud ahead."

Miss Dembe joined him at the window. "The witch doctors of my people have power over weather," she stated with calm certainty. "If our foe has become an exponent of that magic, then this is their doing."

Colonel Maltby and I went to the window, too. Ahead of us, the top of the valley slope was already covered by dense, black cloud. Thunder rumbled and a moment later heavy raindrops began to strike the carriage roof.

Holmes remained seated at the table. He'd occupied that same place for the last hour, eyes closed, deep in thought, preparing himself mentally for the battle to come, and seemingly oblivious to our conversation. Of course, Holmes listened. I've never known a man so aware of what was happening around him. He noticed everything. Missed nothing. Always as alert as a cat hunting its prey.

Then:

"My good God!" exclaimed Maltby.

Nolan pointed. "Did you see that?"

Holmes opened his eyes, though remained calmly seated.

"By jingo," I added in astonishment, for we'd just seen a dazzling bolt of silver lightning strike the top of a tree not fifty paces from the train. Smouldering branches cascaded down to the ground from the exploded tree trunk.

Miss Dembe's eyes gleamed with undeniable intensity. "They are demonstrating their power."

Maltby stared at the young woman in alarm. "Are you saying that those fiends can hurl lightning at us as if ... as if ..." The man struggled for the right words. "As if hurling spears?"

"Indeed, Colonel. Our foe commands this storm. Lightning bolts are their weapons."

Maltby retreated from the window before sitting heavily on a bench. "Then we cannot defeat them, can we?"

Nolan shouted as he pointed: "There! Another one! Just look at that!"

This time the lightning bolt struck a water buffalo that waded in the marshy fringes of the river. The animal arched its back until its spine formed what must have been an agonizing U-shape. Its muzzle pointed upward, its mouth opened wide in pain, eyes bulging in shock at this death-strike from the sky. A second later, the big bovine fell lifeless, its hide steaming. The skin had split open from neck to haunches to reveal blood-red flesh.

Maltby cried out, "We'll be next—mark my words! That devil will kill us next!"

Holmes spoke with serene authority: "I think not."

Nolan shouted, "Open your eyes, man! Lightning bolts are striking the ground at either side of the train. There … there! Another tree has been struck. My God, it's been split down the middle from top to bottom."

"We're next," wailed Maltby, pressing his hands to his eyes, so he would not see the spear of electricity that he knew would strike our carriage at any moment.

"Our enemy toys with us," Holmes said. "If he or she had wanted to hurl lightning bolts at our carriage, they would have done so by now." He glanced at Miss Dembe. "Is that not true?"

"Yes, Mr. Holmes. So far, the intention has been to terrify us."

I glanced at Maltby cowering on the bench. "In part, they are succeeding."

Holmes nodded. "Like a cat playing with a mouse that it has caught, our foe intends to torture us mentally. Where we live in a constant state of anxiety, where we believe we might be fatally struck down at any moment."

Just then, lightning savagely blasted a dead tree beside the track, causing the dry wood to burst into flames—a tower of fire that blazed with Biblical symbolism. A warning to go back? Or to surrender to our enemy's will? Did they believe that we would fall to our knees, begging for mercy?

Holmes, of course, was, as the saying goes, made of stronger stuff. He remained sitting there calmly, observing that unnatural storm. A bolt of electric blue even struck the river, making it foam up all white. Crocodiles opened their long jaws, studded with sharp teeth, and roared up at the threatening sky—the reptiles could have been shouting "HURRAH!" at that demonstration of occult power.

I went to the window, and Holmes joined me— we looked out at the burning tree as smoky branches detached themselves from the trunk.

Holmes murmured. "Curious."

I turned to him. "A dashed sight more than curious," I exclaimed. "The sheer force of lightning! The way it can ignite a tree in less than a second!"

"No," murmured Holmes. "The sign nailed to the tree." He read what was written on a wooden board in white paint. "Charlington Crossing."

I looked at the sign and echoed, "Charlington Crossing. Possibly the name of the ford that allows travelers on foot to cross the river." I frowned as I noticed that Holmes appeared to find the name compelling for some reason— and so compelling he could not take his eyes from it.

"Holmes," I asked. "Charlington Crossing? Is the name significant?"

"Hmm, let us see … as yet, I have insufficient data."

A moment later a heavy branch, afire with purple flame, fell from the tree trunk, smashing the wooden sign into oblivion.

Then a terrible sight. My beloved wife ran from the bushes as the train rumbled by. She gave a scream that vibrated with such horror. Then the blue flame of lightning struck her head. Her entire body vanished in a burst of steam.

Clenching my fists, I growled, "That did not happen. My wife is in London. I am being forced to see something that is not there." Yet my heart ached painfully at such a sight, even if it had been perniciously delivered to my mind, not my eye.

Holmes immediately put his arm around my shoulders, concerned for my wellbeing. "Watson, sit down old fellow. You look ghastly."

"I'm all right, Holmes."

"Do you believe you hallucinated?"

"Something of the sort, Holmes … my dear wife … she was there…." I rubbed my face, shuddering. "Of course, she wasn't … not really. My wife is at home in England. No doubt sitting in our living-room and grumbling about the London rain, while …" I'd attempted to make light of

191

what had happened, yet I simply could not find sufficient words. The way her body had seemed to vanish in a gust of white vapor had appeared so distressingly real that my throat muscles had tightened to the extent I could not speak properly.

Miss Dembe clasped my hand in hers. "Doctor, we must take care. Our enemy will show us scenes, possibly dreadful scenes, that aren't real. This is all part of their plan to destroy our peace of mind."

"Before the devil destroys our bodies," added Colonel Maltby with a bitter laugh that suggested his mind might not be as well-balanced as it was a few days ago. "Great Scott. I wish I was back in England now, enjoying a tankard of cool ale in the Woodley Tavern...." His eyes became distant in the way that happens to us when we realize that something is amiss. "No ... not Woodley Tavern. Whatever made me say that? The White Stag Tavern. That's where I meet my friends. Ah, this damn heat—it melts the memories right out of one's skull. I even forgot the name of my favorite watering hole. Woodley Tavern ... where on earth did I get that name from?"

"Where indeed?" murmured Holmes, and I could tell that he mentally stored the words that Maltby had uttered about the tavern, as if they had become a valuable clue.

Seeing the horrible vision of my wife being struck by lightning was so ghastly that my mind was swimming with all kinds of troubling thoughts, and I couldn't concentrate on any one thing—nevertheless, I did find myself intrigued by Holmes' apparent interest in the sign on the tree, spelling out 'Charlington Crossing', and Maltby believing that his favorite inn was the Woodley Tavern and then correcting himself by saying it was actually the White Stag Tavern. Now, this was a mystery indeed. What had Holmes noticed that I had not? And were those names relevant to what faced us now?

I didn't have time to dwell on that puzzle for long, because Nolan said: "The lightning strikes are getting closer. We should sit on the carriage floor."

I responded somewhat pessimistically: "I doubt if sitting on the floor would protect us to any degree."

"Besides," Holmes added, "my belief is that our witchcraft-toting enemy no longer wishes to kill us here, otherwise they would have done so already. No. They have something else planned for us—something absolutely vengeful—and they want to be there in person when they spring that fateful surprise on us."

Holmes had barely finished speaking when I noticed that the clouds above were changing.

"Look," I said, leaning toward the window. "The clouds are parting directly above the railroad track. See, it's like a road of clear blue sky above us."

"Which bears out what I have just told you." Holmes nodded with satisfaction. "Our decidedly unholy enemy is creating a zone of clear sky for us. They do not want inclement weather to impede our progress—even if they were responsible for that oh-so dramatic storm, which we have just experienced." His expression became even more tense, even more worried. "Clearly, someone prefers that we arrive safely at our destination."

Maltby spoke up, his voice shaking with fear. "The devil has made an appointment with doom for us. They are sadistic! They want to enjoy watching us suffer before we die."

Holmes gazed out at the clear air above us, which was now free of rain and lightning. "Without a shadow of doubt, that's what they intend. We are the actors in a tragic play they have devised for us." The train began to slow. "And if I'm not mistaken, the curtain is just about to rise on the final act of our drama."

Chapter 24

The train stopped just twenty feet or so from a brilliant green wall of densely packed vegetation, consisting of thorn bushes, mahogany trees, crabwood and towering red ironwood.

Holmes and I swiftly climbed down from the carriage to stand beside the railway line, just a little to the rear of where the locomotive stood wheezing softly, grey fumes rising from its smokestack.

Nolan jumped down from the carriage. "This is literally the end of the line," he told us. "So many men were dying in the construction of the railroad, a halt had to be called to the works."

"Then, I take it," I said, "that the rest of the way will be on foot?"

"I fear so, Doctor Watson."

Nolan had brought that straw hat, the one with the amazingly broad rim. He now placed it on his red head to shield his pale face from the blazing sun. Meanwhile, Colonel Maltby was marshalling his troops. The squad of thirty or so men were donning backpacks and checking rifles before forming a line beside the carriage. The head of the porters, a tall Scotsman, with gold teeth glinting prominently in the front of his mouth, called to his own men to gather up the bales of supplies that they would carry on their backs. There were nigh on twenty porters—all powerful young fellows with broad shoulders. They wore the blue jacket with the red X motif, identifying them as prisoners who had been shipped here from British jails to start their lives afresh. I could not help but notice the way they cast fearful glances in the direction of the forest ahead of them.

"Foreman," Colonel Maltby said to the head of the porters. "Tell your men not to be afraid. My soldiers will protect them."

The porters exchanged large-eyed glances that told me plainly enough that they doubted the value of the soldiers' protection. They, too, had witnessed the thunderstorm earlier. Those lightning strikes, some destroying objects just a few short yards from the train, must have told them that uncanny forces had been at work. *Rifles against lightning bolts,* they would have been thinking. *We know which of the two is the most powerful weapon.*

Miss Dembe stepped down from the carriage to join us. The woman carried a leather satchel on her back.

"Gentlemen. We have no time to lose." She spoke in a firm and self-assured manner. "The longer we delay in confronting our enemy, the stronger they will become." Then her next statement sent a shiver of both excitement and trepidation down my spine. "They must be stopped today."

Nolan frowned. "That is, if we can find them—the jungle covers hundreds of square miles."

Holmes gave a grim smile. "Indeed, we will find them, Mr. Nolan, or, rather, they will soon find us. I suspect that a vengeful soul wishes with all their heart to see me suffer."

"Holmes," I said, "you know the identity of our enemy, don't you?" I paused, remembering what had piqued Holmes' curiosity earlier. "By Jove! Something to do with the sign attached to the tree, the one that read Charlington

Crossing. And when Colonel Maltby mis-remembered the name of the inn as the Woodley Tavern."

"The names do ring bells, don't they, Watson?"

I thought hard, striving to remember. "Frankly, Holmes, they do not."

"Keep casting your mind back by a few years. Then your own bells of memory might start to peal a little."

"Holmes, this is hardly the time to make a joke of all this."

"I am not making any jokes whatsoever," said Holmes somewhat sharply. "I have insufficient data; therefore, I have no intention of making haphazard guesses." He paused, smiling a little. "Let me just say that, finally, my chain of thought has engaged with the cogs of my brain."

I stared at my friend in absolute puzzlement. "Holmes. If I didn't know you better, I'd declare very loudly that you are talking in riddles. But intuition tells me that you can put a name to the mendacious scoundrel that has been toying with us."

Holmes' smile broadened; however, it was a tense one, and somewhat grim. "Correct, Watson. Mentally, I have compiled a list of suspects, but I require to glean a little more information before I can accurately identify the reprobate."

I couldn't resist asking a somewhat obvious question: "Then we have met the reprobate before?"

"Yes."

Any further discussion of the matter came swiftly to an end as Colonel Maltby bustled toward us, not walking in that purposeful way of the officer I'd first seen at the railway station yesterday. No, he appeared to shamble along, stubble darkened his lower jaw, perspiration stained his brown uniform around the armpits. And his Adam's apple bobbed in his throat as he swallowed. The man was nervous, very nervous.

He turned to his squad of soldiers. "Men, keep your rifles at the ready. But only fire on my orders. Understood?"

The men chorused a "Yes, sir!" I noticed that they held their rifles in such a way that the first finger of their right hands rested on the trigger.

And so, we entered the forest. The engine driver and the stoker remained with the train, with a soldier to guard them. Gradually, the locomotive's gentle hisses and whispery sighs faded as we made our way into the gloom beneath the trees. Colonel Maltby divided his men into smaller groups. Two groups of six men flanked the line of porters. Another eight men, or thereabouts, moved at the head of the column and a similar number formed our rear-guard. Meanwhile, Miss Dembe repeatedly glanced around her, alert to the first signs of danger.

At one point, I heard a soldier mutter a quote from John Dryden: "There is a pleasure sure in being mad, which none but madmen know ..." The other soldiers glanced uneasily at their comrade, perhaps wondering if his nerves were near breaking point. Then the soldiers became even more anxious when the man who had quoted Dryden murmured, "What if the Lucifer Vine had done for us? I mean, what if we have gone and lost our wits ... and our sanity is beached and broken on shores of madness ... what if, in reality, we're all sitting on the riverbank back there, mad as hatters, and just hallucinating we're here in this jungle?"

A sergeant, walking just behind the mumbling fellow, growled, "Shut your mouth, Cromby, or my boot up your backside will prove to you enough that you aren't dreaming—and that you really are taking this little stroll through the blooming Garden of flipping Eden."

The sergeant's no-nonsense remark to the Dryden-quoting soldier did the trick, because the man stopped uttering his disturbing speculation that we all might have gone mad. Even so, I pinched myself firmly enough on a fleshy part of my arm, hoping the sting of such a pinch would reassure me that being in this jungle was the stuff of reality, not a Lucifer Vine-inspired fantasy.

We continued walking through the underbrush. Insects

buzzed around our ears. Lizards with bright green scales scurried up the trunks of trees. Above us, unseen, yet very vocal, monkeys announced to the forest in tremendously loud voices that strangers were trespassing in this forbidding realm of venomous snakes and savage beasts.

A crashing sound from our left caused the soldiers to raise their rifles, ready to fire. Such was the density of the vegetation, however, we could not see what blundered so loudly through the greenery nearby. Nevertheless, my ears told me that the large creature, whatever it was, now moved ahead of our group.

"A buffalo," suggested Nolan.

"More like a bally elephant," I said, hating the sensation of perspiration trickling beneath my shirt and down my back.

The crunch of a heavy body smashing through underbrush grew louder. One of the soldiers cried out in alarm, and Maltby's squad hurriedly pulled back the bolts of their rifles.

Holmes spoke in a stern voice: "Do not fire. Gunshots will only tell our adversary that we're ready to shoot on sight, which might prompt them to fire on us before we even catch sight of them."

Maltby shot Holmes a fierce glance. "These are my men, sir. You will not give them orders."

"Colonel, you must not forget ..." he gave a tight-lipped smile; "... I am the Lord of Damnation. That means I have overall control. Therefore, I forbid your men to fire until I give the order."

Though Maltby's face flushed red with fury, he said nothing.

The crunch of vegetation suddenly became softer, more distant.

I sighed. "I do believe our heavyweight visitor is leaving."

For a moment, we stood absolutely still, listening to the creature's blundering crashes recede as it moved away from us. Slowly, we began moving forward again.

I muttered, "If only we knew which direction we were headed. We might be going around in circles for all we know."

Then a funny thing happened. Ah, I use the word 'funny', but I should have inked the words 'absolutely disturbing' because Holmes pointed out two signs nailed to a tree—both signs bore words and an arrow pointing the way.

Holmes' did not speak in jest when he told me, "Your wish came true. Two signs pointing two different ways. Which one do we follow?"

The soldiers all stopped to watch me as I read aloud what was written upon the signs in bloodred paint. "'Williamson Way', and ..." I gave a grunt of annoyance as I realized that I was the butt of a joke. "'Watson's Folly'."

Holmes pointed to the right. "The sign tells us that Watson's Folly is in that direction. And Williamson's Way is straight ahead."

Colonel Maltby's anxious, darting eyes constantly scanned the jungle—the man expected an ambush at any moment. "So, Mr. Holmes. Which way? Watson's Folly, or Williamson's Way?"

However, it was I that answered. "Watson's Folly is clearly an insult directed at me."

Holmes nodded. "Then Williamson's Way, it is. We proceed straight ahead."

Miss Dembe had said nothing through all this. Now she took a deep breath and addressed everyone there. "Please listen carefully to me. It is possible there may be sudden storms. Or you might see strange creatures that aren't really there. You may be attacked by wild animals. All of this will be the sorcerer's doing." She patted the bag she carried over her shoulder. "I do have certain items that will help counteract any witchcraft that might be inflicted upon us. Be warned, though. In my youth, I only learned the rudiments of witchcraft before I turned my back on such things. Undoubtedly, our foe is stronger than me. Our only hope of overall success lies with Mr. Holmes, here. His rational mind is the most powerful weapon at our disposal."

Holmes gave a single nod, his face grave. "Then my own powers are to be tested to their fullest. So bet it. Let's press on—our destiny awaits."

We continued ever deeper into the jungle. This was wilderness in its purest, most total form.

I murmured to Holmes so that the others would not hear: "Watson's Folly—pah. The scoundrel is goading me, isn't that so?"

"Indeed, they are. And what of Williamson's Way?"

"The name Williamson is significant?"

"Absolutely."

"Then we have met a Williamson in the past? He is a criminal you have tangled with?"

"He is."

"Dash it all, the heat is so formidable that it blurs one's memories. I simply do not remember a Williamson."

"You wrote about him with regard to one of the cases we investigated."

In that suffocating heat that smelt of exotic blooms, I searched my memory as I walked beside Holmes. And I searched in vain. Simply, I could not recollect a wrongdoer I had met by the name of Williamson.

Now, apart from the soft tread of our group's feet on soft earth, there was silence. Even the animals had become hushed. Presently we entered an open glade. The heat caused steam to rise from the damp earth to form a pale mist in the center of the clearing. Miss Dembe held up her hand.

Holmes whispered to her, "What have you seen?"

"Nothing. But I sense danger here."

The soldiers glanced about themselves, rifles at the ready. The men were jittery—as were the porters, who carried our supplies. Nolan removed the straw hat from his head in order to use that extravagantly large headgear to fan his hot face.

Colonel Maltby pulled his revolver from its holster.

"Even the damn monkeys are quiet. They must—"

Holmes placed his finger to his lips, a demand for silence. This pause lasted a full twenty seconds. Then Holmes spoke out in a clear voice, attempting to address someone who was not visible to us: "Why don't you show yourself, so that we might speak face to face?"

Holmes' invitation was met only by silence. He moved deeper into the clearing. I remained at his side, my revolver drawn. The hot air pressed against my face, filling my nostrils and my lungs with such humidity that even to breathe became difficult. My heart pounded, my face grew slick with perspiration, and even holding the butt of the revolver was far from easy—my hand perspired so much, holding onto the weapon was like holding tight to a bar of wet soap—the gun felt as if it would slip from my grasp at any moment.

Miss Dembe's keen gaze cut this way and that, fixing on the way grass stalks had been trampled down, or where raw earth had been disturbed by the passage of animals. No doubt, she searched for clues that would suggest to her that we were in danger of ambush. Because clearly our position here was extremely vulnerable. Snipers, concealed in the underbrush, could begin knocking us down one by one.

"Gentlemen. See?" Miss Dembe pointed to a wooden cross that had been set into the ground—something, frankly, I had not noticed, partly due to perspiration running into my eyes, blurring my vision, and that ocean of lush vegetation that almost overwhelmed my senses. Holmes looked at the wooden cross, which stood as high as my shoulder. Fixed to its center, where the two lengths of wood intersected, someone had hammered a nail through a Bible, so it was fixed to the cross.

I grunted, feeling increasingly breathless. "A rather obvious blasphemy," I said. "Crude. Direct."

Miss Dembe nodded. "Obviously intended to unsettle us. Our enemy telling us that they do not even fear the Christian God, so they most certainly won't fear us."

"Agreed," murmured Holmes. "Moreover, I do believe that whoever nailed the Bible to the cross is giving me a rather overt clue as to their identity."

Maltby's eyes bulged—a combination of physical discomfort due to the heat and nervous stress. "Sir, you know the name of the devil who is playing these evil games with us?"

"I believe I do," said Holmes. "Watson. Have you remembered who it is, yet?"

I shook my head so firmly that drops of sweat were flung from my chin. "No. Other than ... other than ..." I dragged the back of my hand across my forehead, trying to prevent perspiration from rolling down into my eyes. "Other than the name must be Williamson ... the sign back there. The one paired with Watson's Folly."

"Ha!" Holmes' face tightened into the grimmest of smiles. "Williamson. You have the name of the scoundrel all right. A minor player in one of our cases. However, though he played a small part in a dreadful crime, he has harbored a prodigious grudge against me, which had grown malignantly into an unholy lust for revenge."

The soldiers and the porters listened to what Holmes was saying with absolute attention. I sensed that not only his confident manner of speaking, but his commanding presence reassured them. They knew that Mr. Sherlock Holmes was assembling clues, interpreting them, reaching conclusions—and every man there knew that knowledge is power. Therefore, Holmes' forensic accumulation of knowledge empowered him, and reassured those people around him that he was the man to defeat their enemy. The soldiers straightened their backs, standing taller, as they felt their courage grow, and their resolve become stronger.

Nolan spoke in an imploring way: "Mr. Holmes, won't you tell us what you have discovered?"

Holmes consented with a nod. "Our enemy is a man by the name of Williamson. He is a victim of his own unbridled vanity, because he wanted me to discover his identity, even though he pretended to remain anonymous. It is certainly a truism that people who intend to wreak vengeance on their enemy absolutely want their enemy to know who is making them suffer. After all, where is the satisfaction in vengeance, if your enemy does not realize that it's you who inflicted the painful wound?"

I frowned. "Then, I take it, the names on the signs you saw as we travelled here revealed the identity of our foe?"

Miss Dembe recited the names we'd read on the signs: "Charlington Crossing, Watson's Folly, Williamson's Way."

"And," I pointed out to Holmes, "you seemed especially interested when the Colonel here misremembered the name of his favorite inn as the Woodley Tavern. "

She added, "Those names clearly mean something to you, Mr. Holmes, but, other than Dr Watson's name, we are unfamiliar with them."

"As am I," I admitted with a flush of shame at being unable to remember what was clearly a significant name amongst the cases we had investigated.

Holmes nodded in the direction of the cross with the Good Book nailed thereto. "And that blatant example of blasphemy—a Bible crucified, as it were, hints that we seek an individual with an ecclesiastical background."

"Then a clergyman," suggested Miss Dembe, her mind clearly working more efficiently than mine.

Maltby's red face twitched—the man must have anger perpetually flowing in his veins, not blood. "So, a wretched parson is responsible for all the mayhem we have experienced." Maltby's bulging eyes appeared to become even more prominent. I could even see red veins glaring from the white substance of his eyes. "You are telling us that you once had a priest or clergymen arrested, and now he has followed you to this island to extract his pound of flesh?"

Holmes said, "I'm sure Williamson was already here, as a convict who had been shipped to Yagomba."

"Then clearly he has returned to his criminal ways," said Nolan. "He has caused many deaths."

The sweltering heat had melted my patience. "Holmes. For Heaven sakes! Who is Williamson? In which case did he play a part?"

Then sounds from the jungle—the spell of silence broken. But what strange sounds. Not the howl of a monkey, or screech of a bird, or roar of a lion. No, this was the loud ratcheting of a chain driving a cog—of wheels on a road—of metal striking metal: *ding, ding, ding.*

Nolan shouted in astonishment: "Bicycles! I hear bicycles!"

"Impossible," snarled the Colonel. "How can there be bicycles? This is thick jungle."

Nevertheless ...

I heard the swish of wheels, the clicking ratchet of pedals driving a chain, which in turn drove a rear wheel of a bicycle. And that bright *ding, ding, ding* melody of ...

I gawped at clouds of mist moving swiftly through the trees to emerge into the clearing.

And that noise: *ding, ding, ding* ...

"Great Scott," I exclaimed. "That sound? It's the sound of bicycle bells!"

The cloud of mist moved swiftly toward us above the long grass of the clearing. And that is when the mist began to shrink into a concentrating clump of vapor that swiftly ceased being a diffuse, blurry smudge of white mist and became ...

I gasped with astonishment. "A bicycle. Upon my soul! A bicycle!"

Ding-ding-ding-ding. The striker hit the bell at a faster rate—a speeding metal heartbeat. As eerie, in this setting, as it was utterly disturbing.

One of the soldiers took a step backward, the shock of what he saw almost overwhelming him. "A phantom cyclist!" he shouted, his eyes bulging in shock.

"No," shouted Holmes. "Watson, tell them what you see!"

Then I remembered. "I see a ... a solitary cyclist!"

A woman in long white skirts, a hat tied to her head

by a pink ribbon beneath her chin, came cycling toward me across the jungle clearing, energetically ringing the bell fixed to the handlebars as she pedaled hard. Wheels turned, pedals clunked and squeaked as they drove the chain. All the sounds were there—the ratcheting click-click-click of the chain, the sound of the bell. Yet the tires did not touch even the upper tips of the grass.

The bicycle flew along, some three feet above the ground. The woman's eyes were fixed straight ahead, her face serious, wisps of hair blowing from beneath her hat.

Holmes gripped my arm. "Now you remember?"

"The case of the Solitary Cyclist," I cried. "Yes, it all comes flooding back! How could I have forgotten? A Miss Violet Smith came to you because, as she cycled through the countryside, a mysterious figure followed her on a bicycle. You later discovered that she had been kidnapped by rogues by the name of Woodley, Carruthers and Williamson. Oh, good grief!"

The cyclist sped past us, pedaling hard—the soldiers and porters flung themselves to the ground to avoid being struck—however, the lady cyclist was flying above them now, and the bicycle rising skyward, as if climbing an invisible hill.

"You understand the relevance of the names?" asked Holmes. "Woodley, Charlington, et cetera?"

"Yes." I nodded vigorously. "Charlington Hall was the scene of the kidnap. Woodley was the vile bully who intended to force Miss Smith to marry him, and Williamson was the defrocked priest who conducted the marriage ceremony. Williamson was given a prison sentence of seven years. Therefore, he may well have been sent here to—"

I didn't get chance to finish the sentence because, explosively, a dozen cyclists erupted from the trees at the far side of the clearing. However, these cyclists were absolutely not mortal men and women. Some of the bicycles were ridden by demons—their eyes blazed red, like burning coals in a fire. Their skin was ridged and segmented, resembling that of a crocodile, and their mouths yawned open, revealing hook-shaped teeth. Other machines were pedaled by what appeared to be men and women. Yet their faces resembled those of corpses. Their eyes bulged until they resembled hens' eggs, protruding whitely from the sockets.

And they all rang the bells of the bicycles as they flew through the air toward us, above the long grass of the clearing. *Ding-ding-ding-ding.* And every single one of those uncanny riders laughed—a demonic laughter that vibrated with a mocking hatred of us. A laughter so loud we all clamped our hands over our ears, lest our eardrums be ruptured by the sheer enormity of the sound.

The bicycles whooshed above our heads, gaining height all the time.

A moment later, two cyclists appeared—they moved slower than the rest, and much lower toward the ground than their brethren, so the wheels of their machines were at the height of my head. On one bicycle sat my wife. Her eyes flashed with anger when she saw me.

She yelled, "You should have killed Sherlock Holmes while you had the chance! Now I have paid the forfeit. They have taken my life because you did not take his. I lie in my coffin back in London, my dear, stupid husband." She began laughing in the same way as those other unearthly cyclists. And, as she did so, blood sprayed from her mouth, yet she never took those blazing, hate-filled eyes from me.

Then she pedaled away, rising higher and higher into the sky, scattering a flock of vultures before her, and the sound of the bell being rung at a furious speed still reached me.

After that extraordinary and profoundly shocking departure, the last cyclist approached. A woman wearing clothes made from leopard skin and carrying a spear. Halting the bike directly in front of us, she grinned at Holmes. "Remember me, Mr. Holmes," she hissed. "How easy it would have been to kill you."

Miss Dembe stepped forward, staring up at the cyclist as she floated above the ground. Miss Dembe pointed at the warrior. "You are of my blood. You are from my ancestral line. How many generations gone, though?"

"You are correct, my great-great-granddaughter. And I have been called back from our cave of bones to rid the world of the interfering busybody, Mr. Sherlock Holmes. Yah!" With that shout, she hurled the spear at Holmes.

Miss Dembe flung herself forward, attempting to shield Holmes with her own body.

However, she was too late; the spear moved so swiftly— the shaft, tipped with a sharp metal point,sliced through the air with a hiss.

A second later, the spear struck the ground between Holmes' slightly parted feet, the point deeply penetrating the soil and the shaft still quivering from the force of the impact.

Miss Dembe held up her hands above her head and began to cry out words—possibly an incantation—in a language I did not understand.

The warrior, gripping the handlebars with one hand, leaned back as if she rode a stallion that had reared up onto its hind legs, and she released a roar of laughter from her lips. "Until we meet again, Mr. Holmes. Farewell!"

She didn't pedal the machine, then. I don't believe she even had to, because some occult power caused the bicycle to accelerate to an impossible velocity. It moved upward like a skyrocket, following the other cyclists into the clouds where they all, one by one, disappeared into grey cumulus. Even though the phantom cyclists were no longer visible, faintly, I heard the *ding-ding-ding* of bicycle bells high above us. A mocking refrain, yet one that contained, perhaps, a warning of mortal danger for us here, down on the ground.

Colonel Maltby strode forward where he pulled the spear from the earth. He said: "That was close, Holmes. She only just missed you."

"On the contrary, Colonel Maltby," Holmes said in cool

tones. "She hit the target she was aiming for—specifically, that patch of dirt between my feet. If she'd intended to plant that spear into my chest, she would have had no difficulty in doing so."

I turned to Miss Dembe. "That woman did resemble you to an uncanny degree."

"I have no doubt," she began, "that the woman is an ancestor of mine. Though it troubles me as much as it puzzles me why she has returned from the dead to join with our foe, this Williamson individual you spoke of, in order to torment us."

I glanced at Holmes. "Yes, I remember Williamson now, the defrocked clergyman, who was part of a vile conspiracy to force a lady to marry Woodley, so he could get his hands on what was a considerable inheritance of the young lady's."

Holmes nodded. "Williamson was jailed for assault and abduction. One can imagine that he was sent to here to this penal colony to serve his sentence. At some point, he learnt from an errant witch doctor how to wield certain occult powers. With that ability to control minds and weather, and no doubt other supernatural chicanery, Williamson decided to become the ruler of Yagomba. Of course, first he needed to undermine the authority of the government here before he and his band of outlaws, who'd squirreled themselves away in the jungle, could violently seize control of the island. Then Williamson could appoint himself as the new Lord of Damnation."

Nolan fanned his hot face with the straw hat. "Rather rum, though, a man of the cloth to have such an ungodly craving to become the worst kind of despotic ruler of thousands of men, women and children."

Holmes smiled. "All clergymen and priests must derive some satisfaction from being the center of attention in church. They enjoy the respect accorded to them by their congregation. And to a certain degree they are the Earthly representative of the Almighty—which is a decidedly high-status position of power. Of course, in the main, the priesthood is a benevolent fraternity. However, a disgraced and defrocked priest may well find that their loss of authority and the ability to command respect pains them, just as the opium addict is pained when he or she is deprived of the drug. Williamson, therefore, decided to reinstate his power over others—even if that meant using the power of the occult and the brutal persuasion of the gun."

I said, "And so he must have been delighted to hear that you were coming to Yagomba, Holmes. You had the fellow arrested, which resulted in him being sent to jail. Therefore, he decided to wreak his revenge on you, too."

"Absolutely. And no doubt he wishes to cause me a great deal of pain and torment before despatching me into the hereafter."

"Then Williamson is evidently a loathsome creature," declared Miss Dembe. "And I suspect he has effectively enslaved the spirit of my ancestor to do his bidding. After all, like me, she will have been of a priestly caste."

The soldiers, by now, had recovered their composure and formed a circle around the porters and Holmes, Miss Dembe, Nolan and myself, their rifles pointing outward, as if imitating the spines of a hedgehog. Ready for any ambush that might be sprung on them.

By this time, the unearthly sound of the bicycle bells had faded, and Holmes, after gazing up at the sky for a moment, declared, "I don't think the phantom cyclists will be coming back for a while—if at all. I rather suspect their purpose was to alarm us, rather than cause physical harm."

Nevertheless, the soldiers still glanced skyward with deep unease, the tension on their faces plain to see.

Holmes called out across the glade: "Williamson. I know that you are close. Why are you so shy about speaking to us? After all, your tricks with the lightning and the flying bicycles were really quite impressive."

Suddenly, the smallish figure of an elderly man walked briskly from the cover of the trees on the far side of the glade. Bizarrely, he was clad in a white suit, which was complemented by a priest's dog collar—yet this dog collar was made of black material.

"By Jove," I uttered in surprise. "The fellow resembles a photographic negative of a priest. Instead of dark clothes, he wears white, and instead of a white collar it is completely black."

Holmes' clear voice rang out: "Williamson. I see that you are making a virtue of being an defrocked priest. You have reversed the colors of the priestly garb. You have crucified a copy of the Bible by nailing it to a cross. All very droll to some, yet as vulgar and as ugly as the content of your mind, no doubt."

Williamson spoke with the easy authority of someone used to preaching from the pulpit: "Mr. Holmes, you have ambled quite sedately into my trap."

Holmes watched the man's face, no doubt reading his expressions with exquisite accuracy. "Williamson, you could have destroyed us at any point during this journey. Indeed, I suspect you could have murdered us when we were asleep in our beds, back in New London. You brought us here for a reason other than slaughter."

I glanced at the soldiers. They, in turn, looked to their commanding officer, Maltby, for orders. Obedient to Holmes' own orders, Maltby remained silent, listening carefully to the conversation between Holmes and the strangely attired figure, standing waist-deep in long grass—a white-clad scoundrel amid a lake of green vegetation. How I longed to wring the devil's throat.

Sherlock Holmes took a step forward, showing no fear. "You no doubt wish to see me suffer, in order to satisfy your lust for revenge, but I have no regrets in having you arrested for abducting the young woman in England all those years ago. You really did deserve that prison sentence."

"Holmes," I whispered so that Williamson wouldn't hear. "Permit me to put a bullet in his heart. After all the deaths he has caused, it is what he deserves."

211

"I wish it was that simple," Holmes whispered back. "However, firing at him will likely result in a battle that we cannot win. Williamson isn't all that he seems."

"How so, Holmes?"

"Look at the tracks he has left in the long grass."

"There are no tracks ... ah ..." Shivers ran down my spine. "No tracks: then he isn't really—"

"Williamson." Holmes spoke in a loud voice, deliberately ending our conversation, lest our enemy suspect we were plotting some attack on him. "Clearly, you have an unrelenting craving for attention, and a burning need to be admired, though there is nothing admirable about you."

Williamson erupted, his voice thundering a string of the most vulgar oaths that I've heard in a long time, his face blotching red with fury. Then, taking a deep breath, he contrived to speak in a way that was excessively polite. "My good sir, you have such a pleasant sense of humor to tease me the way you do. However, I have considered an array of delicious scenarios that involve you, Mr. Holmes. What if I set you down on a remote island, where you would live alone for a year, just to see how you fared? Believe me, I have the occult power to do just that. Or how about placing you in a cauldron with water up to your neck ... oh, to light a fire beneath the pot and sit and watch the marvelous way you devise a means of escape before the water boils you like an egg."

Holmes took another step forward. At the same time, from the mist emerged dozens of men, armed with rifles.

Miss Dembe sneered. "So, the vile creature isn't as brave as he pretends? He has brought his partners in crime to protect him."

"Young lady, you and Holmes, and that dimwit Watson, have your own ... ha! ... Praetorian guard," remarked Williamson, pointing at the soldiers.

Holmes held out his hands to indicate that he spoke with simple honesty. "What if we negotiated a peaceful settlement to our differences, instead of resorting to yet more violence?"

"You would never agree to my demands."

"And they are?"

"That I am appointed governor of New London."

"You do realize that the British government will despatch naval ships here to regain control of the island?"

"All enemy vessels will be destroyed by the lightning that I summon from the sky. Yagomba will be an island fortress. Impregnable. Unassailable."

"What will you do to its people?"

"In the main, they will continue to live as they have done so before, however ..."

"However?"

"However, certain individuals," Williamson said, "shall be punished for what they have done to me."

Holmes nodded. "I expected that would be the case. And I am to be punished, too?"

"If you appoint me as your successor, you will be free to leave the island. Though I reserve the right to have you publicly flogged before boarding the ship to England."

"And what of the witchcraft you now practice? Will you give that up?"

"When one acquires power, one never willingly surrenders it."

Holmes sighed. "Williamson. What is more important than the flesh on my back, which you wish to flay with a whip, is the safety of the island's population. I know that if I refuse your demand to become governor then you will violently overthrow the government here, and there will be much bloodshed. Innocent citizens will die. Therefore, if you agree to an immediate ceasefire, I will hand the governorship to you."

I whispered with some force: "Holmes, I do not trust the fellow."

"What choice to do I have? What use are bullets against the occult power that is at this man's disposal? You saw how he uses the very lightning from the sky as a weapon."

"Holmes," I hissed. "Find another way. Do not surrender New London to him."

I'd reached out, placing my hand on his forearm, as I whispered the words to him with such heartfelt intensity. Holmes shrugged off my hand.

Holmes spoke loudly: "Very well, Mr. Williamson. I will see to it that the governorship is signed over to you."

"Traitor!" This word was screamed by Colonel Maltby, whereupon he pointed his revolver at Holmes. Yet, instead of shooting Holmes, he swiftly spun around to aim the weapon at Williamson. Maltby fired three times into Williamson's chest. The man looked down where the rounds had struck. They left no bullet holes, and no blood seeped from the white jacket. With cold fury, he raised his chin to stare with absolute hatred at Maltby.

Williamson's contempt for the Colonel was plain to see. "So, you thought I could be distracted with talk of peace in order to kill me? But I am not in this glade, gentlemen. I never was."

Williamson's body became misty, indistinct. Soon, I gazed through his flesh, as if he consisted purely of thin vapor.

Then, before he faded entirely, his voice rang out in priestly tones: "It is time for the great experiment to begin, Mr. Holmes. Do try your hardest to be an interesting subject."

Maltby's soldiers could no longer restrain themselves. They fired their rifles at the outlaws. These, unlike Williamson, were mortal and many fell with blood spurting from bullet wounds. Those that survived the first onslaught of bullets stood their ground and immediately fired back. Colonel Maltby sank to his knees, clutching his throat, liquid crimson streaming over his hands. Meanwhile, the porters had ducked down into the long grass to avoid the speeding bullets, some of which struck soldiers who screamed, arching their backs in agony, as they toppled to the ground, blood gushing from a profusion of wounds in their torsos, limbs and, most shockingly of all, faces. For I confess, even though I have served as a military man, and continue to practice as a doctor, witnessing the effect of gunfire on a human face still has the power to render me sick to my stomach.

The death of their commanding officer broke the nerve of the soldiers, and that of the porters, too, and every man jack of them fled into the underbrush.

Miss Dembe seized my hand. "Come with me!"

I ran holding Miss Dembe's hand. Holmes ran, too; as did Nolan. Thereafter, the jungle engulfed us as we left the scene of slaughter behind.

We'd only been running through the jungle for two or three minutes, at the most, when the strangest of sights met my eyes.

"Good grief," I cried. "We are back home!"

Chapter 25

My astonished exclamation, "We are back home!" continued to resonate within my skull as we stood there amongst the trees, gazing at buildings that were of the strangest construction I have ever seen.

Nolan shook his head in amazement. "It's like a London Street ... *old* London, at that."

Miss Dembe stared in astonishment, too. "Yet one deep within a tropical jungle."

"Not any London street," Holmes stated in that forthright way of his.

"Holmes ... this place ... my God." Shock had rendered me breathless. "This is Baker Street!"

Sherlock Holmes stepped from beneath the canopy of trees onto open roadway formed from bare earth. "Yet a Baker Street ..." said he, "... conjured by unknown forces. Behold." He pointed at the row of four-story buildings in front of us. "There is not a single clay brick in its construction. Not so much as a splinter of stone, nor even a bucketful of mortar has been used. It is woven from plants. Vegetation has been employed to ape the very house and the very street I call home."

With that, Holmes marched briskly forward, heading

for a doorway that was in some ways so familiar, yet now so alien.

Miss Dembe hurried after him. "Mr. Holmes. The buildings consist of Lucifer Vine. You must not go any closer."

"Clearly, this copy of the house where I live has been purposefully conjured out of the jungle by Williamson for me. He expects me to visit my rooms."

Nolan gripped the straw hat in both hands, his eyes bright with anxiety. "Sir, to enter a building consisting entirely of Lucifer Vine will drive you insane within moments."

"He's right, Holmes," I said. "Williamson has set a trap."

Holmes paused, nostrils flaring, as if he could smell a delicious mystery in the air. "Would that reprobate set such a poor trap as this? We know all too well the plant is toxic to the human mind. Surely, he would have disguised the appearance of the plant, if he wanted to render us insane?" Holmes walked in the direction of the green house that was a parody of 221B Baker Street. "It is my belief that Williamson intends us to enter 'my' apartment. He has, I do not doubt, installed something there of particular interest to me."

Miss Dembe grasped his arm to prevent him from getting any closer. "Sir. What you say is true. But what that devil Williamson has placed within those sham walls is madness ... your madness. Do you understand?"

Holmes glanced down at the leather satchel the young woman wore. "You have something that will protect us from Williamson's magic?"

"I do," she replied. "Yet I do not believe you will use it."

"Oh? Pray, why?"

"Because what will grant you at least a degree of immunity from his occult power is of a repellent nature."

As she spoke, three soldiers from Maltby's squad emerged from the forest behind us. These men, I suspected, might be the only survivors of the battle fought in the glade just moments ago. They, too, stared in awe at the replica of the London street, formed from living vines. The green walls rippled—such a peculiar effect—as the breeze stirred the leaves that grew from the stems. One of the soldiers, a young man of perhaps seventeen, with softly curling blond hair, had lost his helmet in the battle, and his face bore vivid red scratches, either as a result of hand-to-hand combat or running through the thorny undergrowth. His large blue eyes were boyish, as he stared at the green structure in front of him in nothing less than fear. As he gripped his rifle in one hand, the other hand rose to a silver crucifix that hung on a chain outside his brown tunic. Trembling, he took hold of the cross of glittering silver, raised it to his lips, kissed it, while murmuring words that must have been a prayer, beseeching protection from the Almighty.

My gaze now strayed to an upper floor where Holmes had his rooms, or, rather, where his rooms would be, back in the *real* house, back in the *real* Baker Street. Just for a moment, a face appeared there. A familiar pair of sharp eyes stared unflinchingly down at us, as we stood on bare dirt, which had been pounded flat to resemble a roadway. The power of that stare robbed me of the ability to speak. Then I caught the pungently sweet aroma from the Lucifer Vine's pink flowers. The plant's mind-poison, I feared, had already begun to intrude upon my brain; so, how long before I found myself vine-struck? Then I would become lost in a maelstrom of insanity; a babbling lunatic whose longevity could be measured in days, not years.

The three soldiers moved forward to join Holmes, Miss Dembe, Nolan and I. Two of the soldiers were in a daze—they dragged their rifles so that the muzzles ploughed the soil, as it were, leaving little furrows. The shootout evidently had had a detrimental effect on their nerves. What they saw now, in the form of houses apparently fashioned from vine by occult forces, must have threatened to overwhelm their reason entirely.

The shock (or was it the early effects of the Lucifer Vine?) had left me somewhat dazed, too, for I became aware that Miss Dembe was still speaking, though I hadn't heard her words. She opened the satchel in order to hand Holmes, Nolan and myself some morsels of food that were pale orange in color.

"Eat this," she instructed. "It will mitigate the effects of Williamson's power. Be warned, though, its protection, such as it is, will last no more than an hour."

"What is it?" asked Nolan, gazing at the fibrous shreds of that pellet of matter in the palm of his hand.

"Oh, my dear Lord." My exclamation came with such loudness that the soldiers glanced at me in shock. "Cured meat ..." I turned to Holmes, my heart pounding. "Flesh from a human being." In utter horror, I stared at the object in my fingers. "This is a human ear."

Miss Dembe nodded. "Harvested from those who have died of natural causes. However, unlike the tincture I gave you earlier, when Lucifer Vine invaded our train carriages, this flesh will not grant you absolute protection from the effects of the vine, nor Williamson's sorcery—but it is better than nothing. Now ..." She spoke firmly: "You must eat it."

Nolan shook his head. "Never."

"I agree," I declared. "I will not eat human flesh."

A sudden rumble of thunder seemed to comment on my ardent refusal to turn cannibal.

Holmes glanced up at gathering clouds that were nearer purple than black. "There is another storm coming. One, no doubt, summoned by Williamson. And the only shelter I spy is that house of vines. And possibly our only protection from evil sorcery is ..." His sharp-eyed gaze alighted on the vile matter lying there on the palm of Miss Dembe's upturned hand.

"But, Holmes ..." I daresay my eyes bulged with horror. "I am not squeamish. But I refuse to eat the flesh of my fellow human beings."

Miss Dembe spoke with absolute conviction: "It's

the only way you can lessen Williamson's power. If he has become truly adept at using the sorcery, which is employed by the witch doctors of my people, then that power that will certainly harm you. The man-flesh will protect you—albeit for barely an hour or so—from the worst effects of the Lucifer Vine. Though be warned: the poison of the vine is strong; therefore, you are still likely to experience confusion of thought—moreover, you might see and hear things that do not exist in reality."

Again, thunder grumbled in the heavens—a deeply ominous sound.

Holmes said, "Needs must, Watson. That goes for you all." He glanced at Nolan and the soldiers. "Swallow the flesh. Yes! It is vile. It is also a necessity."

Miss Dembe gave a resolute nod. "Mr. Holmes is right." With that, she quickly handed out more nuggets of flesh to the soldiers.

Nolan pushed the orangish meat between his lips. Screwing his eyes shut, he chewed with grim resolve. Although, it must be said, the man's face twitched with revulsion. With a huge effort, fists clenched tight, he endeavored to swallow that pellet of ungodly food. He failed, however, and appeared close to spitting it out.

"You must get it down," insisted Holmes. "You must!"

I glanced at the ear in my hand, seeing small hairs on the lobe, and white pearls of fat embedded in the part of the flesh where it had been sliced from the cadaver's head.

"Holmes," I gasped. "This is intolerable."

The soldiers shook their heads. They were refusing to turn cannibal, too.

That's when the lightning struck. A bolt of pure electrical power sped down from the clouds to smite one of the soldiers—a man of about fifty with short-cropped white hair. The abrupt surge of heat boiled the blood in his head so quickly that the skull exploded with a shockingly loud bang. Headless, steaming, bereft of life, the man fell to the ground.

Thunder roared with what seemed like vicious triumph at killing the man.

"Eat!" Miss Dembe commanded. "Eat if you value your lives!"

Holmes placed lacy strands of human flesh onto his tongue. Then he devoured the meat as easily as swallowing nothing more troubling than a piece of bread. Nolan clenched his fists again, forcing the knot of dead flesh down his throat. This triggered a bout of coughing and he quickly reached for his water bottle before drinking deeply, sluicing the vile morsel down his gullet. The two surviving soldiers pushed the foul nuggets into their mouths, grimacing, shuddering, moaning in horror as they did so. Eventually, with a supreme effort, aided by gulps from their water bottles, they all succeeded in swallowing the flesh.

Quickly, I put the ear between my teeth, whereupon I tore a piece off that tough organ. I tried not to do so. Yet my tongue roved over that part of the ear that I'd bitten off. I felt its contours with my tongue, the swelling bulge of the earlobe.

The taste ... dear God, the taste ...

Then came one of the greatest horrors of my life as the flavors of that cured piece of human flesh washed through my mouth. I have tasted dried beef before in the form of what some call 'jerky' or 'biltong'. This tasted much smokier, much stronger. A savory flavor that flowed over my tongue, tingling the skin inside my mouth, before running down my throat, down into the deepest part of my gut.

"The taste ..." I muttered, my eyes watering. "The taste ... it is ... delicious."

I slapped my hand over my mouth, disgusted with myself. By all that is holy, I had actually confessed to liking the flavor. No ... no. I didn't like the taste of human flesh. *I loved it.* What's more, energy surged through my limbs. My mind became clearer than ever before. When I looked around me, colors were brighter.

No, not just brighter—they were scintillating, iridescent, coruscating, shouting colors—greenery blazed, my pink fingernails became luminous, the gold ring on my finger enchanted my eye with such brilliance I sighed with ecstasy. Normally, I require glasses to see clearly. Now, even though I hadn't donned my spectacles, I saw the trees, the human faces around me, the tiny butterflies hovering above wildflowers, with perfect clarity. Could that heightening of my senses be attributed to the simple fact I had eaten part of a human body? I must answer in the affirmative ... unless the meat had been steeped in some mind-enhancing drug.

Thunder barked again. Lightning struck a mahogany tree in the forest behind us. The massive trunk shattered at its base and the tree toppled in our direction.

"Run!" shouted Holmes.

He raced toward the bizarre growth of vines that mimicked the facade of Baker Street, right down to the doors, windows, and boot-scrape beside the step. The falling tree certainly encouraged us toward the building, for the uppermost branches crashed down to earth not twenty paces behind us—thankfully, missing us by a goodish margin. Nevertheless, the felling of the tree by lightning bolt was clearly Williamson's doing once more— evidently, he had grown impatient waiting for us to enter the building that he had conjured from the jungle. That vile specimen of a human being wanted his amusement to begin.

Holmes reached the front door of the house. Then the strangest thing: the door did not swing open on hinges, it simply parted down the center like two halves of a curtain being draw apart, the vines squirming back toward the frame.

A moment later, we had rushed into the hallway.

"There are stairs," I panted. "And walls. They are all made from tightly woven vines."

No sooner had I spoken, than a female voice issued from the landing upstairs. A familiar voice at that.

"Good afternoon, Doctor Watson. You are all well, I trust?"

"Mrs. Hudson," I gasped.

"Welcome to Baker Street," said the woman. "Mr. Holmes will see you now."

Chapter 26

Sherlock Holmes climbed the stairs to the floor where he would normally find his rooms. This bizarre structure imitating the building that contained 221B Baker Street had been formed from thousands of strands of Lucifer Vine. The vines, themselves, were in constant motion: squirming, writhing, worming their way up and under their fellow strands in order to weave the fabric of the building. The steps beneath my feet were made from the same plant. The risers would sag, just for a second, when I put my weight on them, then they would immediately firm up to take the strain. The tentacle-like stems of the plant acted like a muscle, tensing themselves into hard sinews to bear the weight of visitors to this strange abode.

Mrs. Hudson spoke again. "Can I get you some tea? I baked today. Would you care for a slice of Dundee cake?"

"Williamson is taunting us," I muttered. "He has made this vile plant resemble Mrs. Hudson."

"Pay no heed to the figure," Holmes told us. "This is just another bit of mischief."

"And expect more mischief like this," warned Miss Dembe. "Much more ... and much worse."

Holmes turned right at the top of the flight of stairs. He ignored the disturbing figure that protruded from the wall.

"Miss Dembe," shrilled Mrs. Hudson, or the thing that resembled her. "Miss Dembe. Would you prefer milk or a slice of lemon in your cup of tea? Oh, Doctor Watson. I know what you do love in your tea. A nice tot of whisky. Keep the chill out of old bones."

Despite Holmes' instruction to "pay no heed to the figure," I found I could not simply walk by without taking a closer look. Yes, the figure was an approximation of Mrs. Hudson. Same height, same build, similar features, and a voice that disturbingly resembled the woman that both Holmes and I were so fond of. Yet the body of this Mrs. Hudson had been fashioned from more of the Lucifer Vine—a living tapestry of slender fronds that extended out from the wall and were still firmly connected to the self-same wall. The vine's flowers clustered into an oval, thus resembling Mrs. Hudson's face. Pink petals echoed the color of her skin. Tightly concentrated groupings of tendrils had been made to imitate her eyes and mouth. Plump buds bulged from the center of the face to form "her" nose.

Mrs. Hudson—more accurately, that hideous mockery of her—pointed at a door. "You will find Mr. Holmes and Doctor Watson waiting for you in the sitting-room. They are most eager to see you."

Holmes, without hesitation, stepped across the threshold. I was close behind him. Miss Dembe, Nolan and the two remaining soldiers followed us into the sitting-room.

Once again, I noted that the room had been formed from densely packed vines. Daylight penetrated the plant-growth to a certain degree, making the heart-shaped leaves glow green in a way that was decidedly eerie. In fact, that luminescence filled the room with light that was emerald in color. The soldiers stared in amazement at their surroundings before glancing at one another, as if to

226

reassure themselves that their comrade also bore witness to the same remarkable features of this structure, for I'd not doubted for one second that the soldiers feared that this lush, green sitting-room might be the product of some pernicious hallucination.

"Goodness," I breathed. "Holmes. This is a replica of your room in London. Look … the sofa, the table, even the fireplace and coal scuttle—all resembling those where you live."

"Although you will note the contents of the room are over-sized by at least half again. Even the letters 'VR' on the wall, which I picked out with pistol shot, are the same, if somewhat larger." Holmes appeared impressed. "Should I consider this as an attempt to honor me, or to mock me?"

Holmes, several years ago, had, during a fit of boredom, fired his revolver at his sitting-room wall in a deliberate pattern, so that the bullet holes inscribed "VR" in the plasterwork by the fireplace. "VR," of course, is the royal cipher for Britain's late monarch, namely Victoria Regina.

I said, "When the officials of New London decorated your accommodation to resemble your home back in London, that was most certainly intended as a warm-hearted gesture to make you feel at home, as you were their esteemed guest. This …"—I waved my hand at the counterfeit room—"… this is a demonstration of Williamson's power in an attempt to make you feeble in comparison to him."

"You are correct, Doctor." The clear voice rang out so suddenly that I flinched in surprise—for the voice, issuing from a person unseen, was identical to the voice of Holmes, but he had not spoken. "Welcome to my abode."

Hitherto, I had believed the room unoccupied, apart from our little group, comprising Holmes and I, Miss Dembe, Nolan and the two soldiers. However, a high-backed swivel chair, facing the window, caught my attention as it appeared to tremble slightly. Because the chair was also fashioned from tightly woven vine, I was inclined to

... a purple dressing gown identical to the one that Holmes favored ...

fancy that the trembling was on account of the incessant writhing of those green tendrils. But, at that moment, the swivel chair turned to reveal that this strange item of furniture had an occupant—a most singular occupant at that, and one glimpse of the extraordinary individual gave me cause to flinch back in shock and horror.

A long, thin figure sat there with casually crossed legs. I noted immediately that the figure wore a purple dressing gown identical to the one that Holmes favored when in the privacy of his rooms.

The figure waved a languid hand in the direction of Holmes. "Do take a seat."

"Good grief," exclaimed Nolan.

I said, "Surely, the time has come when I should no longer be shocked at what I see in this bedevilled place, but this ... this...," I pointed at the figure in the swivel chair, "... this revolts me to the core."

Holmes stepped forward to speak to our seated host. "Thank you, sir. I prefer to remain standing."

"Sir?" I echoed. "How on earth can you address that horror as 'sir'?"

Rather than answer my somewhat rhetorical question, Holmes said: "You're right, Watson. We should no longer be surprised by what we encounter here. Then again, who else did you expect to meet in 221B Baker Street, other than Mr. Sherlock Holmes?"

The figure rose from the swivel chair, the long dressing gown swishing as the limbs moved. My blood ran cold as I stared at the massive figure in front of me. Fully seven feet tall, it possessed the body of a thin man. The head, however? The head was simply awful.

You may have seen paintings or carvings of the mythical creature known as the Green Man, sometimes known by another soubriquet, Jack-in-the-Green. Images of the Green Man dating back to medieval times are often located in European churches—indeed, images of the Green Man have been found in Roman mosaics over two thousand years old. The Green Man is often depicted with a human face, yet with hair and beard of lush grass. Other images show the Green Man's face to be entirely composed from leaves, with strands of ivy sprouting from between the fantastic creature's lips. Here, Williamson had once again created a copy of a human being, formed from the stems, flowers and leaves of the accursed Lucifer Vine. We had encountered the copy of Mrs. Hudson on the stairs—a creature formed from vine. However, the figure standing here had clearly been the subject of much greater endeavor and attention to detail, to create something which very, very closely resembled a human being.

Before me was the body of an unusually tall man. On those apparently human shoulders had been placed a large head that appeared to me to be formed from strands and leaves of Lucifer Vine that had been fused together under so much pressure that the face resembled a living human face. Smooth skin. Eyes turned in their sockets. Eyelids blinked. A tongue extended to run along the upper lip as we would see in a *bona fide Homo sapiens*. Strangely, what revolted and horrified me so much was that the face before me was nine-tenths flesh and blood, or seemingly so, but the one-tenth that was clearly vegetation disturbed my mental equilibrium to the extent that I flinched back in terror. You see, whatever forces held the plant in compression to form the near-perfect human face would momentarily lapse, then a bulge would appear in the forehead, for example, and leaves would burst out, green and wet—stickily wet, or so their appearance suggested. When the Lucifer Vine had been compressed, Williamson (for surely he was responsible for this abomination) had neglected to remove insects and other creatures, so when the face bulged and the leaves ceased to be compressed and became loose fronds of green suddenly erupting from the forehead, or jaw, or a cheek, ants would scurry out from the green matter, and run in that hither-thither manner of ants down the face and throat of the man to disappear back inside the purple dressing gown. In one instance, the side of the 'man's' head bulged until the skull almost doubled in size as the growth distended—cohesion was lost, strands of Lucifer Vine unravelled moistly from the side of the head above the ear and a small yellow lizard ran out from the chasm that appeared in the side of the head, the creature then scurrying down the man's arm before dropping to the floor and darting away through the open door.

You will agree, this was a sight that would revolt even those with the firmest of resolve. When the forces that created this human-like figure reasserted themselves and the face became smooth again, and the leaves lost their green tints and once again resembled pale skin, that's when everyone there could see that the skin tone matched that of Holmes. The vegetable matter at the top of the head had split into thousands of fibres to leave a small topknot of hair, like Holmes' own hair.

Somehow, that hard mass formed from tendrils, leaves and petals had been sculpted so that a protrusion in the center of the 'face' had become a prominent hawk-beak of a nose—again a replica of the nose of my friend Sherlock Holmes. The effect made one sick to one's stomach. At that moment, the face suddenly contorted, causing the lips of the mouth to slide back to reveal white teeth set in greenish gums that glistened wetly in the light filtering through the wall. I must stress that what made one's stomach churn was that the face was constantly in motion—one moment a smooth face that was an echo of Holmes' face, then the chin, for example, would swell, loose cohesion, leaves bursting from flesh, revealing that the monster was made from vine. Or one of the eyeballs would split vertically, and green tendrils would pour out down one cheek. And a moment later, occult forces would regain control of the matter they had possessed, and I would find myself gazing at a near-perfect copy of a human face again. The horror! The absolute horror! If I lived to be hundred years of age, I knew only too well what

231

would forever haunt my nightmares the moment I fell asleep.

The creature's lips tightened again, revealing green gums and slippery green tongue.

"Dear God in heaven." I slipped my hand into my pocket to take hold of my revolver. "That abomination is smiling, Holmes ... *it is actually smiling.*"

"Watson, whatever you do, do not take that pistol from your pocket. We don't want to bring matters to a head ... not just yet, anyway."

The figure that (to a degree) resembled Holmes went to stand with its back to the fireplace, hands clasped behind its back in a way that Holmes favored. Despite the ghastly head upon human shoulders, the vine creature's manner, and way of holding itself, was indeed identical to Holmes. The voice was remarkably similar, too.

Now, I must confess to the reader, that to make it clear which is the real Holmes and which is the mocking fake, I am compelled to select a name for the disturbing copy of my friend. To avoid any confusion in this narrative about to whom I am referring, I will, henceforth, refer to the copy of Sherlock Holmes as "the Ogre." Indeed, Ogre is apt, because that is a mythological creature in the shape of human being, with a fondness for committing evil acts. I did not doubt that the Ogre that stood in front of me was evil to its poisonous core.

The Ogre gazed at each of us in turn with those large, grey eyes set in the massive face. "Mr. Williamson had told me to expect an invading army. You have arrived here, Mr. Holmes, with just two soldiers, who are clearly scared out of their wits."

Despite this comment, the pair, to a man, raised their rifles, pointing them at the Ogre.

The vine creature gave a loud grunt. "Gah! Put your rifles down, sirs. It's frightfully bad manners to point guns at your host."

Holmes gestured that the men should lower their guns.

232

"Thank you, Mr. Holmes. Now, isn't this a remarkable state of affairs, bearing in mind that as well as sharing the same name we look so very much alike?"

Despite the dangerous situation, I laughed with derision at this comment.

"Ah," boomed the Ogre. "Doctor Watson—Sherlock Holmes' faithful friend and biographer. Allow me to introduce to you my very own loyal companion." He called toward a doorway. "Doctor Watson, please join us."

My stomach muscles tensed at the Ogre's invitation to some unseen individual. I fully expected to see a creature fashioned from pond slime or something of the sort, grotesquely moulded to resemble my features, to step through the door. The figure that did enter through the opening, created when the screen of vines parted, was not some fantastic amalgamation of vegetable matter. No, this was not a vile chimera.

The name burst from my lips. "Bullman!"

The huge man, he with the bald head, entered the room, clad in a cream linen suit, a scarlet handkerchief neatly arranged in the breast pocket. Politely, he nodded to us. Previously, the man's eyes had burned with the fires of utter insanity. Now his gaze was cool, and not at all unfriendly.

The Ogre held out his hand—a gesture to introduce his companion. "This is my friend and assistant, Doctor Watson."

"Impossible," I protested. "Bullman doesn't even look like me."

Nolan shot me a sideways glance before snapping somewhat contemptuously, "Don't tell us you feel insulted that no attempt has been made to replicate you?"

"No, of course not. But, good grief, look at the fellow. He is a mindless brute."

Miss Dembe spoke up. "Doctor Watson, Mr. Nolan. Take care. This is exactly what Williamson craves: to sow disharmony in order to weaken us as a group."

Bullman (for I point-blank refuse to refer to him as 'Doctor Watson' in this narrative) bowed to us in a decidedly courtly fashion. "Miss Dembe. Gentlemen. You are here to consult Mr. Holmes about a matter that vexes you." Bullman had nodded in the direction of the Ogre rather than the real Sherlock Holmes when he uttered the name 'Mr. Holmes'—that done, he turned back to us. "Please explain to Mr. Holmes the nature of the mystery you are attempting to solve."

"There is no mystery," Nolan declared stoutly.

"I agree," I said. "Our aim is to prevent that scoundrel Williamson from overthrowing the government in New London."

"Come now," said the Ogre, mimicking Holmes' own voice with undeniable accuracy. "I am the greatest detective in the world. You, Sherlock Holmes, have come a long way to bare your soul to me. Is that not so?"

"Mr. Sherlock Holmes, the *bona fide* Mr. Sherlock Holmes, has not come here to consult you," I said, anger heating the blood in my veins. "You are not real. You are a conjuring trick!"

"Doctor," the Ogre purred. "You really must allow Mr. Holmes to speak for himself."

"Of which I am perfectly capable," said Holmes with just a small trace of annoyance directed at me.

The Ogre studied Holmes for a moment. "So, Mr. Holmes," it began in soft tones. "I see that you planned to hand over the governorship of Yagomba to your friend, Doctor Watson." It pointed a long finger at me. "You intend for this fellow to be become the new Lord of Damnation."

For many a year, Holmes' deductions have amazed me. The man possessed what seemed like an uncanny ability to read people's most secret thoughts. Now I experienced that amazement all over again when the Ogre appeared to divine the content of Holmes' mind.

I turned to Homes. "Can this be true? You wished me to replace you as governor?"

Holmes' expression was that of a trapped man. His eyes darted toward the doorway as if contemplating dashing from the room.

I grabbed Holmes by the arm. "Holmes, does this creature speak the truth?"

"Damn it all, Watson! Yes, it does!"

Holmes looked away from me, his face burning crimson with shame.

Miss Dembe appeared puzzled. "Mr. Holmes, what does this mean?"

"More to the point," snapped Nolan, "how does this creature know that Mr. Holmes intended to give up the role of governor, and we do not?"

I turned back to the Ogre. "How can you know anything of Mr. Holmes' plans? Who told you?"

The Ogre gave a knowing smile. "The deduction is childish in its simplicity."

"Do please share it with us," I growled, feeling angrier at Holmes than at that creature with the palpitating face, and the infuriating cocksure smile of someone who knows they have got the better of their adversary.

The Ogre, standing tall before the fireplace, thrust its hands into the pockets of the purple dressing gown. Clearly, it enjoyed Holmes' embarrassment.

And my confusion.

Bullman grinned, too. "Looks like you've baffled the great Mr. Sherlock Holmes." The smile became an expression of foul gloating. "Though not so great now, is he?"

The Ogre began to speak in the manner of a teacher lecturing their students: "Very well. I will explain how I reached my deduction that Sherlock Holmes planned to make Doctor Watson the governor of this island ..." He paused. "And that Holmes will, even now, cruelly abandon Watson to rot here."

"You're inventing this," I said, hoping to find some way to expose the Ogre as a liar.

The Ogre shook its massive head, its grey eyes momentarily turning green as it locked that fierce gaze with mine. "As Sherlock Holmes often hints: you, Doctor Watson—although a faithful friend of the man beside you—well … he really does see you as being utterly stupid."

Holmes turned away, unable to look at me, lest those deep-set eyes reveal that he agreed with what the Ogre had just said.

Miss Dembe, Nolan and the surviving soldiers watched this grim scene play out before them—fascinated yet horrified.

The Ogre smiled. "Let me put you out of your misery, Mr. Holmes, by swiftly revealing the clues that led me to this conclusion. One: you, Mr. Holmes, have repeatedly and surreptitiously checked that the inner pocket of your jacket is buttoned shut."

Holmes glared at the creature, loathing the fact that someone had now turned their forensic scrutiny on to him.

Holmes said: "I do not see what is relevant about my jacket pocket."

"Every relevance," declared the Ogre, employing a perfect imitation of Holmes' gestures and speech that could become so masterful when explaining one of his deductions. The Ogre continued briskly: "You are clearly anxious about the contents of that pocket. It can't be a bag of gold coins, or a weapon, because what resides in your pocket is not bulky. So … clue number one: whatever it is that's contained within your pocket, you value it highly enough to repeatedly check it is still there. Two: forty-eight hours ago, you were observed visiting a shipping office in the port of New London. Three: you bought a ticket for passage, for one traveller, back to England on the SS *Magdalen,* sailing on the midnight tide tomorrow. Four: I surmise that ticket is in your jacket pocket now. Five: if it is, you do not even intend to return to your accommodation in New London. Instead, you will immediately board the ship, fleeing like a coward who fears for his life. Six: you intend to leave your old friend, Doctor Watson, behind, who you know full well will agree to become the governor of the island to try and prevent the catastrophic collapse of law and order, which, however, will surely occur upon news reaching the populace of your cowardly departure."

Holmes tried to put on a brave face. "That is an absurdly simple deduction based mainly on spying on my movements."

"Ah, I should have made you sign a document that testified you were astonished by my insight, prior to explaining how I discovered that, like a rat, you intended leaving the proverbial sinking ship. My dear fellow, what do you say to that?"

Miss Dembe said: "What I say is that you have paraphrased lines from Doctor Watson's famous accounts of Mr. Holmes' cases."

Nolan took an aggressive step toward the Ogre. "Not only do you attempt to be a malevolent copy of Mr. Holmes, but you also plagiarise Doctor Watson's writings."

Nothing less than cold wrath crept through my body. "And what I say is this." I turned to Sherlock Holmes, a man I had counted as my closest friend for many a year. "What I say is, how dare you, Holmes? I've always trusted you, now this!" I lunged toward him, flipped open his jacket, tore the lining of the pocket away, and snatched an envelope from the ripped material. "Let us see if the monstrosity that imitates you, Holmes, speaks the truth!" I opened the envelope. "A single ticket!" I shouted both in triumph and dismay, as one who thrills at discovering the truth, and who also experiences the bitterest disappointment in a friend who has, to put it bluntly, betrayed a hitherto precious trust. "A ticket in your name—for the SS *Magdalen* sailing for Portsmouth, England, tomorrow night." My eyes watered with a powerful emotion that threatened to send me into a fighting rage. "Treachery, Holmes! Treachery! You planned to sneak away and leave me here in this God forsaken place."

Holmes flinched before my anger. For once, his eyes were so wounded looking, so pitiful. "Even without me, Watson, you would have done the right thing."

"What? To become the new governor? To try and prevent New London descending into anarchy, riots, bloodshed!" At that moment, I so longed with every atom of my being to crash my fist into Sherlock Holmes' face. "You intended to abandon me here!"

"My friend—"

"Friend?" I echoed in horror. "You have betrayed our friendship. What is more, you have become a coward! A cringing yellow-back."

Holmes whispered, "See here, my good fellow. There are forces here that cannot be defeated by the likes of you and I."

I flung the ticket back into his face. "Take this. Board the ship. Scurry back to Baker Street. Cower and cringe there like the pathetic wretch you are."

Frantically, Holmes scooped up both the ticket and the envelope and, eyes bright with terror, stuffed the envelope and that shameful square of paper into a side pocket of his jacket. Then he pressed his hand there against the pocket, as if he now lived in fear of losing his means of escape from Yagomba.

The Ogre and Bullman smiled with pleasure, evidently enjoying my ferocious verbal attack on the man who had once been my friend.

Abruptly, the silence that followed my outburst at Holmes was broken by a shriek. One of the soldiers had run at the wall made from Lucifer Vine. Screaming, he attacked the wall with a dagger—slashing, cutting.

Nolan and I rushed across to the man, who raved as he hacked the greenery.

Miss Dembe called out, "The Lucifer Vine has driven him insane."

Nolan glanced back at Miss Dembe as he wrestled the soldier to the floor. "You gave us … *things* to eat that conferred protection."

"He must not have eaten the flesh, otherwise he would not have been affected to this extent."

Nolan checked the man's pockets in his uniform. A

moment later, he pulled out a pellet of orangish matter. "You are correct. He did not eat the flesh. Instead, he concealed it."

The solider lay on the floor, writhing: his mad eyes glittering upward at the ceiling.

That was when another figure gracefully stepped into the room.

"My dear heart." I shivered. That beautiful face of hers had become gaunt.

Miss Dembe fixed her gaze on me. "Doctor, what do you see?"

"My wife."

The phantom-like figure glided toward me, hands reaching out, imploring me to embrace her. "John," she whispered, "I don't have much time left. Come home to me so that I might see you before it's too late."

"My dearest love, what has happened to you?"

"I'm sick, John. There is no hope."

I held out my hands to the apparition.

Miss Dembe called across the room to me. "Doctor. Did you eat the flesh I gave to you?"

"Yes."

"Then, for a while at least, you still have a modicum of protection from the effects of the Lucifer Vine. However, the protection I gave you is not wholly effective against all the powers of the occult."

Although almost mesmerised by what seemed to be the miraculous appearance of my wife, I did manage to gasp out, "Then pray tell me ... what I must do to banish this ... this shade ... this ghost."

Miss Dembe spoke firmly—calmly. "You tell me you see your wife. Believe me, sir, she is not here. Williamson has conjured an apparition to torment you."

Dazed, I uttered, "I see her as if she has become a spirit ... insubstantial, translucent ... her feet do not touch the floor."

Miss Dembe's voice became stern. "Your wife is still alive?"

"When I left London, yes."

"Then I believe she is still alive, Doctor. What you think you see is a phantasm projected into your mind, because I do not see her. Do you see another woman in this room, Nolan?"

Nolan shook his head.

"I see her," I breathed, my heart pounding, my head spinning in a dizzying whirl. "Nolan ... Nolan, my boy ... confess to me that you see her, too."

"I see nobody that wasn't here just a minute ago."

"A lady in long brown skirts? A pearl-studded brooch, just here?" I touched the left-hand side of my breast.

"No, sir. I see no lady other than Miss Dembe."

My wife's face twisted as pain speared through her body. "John. You are a doctor. I am in such agony. Please make it stop!"

Miss Dembe plunged her hand into the satchel. When she withdrew her hand, she appeared to be clutching something in her balled-up fist. A second later, she hurled a grey powder into the air above my head. With a sharp snapping sound, my wife vanished—or at least the phantom I'd see before me had vanished, leaving no trace other than a faint smell of acrid burning on the air.

Bullman clapped his hands together. "Bravo, Miss Dembe. See? The woman is much more capable than this fellow, Sherlock Holmes."

The Ogre nodded, its upper lip curling into a sneer of contempt. "The so-called great detective has been a *great* disappointment. Look how he stands there—saying nothing, doing nothing. He's a dying dog of a man—of no use to anyone."

On turning to Holmes, I immediately noted that his skin had turned waxy and had acquired an unhealthy pallor. There seemed to be no strength left in his body, for his arms hung limply by his side. He stared at the floor in front of him with an expression of utter defeat—he couldn't even bring himself to look me in the eye.

Miss Dembe's action of flinging the powder into the air to destroy the phantom-like apparition had drawn our attention away from the mad soldier. He had fallen into trembling silence for a while, but now he leapt to his feet. With a squealing cry, he sprinted toward the door. As he did so he brushed against Holmes. By now, Holmes was so feeble that even this slight, glancing contact caused my former friend to stumble to his knees. His torso pitched forward, and he had to put out both hands onto the floor to prevent himself from falling flat on his face.

As the soldier bounded away downstairs, Bullman gave a cruel chuckle. "A once-great detective brought low. See how he kneels before us." Bullman smiled at the Ogre. "You, sir, are now the man to replace Sherlock Holmes. You are not equal to him—you are superior to him in every way."

A voice suddenly cut through the hot, sultry air. "I couldn't agree more."

A vine wall had parted like two halves of a curtain. And, as it did so, Williamson strode through—as before, he wore the negative image, as it were, of priestly garments: a white suit and a black dog collar. Holmes, meanwhile, remained kneeling on the floor. Pathetically, he wrung his hands together, the very image of woe.

"Mr. Sherlock Holmes," Williamson said in a loud, clear voice. "I expected a stronger opponent. You are weak, sir. Weak as water. I anticipated you would fight me using your scientific skill as a weapon. In the end, my sorcery easily prevailed."

"What do you intend to do now?" asked Miss Dembe.

Williamson's grey lips tightened into a smile of utter evil. "I thought that would be obvious, my dear. The remnants of my little experiment here need to be swept away and disposed of forever."

Chapter 27

Sherlock Holmes was a broken man. He remained there, kneeling, his eyes brimming wetly with his shame and his sorrow. Yet the expression of misery didn't move me to pity. His plan to abandon me here in the penal colony infuriated me to the point where I could feel no compassion for him. Nolan and Miss Dembe stood beside me in that room, supernaturally woven from vine, sunlight now shining through the flesh of the plant, producing a bright green glow, which illuminated the scene of Holmes' psychological collapse and our confrontation with Williamson. For there he was: resplendent in the white suit with the black dog collar around his neck—clearly, this was his coarse attempt to mock his former calling as a clergyman, before being defrocked and dismissed from his profession. I dare say that the Church of England was glad to see the back of this vile reprobate.

Meanwhile, the remaining soldier, as quickly, and as surreptitiously as he could, in the hope his foe would not notice, cocked the rifle, then eased his finger around the trigger.

At either side of Williamson stood the Ogre and Bullman.

The trio radiated triumph. They were the winners here. They knew that absolutely.

And I knew, all too clearly, that what would happen next was our certain destruction at their hands.

Bullman stepped toward Holmes before roughly pulling him to his feet. "When I broke out of the cage on the ship, this fellow attempted to fight me with his fists." Bullman looked Holmes in the eye so fiercely that Holmes instantly turned away, his courage failing him. "Mr. Sherlock Holmes ... why don't we have a boxing match now? You and I."

"Why not?" Williamson smiled. "Mr. Holmes, if you succeed in knocking down my servant here, I will permit you to board the ship tomorrow night. There is another condition, of course, and that is you must leave Doctor Watson here to his fate. However, you, Mr. Holmes, can scuttle back to your comfortable rooms in London."

The Ogre, that mocking caricature of Holmes, chuckled. "Sherlock Holmes, sir, do you accept the challenge?"

Holmes managed a feeble nod of his head. Bullman immediately stepped back from Holmes, then adopted the stance of a boxer, clenched fists raised, chin tucked down toward his chest. He jabbed the air above Holmes' head as if warming up for combat.

Williamson's voice rang out. "Gentlemen! Round one, commence your duel!"

Holmes clenched his fists, too, though his boxer's stance was pitiful, shoulder's drooping, face as slack as the features of an opium addict: his fighting spirit had gone. Instead, of attacking, he glanced at the doorway, evidently judging whether he could simply flee from the arena of this contest.

Bullman gently punched Holmes' shoulder. "Come on, old boy. Fight me."

Holmes aimed a pair of half-hearted jabs at Bullman's huge face.

The Ogre roared laughed again; the face lost cohesion, and a froth of leaves burst out from the bottom jaw as if the man had instantly grown a beard of vivid green. "Holmes is as feeble as a kitten. No, a shrimp!" The Ogre's laughter became a huge bellowing sound.

Now, Bullman landed a restrained blow on Holmes' jaw. Holmes staggered, almost losing his balance.

Nolan yelled with frustration. "Holmes! Fight the man!"

"At least make an effort," I snapped in angry tones.

The focus of Williamson's eyes changed, so that he no longer looked at any single individual in the room— rather he appeared to gaze through the wall at some object or person in the distance. The hard rigidity of his features and the drawing together of his grey eyebrows, suggested to me that the man concentrated his mind to an extraordinary degree. Indeed, the muscles beneath the skin of his neck formed into distinct ridges, while his lips parted to reveal those yellowing teeth of his. Then his tongue flickered out between his lips, where it protruded, growing longer and longer—the moistly, fleshy organ quivering like the tongue of a venomous serpent. A sight that was as bizarre as it was disconcerting.

Williamson opened his mouth wide and shouted in a language I did not understand or recognize. And, as if at his bidding, the air began to move in the room, swiftly becoming a vortex of swirling wind. The gusts tugged at Holmes. His jacket flapped; he could barely stand in that sudden hurricane.

Miss Dembe quickly reached into her bag for more of that grey dust, which she flung toward the ceiling. With a series of loud snapping sounds, together with a flurry of blue sparks, the sudden storm in the room blew itself out.

Williamson smiled at Miss Dembe. "Goodness gracious me. Is this young lady actually using magic powder of some sort or other to combat my spells? Then my agents tell me that Miss Dembe, here, hails from a priestly class of her people."

"I will use whatever means are at my disposal to combat you."

When Bullman glanced back at her as she spoke, Holmes seized the opportunity to dart forward to rain punches on Bullman's face.

Bullman retaliated with a single ferocious jab to Holmes' jaw, and Holmes shot back across the room, falling flat on his back, his arms limply flung out. And there he lay, eyes closed, not moving.

Despite my anger at Holmes' intention to flee the country, I could not ignore what had just happened to him. I knelt beside the man, whereupon I pulled him up into a sitting position.

Holmes opened his eyes. "I'm sorry, Watson. I have let you down." Blood dribbled down his chin from the cut on his bottom lip. "I cannot save you. I cannot save our companions. I cannot even save myself."

"My dear fellow, whatever possessed you to decide that you should leave New London and abandon me here? We have been friends for so many years."

"Ah ... that's the nub of it, Watson. What did *possess* me? For the last three days, I confess I have not been feeling myself. Indeed, I have not wholly felt like *me*."

"What are you saying?"

"Watson ... dear friend. I fear that an external force has intruded upon my mind. Directing my actions. Feeding me such strange notions."

"Holmes, let me help you stand. There ... lean against me. I'll support your weight."

"I'm as weak as a man of straw. There is nothing in my armory to fight Williamson. Nothing ... Nothing ..."

His eyes became blank as he started to lose consciousness.

The Ogre, having listened to Holmes' words, gave a throaty chuckle. "Count Mr. Shrimp out." As he finished speaking, his face regained its former cohesion and the froth of leaves appeared to be sucked back into the flesh of the jaw, which turned once more into smooth skin.

Williamson's lip curled with scorn. "No need. I declare Holmes to be the loser."

With no other options available to me and knowing that the threat to our survival was at its greatest, I pulled the revolver from my pocket. That's when the Ogre struck out—it snatched the pistol from my hand and hurled it toward the wall. Instantly, the pistol stuck to the vines. A second later, more vines crawled over the weapon before drawing it out of sight.

To my surprise, the Ogre did not attack me. Instead, that giant of a figure stepped back, grinning.

Turning to Holmes, I shook him, trying to rouse him from his torpor as he swayed there unsteadily. "Holmes, old chap. Do wake up. I rather suspect that matters are coming to a head."

Even as I spoke, Bullman lumbered toward Miss Dembe, his eyes undergoing a chilling transformation as he did so. When he'd first appeared in the room, his eyes were cool, rational. Now they flared with fiery violence again, which I'd witnessed before, when he ran amok on the ship. Miss Dembe stepped back from him as he closed in on her.

"Holmes," I cried, "if we are going to do something to save Miss Dembe and the others, we must do it now. What do you suggest?"

Holmes appeared dazed. "Watson ... didn't Sir Charles Darwin and his son, Francis, state that plants have a rudimentary brain? A brain located in the root apex? And that the brain responds to sensory input from the plant and ... and allows trees and shrubs and grass to respond to threats, and changes in their environment."

"Holmes, why are you talking about this now?"

"I'm sorry I failed you. My mind should have been sharper. I'm so confused in my thoughts." His eyes rolled in such an alarming manner I feared that he might collapse into unconsciousness at any moment, yet he continued to speak about a subject that had irrationally seized hold of his mind: "Sir Charles Darwin tells us that plants have a rudimentary nervous system that enables them to turn to the sunlight or move their stems away from harm."

When Miss Dembe reached into the satchel again, Bullman pushed her against the wall so forcefully, the satchel flew from her grasp, whereupon it fell to the floor. And as she slammed against the wall, she cried out in pain—instantly, vines sped outward and with the sinuous dexterity of octopus tentacles wrapped themselves around her from head to foot. Within seconds, she was firmly trapped there, bound to the wall by living greenery. Although she struggled mightily, she could not break free. Nolan hurled himself at Bullman, swinging punches. However, Bullman effortlessly picked up the man and threw him against the wall. More creepers sprang out to seize Nolan, holding him as effectively as if chained there, his back to the wall.

Holmes' eyelids fluttered and I had to hold him upright, otherwise he would have slumped to the floor.

"Every tree generates electricity," he muttered, as he gazed strangely at the palms of his hands, as one might if a party of fairies danced there, skipping from palm to palm. "Every tree carries an electrical charge of approximately one volt. Not much. Not a great voltage. Now multiply that one volt a single tree produces by a million-fold...." His eyelids fluttered again as he sagged weakly against me. "A jungle like this must have a million trees or more ... that's more than a million volts. Plants are conductors of electricity. Trees in a jungle interweave their branches, touching their neighbors, creepers connect one tree with the next. Roots of different trees interlock. Vines are the circuits of nature. Electricity throbbing through all that greenery, Watson. A million volts moving in lightning-fast torrents through the forest!"

"Holmes, you don't—"

With a piercing scream, Holmes pushed me away. Then frantically seizing the satchel that Miss Dembe had dropped on the floor, he clutched it to his chest. Still yelling, as if deranged, Holmes sped through the doorway. Instead of running down the stairs, he raced upward, shouting words that I could not make out.

The single remaining soldier ran after him, perhaps hoping that Holmes knew of some means of escape from this nightmarish place. Bullman immediately followed, hurrying toward the doorway.

The instant Williamson's voice rang out, with all the force of a priest in the pulpit promising brimstone and fire for sinners, Bullman stopped dead. "No! I will destroy Sherlock Holmes," shouted Williamson. "That will give me at least a modicum of satisfaction after the feeble way he tried to defeat me." He smiled—gloating, somehow unctuous. "And, moreover, seeing him die a painful death will be sweet vengeance for me. After Holmes' interference, all those years ago, which resulted in me, a man of the cloth, being sent to rot in a vermin-infested jail, with all manner of criminals and degenerates, the agonies he will soon endure will heal the wounds in this old heart of mine." His grin was utterly loathsome. "Doctor Watson. For my so-called crime, back in England, I received seven years penal servitude. However, because I chose to take a little walk beyond the prison gates one day, I was sentenced to another ten years in that foul abyss of a jail, which was little more than a tomb for the living. And then, to add to my torment, I was sent to this island with its unbearable heat, and its insects that constantly bite. However, I met a witch doctor here, a woman in exile from the African mainland. From her, I learnt how to wield power beyond the dreams of mere mortals."

I felt my anger increase at the man in front of me, dressed in white, something clearly intended as a blasphemous mockery of the clothes worn by *bona fide* priests. How I longed to grab Williamson by his stick-thin neck, and to squeeze so hard that I would have the pleasure of feeling the neck vertebrae crack and snap beneath my fingers.

I growled: "Williamson. Back in 1895, you assisted in the abduction of Miss Violet Smith, and you took part in a plot to forcibly marry her to a rogue against her wishes. Then, after justly being incarcerated for your crimes, you attempted to cut short your prison sentence by attempting to escape. You, sir, absolutely deserved those additional years behind bars."

Miss Dembe added, "And now you deserve to hang."

"Hear, hear." Nolan's eyes blazed with anger. "And I shall be there, Williamson, when the hangman puts the noose around your neck."

Williamson laughed. "Hardly! Are you forgetting that you are bound tight by the vines to the wall? Ha! You are my prisoners now!"

I stepped forward, fist raised, intending to slam my knuckles into Williamson's repugnant mouth. However, Bullman stepped between Williamson and myself, blocking me from attacking the man.

"Ah, Doctor Watson." Williamson spoke in that gloating way again. "You wrote an account of the case, entitling it 'The Solitary Cyclist,' and caused it to be published in *The Strand Magazine.* I have not forgotten your part in my arrest or the hurtful way you portrayed me as some cowardly, screeching imbecile. You, Doctor, will suffer, too."

With that threat hanging in the air, Williamson swept through the doorway, followed by the Ogre and Bullman. I glanced at Miss Dembe and Nolan as they struggled against their green bonds, though I realized they would never break free of them.

I knew, with the heaviest of hearts, there was nothing I could do to save Holmes now. Nevertheless, despite all that had happened, my own loyalty to him remained as solid as the foundations of a cathedral. I owed it to my old friend to witness his final moments of life.

Chapter 28

I dashed from the room to the stairs. The entire structure—its walls, floor, roof, doors, staircase—were all made from tightly-knitted Lucifer Vine. The steps were firm enough under my feet as I climbed the staircase, following the route Holmes had taken when he'd fled, babbling in that deranged way, clutching Miss Dembe's satchel to his chest, his desperate, searching eyes hunting for an exit from this bedevilled house.

The staircase rose floor after floor. Even though this was a replica of the building that Holmes occupied in Baker Street, it was much higher than the original. By the time I reached the top of the vine-woven building my heart clamored painfully, and perspiration cascaded down my face. At last, however, I reached the top of the staircase, which opened directly into open air. For a moment, I stood there panting, trying to catch my breath. The roof was higher than most of the surrounding trees; consequently I found myself looking down onto treetops some twenty feet below me, despite those trees being at least a hundred feet tall. But how could the building be taller than before? Had this devilish structure actually been growing while we had been inside of it? Apparently so, because the roadway seemed such a considerable distance from me as I looked down.

There, on the roof, I saw Bullman, his eyes blazing with crazed hatred once more. And there was the unsettling Ogre of a creature that had been modeled on Holmes' physical appearance: the creature even wore a long, flowing purple dressing gown (exactly the same as Holmes favored) over day clothes of white shirt, bowtie, grey trousers and black shoes. The illusion of a perfect copy was broken when a swelling bulged out from the Ogre's throat, which burst forth with the heart-shaped leaves and pink flowers of the Lucifer Vine. From the vegetation, suddenly erupting from apparently human skin, a red snake slithered from the interior of the throat before swaying there for a second, the serpent's head rising, dark eyes glinting, and pink tongue flickering out, tasting the air. A moment later, the snake dropped to the roof where it wriggled down into the mat of vine and vanished. And in just another moment, uncanny forces within the Ogre's body caused the froth of leaves and flowers to tightly bunch, before being drawn back into the throat—and once again, the throat appeared to belong to a human being—well, almost, because there was a faint pattern of compressed leaves that created strange stigmata on the skin.

Williamson, meanwhile, stood in the center of the flat expanse of interwoven Lucifer Vine.

The structure had been formed around tall trees, the timber giving the building backbone, as it were. Tree trunks must have supported that dense mass of living vine. Here and there on the roof, the leafy tips of trees, perhaps four or five feet in height, protruded above the vine thatch, to create soft clumps of greenery.

Holmes had, by this time, backed toward the edge of the building. The solider stood beside him, rifle in hand. Holmes, it must be stated, continued to shout in that odd, irrational way. One hand clutched the satchel, the other hand clawing at his own head. Clearly, my friend's sanity had suffered. His eyes darted in panic. And when Williamson moved slowly toward him, he gestured in a most pathetic fashion, as he pleaded with the man to spare his life.

Williamson came to a halt, whereupon he raised his face to the sky, stretched his arms out at either side of himself, his eyes instantly turning fierce with concentration. Once again, he called out in a loud voice. The words he uttered appeared to stem from an ancient language that may well have once flowed from the lips of prehistoric humanity— back when home was a cave, spears were tipped with flint, and men and women roamed the Earth in their nakedness. Within seconds, cloud flooded the blue sky. Thunder began its deep rumbling—a violent sound—that thunder told me that Williamson had once again summoned a storm to use as a weapon against his enemies.

Although I no longer had my pistol, I could not stand there being a mere spectator of the tragedy to come. I ran toward Williamson, one thought roaring through my mind: *Fling the devil from the roof! That will put an end to his mischief!*

Williamson's eyes flashed at the Ogre. "Seize Watson. Hold him still."

The creature smoothly raced toward me, its lips sliding back to reveal a tongue that was colored the same bright green as moss found upon a tombstone. I punched at that face, which was a disturbing copy of Holmes'. For all the effect my blow had, I might as well have punched a tree trunk. The monster hissed with delight as it caught hold of me, enthusiastically locking me in its tight grip. Although I struggled mightily, I could not break free of the inhuman power of its arms. Now, being so close, I felt the powerful exhalation of air from its lungs against my face. A revolting sensation indeed. And the creature's stench filled my nostrils, reminding me of vegetation rotting in some infernal swamp.

Above us, cloud swarmed across the sky, blotting out the sun, casting a forbidding gloom over the jungle.

253

Once again, I heard bicycle bells high above me—*ding-ding, ding-ding.* That, and faraway laughter that oozed with mockery—laughter no doubt directed at Holmes, the soldier and myself on the roof. This time, I saw no phantom cyclists riding their machines through the air. What I did see, however, was a knot of shadows hovering above the roof—shadows that contained purple and red filaments, which squirmed and writhed there between Holmes and me, as I stood, trapped in the viciously tight grip of the Ogre.

Williamson nodded with satisfaction. "Ah, she is here. The one called Yemaya."

I looked toward the stairwell that descended through the thick mat of greenery into the house. Williamson's statement led me to believe that I would see a woman climbing up from the stairwell onto the roof of the building.

Williamson, however, moved his hands in front of his face—a priestly gesture of sorts. Then he said: "Here she is. The source of my beautiful power."

It was then that I realized that the writhing strands of shadow and light had begun to take on a distinct shape—specifically, a human shape.

I gasped with astonishment, for there, suddenly in front of me, was the striking individual I'd seen before in the gallows yard. This was the same extraordinary figure, clad in leopard skin, who had flung a spear, narrowly missing Holmes, just a short while ago. Once again, I was struck how her face was so strikingly similar to that of Miss Dembe's.

"Holmes," I said, "this is the woman that Miss Dembe claimed is one of her ancestors."

Sherlock Holmes, however, remained silent. His eyes were turned downward, staring at the roof, as if he pretended that the bizarre events unfolding here were of no consequence to him.

I directed my next words at Williamson. "I take it this woman is not alive. That she is a spirit, which you have conjured here."

Williamsons' thin lips tightened into a grotesque smile. "Yemaya is—or rather was—a priestess to her people. Though some would term her a witch doctor. Whatever the terminology, she wielded immense power. The witch doctor whom I found in hiding on this island, who taught me the magic of her people, showed me how to draw one of the long-dead witch doctors from the tomb so that I might harness their occult power—a power that still pulsates within their bones."

"Then you have captured a spirit of a dead human being," I said. "Even for you that is a monstrous act."

Williamson merely shrugged, not caring one jot about my accusation. "Doctor Watson, consider Yemaya here to be a reservoir of valuable energy that I can exploit to strengthen my own occult power. I use her as one would use an electrical battery to cause an electric motor to run."

I struggled to break free of the Ogre's grip, vowing to snap Williamson's rotten neck. I struggled in vain. The Ogre's grip on me could not be broken by my own strength alone.

Williamson laughed. "Yemaya. You know what you must do. Summon your gods of thunder and lightning."

Yemaya raised both hands—a gesture of ancient ritual, or so it seemed to me. She then tilted her face up to the sky and called out in words that I did not understand. Yet they had a striking clarity and vibrated with power.

Immediately, the storm grew in intensity. Winds circled the roof, a veritable tornado—the vortex sucking leaves from the vines, drawing them up and up, spinning and fluttering, high into the air above our heads, a blizzard of emerald-green.

That was the moment when the soldier, the youth who wore a silver crucifix, raised his rifle, aimed the weapon at Williamson, and fired. The bullet, revealing itself as a tiny red-hot shooting star, missed his head by inches.

Williamson glared in fury at the man. The soldier's rifle could only be loaded with a single round at any one time. And there, on the vine roof, he tried to reload his weapon, fumbling a cartridge from a pouch on his belt—then, rendered clumsy by both haste and fear, dropping the ammunition. Instantly, vines swarmed over the rifle cartridge, seemingly devouring that little brass casing into itself.

Yet again, lightning painted silver lines of jagged fire across the sky. Thunder followed hot on lightning's heels, crashing about my head so loudly I flinched in shock.

Yemaya raised her arms again, making a fierce gesture of summoning. Lightning split the gloom above, and thunder roared.

Williamson's expression now turned to one of pleasure, for he knew his power over the mortals on the roof was overwhelming. And yet ...

And yet ... that was the moment that Holmes stopped his cowardly begging. Smoothly, and quite slowly, he rose to his full height—and raised his chin with a defiant expression on his face.

My goodness! He was Sherlock Holmes again! The great detective! Intelligence shone powerfully from those clear grey eyes. This was the man whose commanding presence can dominate a room of a hundred men and women. Whose single glance can quell a rowdy gathering into instant silence. Despite being held in the crushing grasp of the Ogre, my heart surged with joy.

"Holmes!" I shouted. "Holmes, you are your old self again!"

Holmes smiled at me. "I trust I always was, Watson, my old friend. Well ... very nearly. For I danced dangerously closely to madness. I confess that the Lucifer Vine nearly stole my wits away." His smile broadened. "Moreover, I admit to being possessed—and willingly so. I was possessed by the questing spirit of the scientist who will never surrender to Bully Superstition and never yield to Tyrant Ignorance."

Hatred glittered in Williamson's eyes. "You fool, Holmes, do not deceive yourself that you will win. You have lost your final battle. You are finished!"

Holmes was once more that towering figure I knew so well as he pulled the white envelope, containing the ship's ticket, from his jacket. "Williamson." The clarity and strength of Holmes' voice was thrilling to hear. "I soon realized that spies were following me in New London. Of course, I did not know then it was you who had sent them after me. What alerted me to the fact I was the target of some as yet unidentified enemy, was when I sat down in my armchair to smoke my pipe. Immediately, after the first puff of my pipe, I noticed my brother Mycroft rush into the room to scream at me that Mrs. Hudson had thrown all my belongings out into the street and had rented out my rooms to none other than Professor Moriarty."

Williamson chuckled. "Oh, how I would have loved to see your expression of utter distress on your face at that moment."

"Ah," sighed Holmes, "what a lamentably cruel fellow you are."

"Pray continue with your tale, Mr. Holmes. Your description of what you suffered is absolutely delightful."

Holmes did continue, but not before awarding Williamson a glance of utter contempt. "Of course, I knew that Mycroft was in London, not Yagomba. Therefore, I concluded that someone had caused me to hallucinate—that is to say, they attempted sabotage my mind. As that hallucination had occurred as soon as I began to smoke the pipe, the source of whatever had infiltrated my mind was immediately obvious. Naturally, I removed the stem from the bowl of the pipe and I found within the hollow stem a ..." Holmes stopped speaking.

"Yes. Yes!" Williamson's eyes gleamed with delight—his ungodly excitement aroused by what he heard.

With a thrill of horror, I shouted, "Holmes! You found a piece of Lucifer Vine in the pipe! Isn't that so?"

Williamson laughed as he clapped his hands together, his expression one of unwholesome pleasure.

Holmes nodded. "Yes, Watson. One of Williamson's spies had evidently crept into our rooms, while we were out, and they had taken apart my pipe, and then slipped a thin sliver of leaf from the Lucifer Vine into the hollow stem. A singularly malicious act, isn't that so?" Holmes continued briskly, "Of course, when I lit the pipe I then, unwittingly, drew warm tobacco smoke over and around the shred of that narcotic leaf, thus releasing its vapor, which I drew into my lungs. And the first lungful of smoke brought a very excitable Mycroft into the room, with a shocking tale of Mrs. Hudson evicting me from my home." Sherlock Holmes smiled. "And one thing my brother is not noted for is excitability."

"Oh, bravo." Williamson clapped his hands together again as he grinned at the Ogre and Bullman. "I told you my plan would work, didn't I just? Ha! Mr. Sherlock Holmes, the great detective, mentally spiked by a shard of greenery. Splendid!"

I said, "Holmes, thank goodness you discovered that fragment of Lucifer Vine before you smoked anymore of the pipe."

"Thank goodness, indeed," declared Holmes in a heartfelt way.

I squirmed in the Ogre's firm grasp, so I could look directly at Holmes. "And then you removed the leaf from the pipe stem."

"Yes, I did."

"Thank heaven for that." The relief was evident to hear in my voice.

Then Holmes said, "And after I had removed the leaf, I tore it in half. And I put one half of it back into the pipe stem."

"You did what?" I stared at Holmes in shock.

Holmes nodded. "I put the much-reduced-in-size shred of leaf back. Then I finished smoking the pipe."

Williamson laughed as he did a little jigging dance of delight. "Mr. Holmes. I cannot begin to tell you how much I am enjoying your account of your descent into madness. Willingly smoking a pipe containing Lucifer Vine? How deliciously insane of you." He wore an expression approaching ecstasy on his face. "Sir, you were clearly deranged before you even arrived here on the island. Isn't that so, Doctor Watson?"

At that moment, I was so astonished by Holmes' act of self-destruction, by smoking a pipe containing that evil plant, that I could not disagree. Yes, it was absolutely insane behavior on Holmes' part.

Holmes held up a hand as he made an important point. "Yes, an immensely dangerous act. After all, I simply did not know if smoking a pipe with even a tiny quantity of vine contaminating the pipe stem would result in me becoming permanently insane. However … desperate times, desperate measures. You see, Williamson, I knew that the spy would report back to their employer in great detail about my mental state and my behavior. So, I gambled that the psychologically destructive effects of the vine would be temporary—this was in order to convince you that any little drama I would then enact would prove to you that I had, indeed, lost my mind. Yes, you will be pleased to know, Williamson, that after smoking the pipe, an entire legion of goblins erupted from the living-room carpet before holding me face down over the burning gas jets of a stove, where I writhed in an agony that seemed absolutely real to me."

Williamson laughed and uttered, "Splendid! Splendid!" However, the man did not appear so pompously sure of himself now. What's more, the grin of delight seemed somewhat forced.

Holmes said, "Naturally, I consider myself to be the master of my mind. Therefore, I convinced myself that I wasn't being roasted alive by goblins on a gas stove, and that it was purely hallucination. However, the peculiar mental state that had been ignited by the vine was my very plausible mask of insanity to convince you that what I did next wasn't a deception on my part, but the actions of a genuinely deranged man. So, with my clothes in disarray, my eyes staring like one possessed, my face squirming with all manner of expressions that would disturb even the most unflappable of individuals, I knew then that anyone who saw me would believe that my sanity had been shattered. Thereafter, I ran barefoot to the shipping office, whereupon I bought a ticket, suggesting to your spies that I planned to sail back home at the earliest opportunity, and that it would be clear to you I intended to abandon my friend here, Doctor Watson, in a city that you hoped would descend into anarchy—a state of affairs that would allow you to seize control of the island with much greater ease. Happily, you believed my deception because of my abnormal behavior. Therefore, I had already manipulated your actions to suit my plans, even when I was still back in New London."

Williamson let out a string of vile curses as he stamped his foot like a spoilt child, his exasperation plain to see, and then he fixed his eyes on Holmes in a way that was now cold and utterly cruel. "Foolish man! Imbecile! Can't you understand that you stand here before me as vulnerable as an ant beneath a raised boot. I can crush you as simply as that?" He snapped his fingers.

Williamson's rage seemed to inflame the storm, for thunder boomed with the ferocity of dynamite explosions. Lightning sped down from the sky to strike the forest. Trees, as close as a hundred yards away from us, burst into flame, casting off their leaves by the thousand, which were drawn up into the whirlwind that had begun to spin around the building. Those leaves formed a green stream that flowed upward into the sky. Holmes quickly ripped the ship's ticket in two; thereafter, he flung the pieces in Williamson's direction—the scraps of paper, however, immediately ascended within the rotating currents of air, where they flew upward and upward—toward the violent storm clouds that still hurled lightning earthward—electric arrows of such brilliance they hurt my eyes.

Then I remembered what Holmes had so often told me in the past. *"Watson, everything I do has a purpose. No action of mine is frivolous. When the situation demands it, every word I speak, every movement I make is a component of a machine I am building that, when I activate its mechanism, will do my bidding."*

"Great Scott," I breathed, whispering to myself so only I could hear. "My dear Holmes, I understand.... Smoking the pipe that contained the shred of vine in its stem, to induce the symptoms of madness. Buying the ticket, the play-acting, running up to the roof with the satchel: everything is part of your plan. But what are you planning to do? What surprise do you have in store for Williamson?"

Williamson's expression of concentration grew more intense by the second. The man exerted his willpower. Veins throbbed in his temples; his grey lips became a hard line that spoke volumes about the cold, unfeeling heart that beat within his breast. And I knew exactly the focus of that mendacious will. Holmes was in Williamson's gunsights, as it were. And Holmes, I very much feared, would be the next man to die. Because that fiend Williamson controlled the storm, summoning a bolt of lightning, which struck a cluster of tree branches that protruded upward from the building's roof to a height of five feet or so. The branches exploded, scattering shredded wood pulp that steamed profusely, such was the heat generated by the fearsome voltage of the lightning.

Holmes' expression changed, too. I could tell that he concentrated with a fierce intensity as he stared up at the sky, seemingly making mental calculations, the results of which would govern his future actions. A fiery bolt of lightning struck a tree fifty yards away, raising a torrent of upward-rushing sparks.

Williamson's laugh was nothing less than a bark of utter contempt. "I know what you intend, Mr. Holmes. You attempt to control the lightning. But such mastery of the elements, sir, is far and away beyond your feeble abilities. Your willpower isn't strong enough to save you or your companions!"

The soldier, meanwhile, had been largely ignored by those on the roof as he quietly struggled to reload his weapon. Terror made the man's hands shake so much that he couldn't slot the cartridge into the rifle—again and again, *fumble, fumble* ... forever dropping the ammunition into the woven greenery. At long last his persistence paid off, because with a cry of triumph he raised the gun.

Bullman had been standing absolutely still, quite impassive despite the storm and the dramatic events unfolding here. Suddenly, like a puppet that has had its strings yanked hard, the giant of a man lurched in front of Williamson, just as the soldier fired. Bullman had become a living shield of flesh and blood, which Williamson used to protect himself.

The bullet slammed into Bullman's mighty chest. Instantly, blood spurted from a hole in the center of his torso. With an expression of surprise on the man's face, he staggered sideways before falling flat onto the roof.

Williamson, shrieking with rage, uttering the foulest of curses, made an extravagant grasping motion above his head, as if plucking an object from thin air. In response to his summons, lightning tore down from the clouds. That fast-moving blade of fire struck the soldier. He fell, a smouldering ruin, his eyes bursting—pink gel weeping from the sockets as the ferocious heat boiled his innards. And, as he shrieked his death-cry, a gush of steam vented from his wide-open jaws. The man convulsed hugely, then lay still.

Williamson made the same gesture again at the sky, while bellowing commands in a language I could not comprehend. Once more, lightning cracked from the sky with dazzling brightness: this time missing Holmes by barely half a dozen feet. The lightning bolt struck one of the treetops that frothed out above the thatch of vine. Shreds of scorched leaf rose into the sky, sucked upward by the vortex of swirling air.

Holmes shouted, "Williamson! Stop this now! Let there be no more killing!"

"Too late, Mr. Holmes, you interfering busybody— you meddler!" His features shone with triumph. "Far, far too late. My magic is infinitely more powerful that your science. Indeed, infinitely more powerful than the creed I once embraced as a clergyman. I will destroy you!"

"Listen to me, Williamson. As governor of New London, I will—"

"Offer me a pardon? Then grant free and safe passage from the island to a destination of my choice?"

"No. You must face the consequence of your actions. However, I will guarantee that you receive a fair trial and the services of a defense lawyer."

"Ha!" Williams eyes bulged as he laughed with utter scorn. "A fair trial? A lawyer? Is that what you offer me in return for my surrender? Pah! You make that ridiculous offer when I have all the power over events here, and you have none."

"Instead of demonstrating your power," declared Holmes, "you should demonstrate mercy."

"Mercy? Did you show me mercy when your testimony at my trial, all those years ago, condemned me to confinement in a meager cell, with little more than the vilest of broth and dry bread to keep me alive?"

Holmes spoke calmly: "You committed a crime, sir. The punishment you received was just."

Williamson scowled. "I will not return to a prison such as that. Not when I have command of nature—and I can do this!" He made that clutching gesture at the sky again, and a lightning bolt seared the air in a great blue flash, striking a tree just fifty yards away in the forest, exploding branches into white fragments of wood pulp that were immediately sucked upward by the whirlwind of air raging around the vine house. "And see this," shouted Williamson, as he grabbed the woman he'd conjured from the grave—the one called Yemaya. "See," he shrieked. "This woman is flesh and blood. She has a beating heart. I learned well from my witch-doctor friend. See, gentlemen! I have the power to put beautiful flesh on old bone. I can make the dead live again! Does Yemaya here not resemble a living, breathing woman?"

... she could not resist his command. Yemaya gestured at the sky ...

Holmes spoke in the coldest of tones: "She lives," he conceded. "And, undoubtedly, you are responsible for how she looks—and that you have concocted a figure derived from your own abhorrent imagination. It is clear to me, also, that she lives in misery. Her eyes tell me that she is in excruciating pain."

Williamson chuckled, a wet, throaty sound that made my flesh crawl. "What do I care about her pain? My resurrected priestess is my puppet. I control her. When I pull the strings, figuratively speaking, she dances as I please. And she is valuable to me. She is even more adept than I am when summoning lighting from the sky." He shook her roughly by the arm. "Yemaya. Show Mr. Holmes how you can carve a highway through the forest."

Yemaya's face revealed no expression, but Holmes was indeed right. Her eyes—and they were truly living eyes—glistened with pain. At that moment, our eyes did meet, and I sensed that she defiantly resisted Williamson's command.

Williamson shook her again—the brutal action of a bully. "Yemaya, do as I tell you. Carve me a roadway through the jungle. Hah! All the swifter for my men to march to New London." He shook her again. "Do it!"

Though resentful, she could not resist his command. Yemaya gestured at the sky, calling out. This time! A dozen—a hundred lightning strikes! They blazed down, one after another—*whoosh! whoosh! whoosh!*—the lightning strikes being so precisely targeted by her that they burned a line through the forest, vaporizing trees in such a way that destructive force carved a clearing through thousands of trees. And when the smoke drifted away on the breeze, I saw that, indeed, an open trackway had been blazed across the forest—along which people could move easily, without having to hack foliage or detour around clumps of thorn trees.

Williamson pushed Yemaya aside, as if he no longer had any need of her—for now, that is. Because I had no doubt that Williamson would force her to invoke destructive powers against the police and soldiers of New London when the time came for him to overthrow its government and impose his own, no doubt, tyrannical rule.

The storm became increasingly savage. Fierce winds tugged at Holmes' hair, and he was compelled to shield his eyes against sticks and leaves that whirled so rapidly around the roof, lest he be blinded by the fast-moving debris. And, once again, another savage updraft of air drew those sticks and leaves skyward with incredible velocity.

Holmes pushed against the torrents of air, moving closer to Williamson. "Yes, the occult forces are strong. But you have a chronic problem. You do not have adequate control over those forces. Neither does Yemaya. They are too unpredictable. That's why you need the services of gunmen and agents, because your powers aren't as strong or as far-ranging as you pretend them to be."

"Is this unpredictable? Ha! Farewell, Mr. Holmes!" He gestured again, and once more lightning devastated a nearby tree, just beyond the building. Williamson scowled in fury at the burning tree.

"There is the proof of my assertion," Holmes shouted. "Modern technology produces the desired result. Magic is *always* unpredictable. Therefore, unreliable. You intended that lightning bolt to strike my body—instead, it struck the tree."

"Soon, Mr. Holmes, it will be you that is struck down."

"How soon? Your ability to control the storm is hit-and-miss. If I may make a comparison. When I press an electric light switch, the circuit is always completed, as the scientist who invented it intended, and the bulb emits light. You use your willpower to direct lightning bolts at me—sometimes they discharge in the air, sometimes they strike a tree in the forest. Therefore, woefully hit-and-miss."

"I have the ability to create unimaginable power."

"No, Williamson, you do not create that power. You attempt to regulate the flow of an already existing power—

you strive to direct it in a certain way to achieve a desired result. But, I repeat, you don't generate that power, nor do you control it effectively. Therefore, science, due to its consistency, must ultimately be more effective than your *absolutely inconsistent* witchcraft."

Holmes slowly backstepped toward me now. As he did so, he opened the satchel that Miss Dembe had brought with her, and which he had carried up to the roof. He then slipped his hand into the bag.

Williamson laughed. "You talk of science but look at you. You are resorting to the use of magic powders that your servant girl brought with her. Ultimately, you do not have enough belief in your science to use it as a weapon against me. But the truth is this, sir: whatever the form of magic your servant girl invoked, it is weak in comparison to mine."

"Let me explain." Holmes took a step closer to where I stood, helplessly locked in the grasp of that infernal creature formed from Lucifer Vine. "Just moments ago, downstairs, you saw me running around in a mad terror. As well as encouraging you to dismiss me as a spent force, I was also investigating the nature of the substance that Miss Dembe threw into the air. When I pretended to stumble, it was so I could drop to my knees in order to press my palms against the floor." He held up a hand to display grey smudges on the palm. "This is a sample of the powder from Miss Dembe's bag."

Williamson tilted his head, curious now. "What is it? Ground crocodile bones? My witch-doctor friend told me that is moderately effective when used to combat the weaker forces of occult."

"No. This substance can be found in my laboratory."

"Some rare chemical, I suppose?"

"On the contrary. It's the most plentiful element within the planet."

Williamson made that clutching gesture again above his head. Instantly, lightning struck a branch that jutted up from the roof just twenty feet away from me. I felt the sting of hot leaf pulp, which had been flung at me by the explosion. The steaming scraps of leaf spattered the face of the Ogre, too; however, the creature didn't even appear to notice, so intent was it on staring at Williamson with a worshipping gaze, like he was a god who had deigned to set his celestial feet on the coarse fabric of our world.

Holmes locked eyes with the man, using that piercing stare of his to unsettle him. "Wouldn't you like to know what this powder is, Williamson?"

"Tell me, if you wish. But I confess it is not important to me, because you and Doctor Watson will soon be dead. After that, I will march into New London and become the new Lord of Damnation." Williamson feigned interest in that scornful way of his. The infuriating wretch! "So? The powder?"

"It is an effective conductor of electrical power." Holmes angled the open bag, so allowing Williamson to see inside. "When Miss Dembe threw the substance into the air, in the room downstairs, the crackle of electricity could be distinctly heard as the powder disrupted the electrical field that your so-called magic depends upon for its power. That's why the image of Watson's wife vanished—the dust broke the circuit."

The Ogre hissed in contempt. "You are now talking nonsense, Mr. Holmes. And doing so won't save your life."

"Must I explain everything in simple terms?" Holmes sighed, disappointed by the creature's lack of understanding. "Each tree of a forest generates one volt of electricity or thereabouts. Now, you will know that the jungle, hereabouts, consists of possibly millions of trees: consequently, that is a huge amount of electricity, which in turn creates a powerful electrical field that fuels Williamson's magic."

Williamson gave a throaty chuckle. "Your scientific explanation of my power is not necessary—it works splendidly, that's all you need to know."

"Ah," remarked Holmes, "but a scientist always desires to know how and why. Therefore, it was vitally important that I learn the nature of this grey powder in Miss Dembe's satchel."

"Oh, yes ... the powder ... then tell me, Mr. Holmes, what is this powder that you foolishly find so remarkable?"

"Believe me, its qualities are indeed remarkable." Holmes took another step backward. "As I have already told you, it conducts electricity. In other forms, it can be used to fashion a lightning conductor or lightning rod. I'm sure that when you were a clergyman, before your fall from grace, such a device adorned the tower of your parish church. And, furthermore, you know exactly the purpose of a lightning rod, which consists of a metal strip running from the top of the tower to the ground, thus protecting the tower from destruction by safely conducting the lightning's voltage down the metal strip, to where it harmlessly discharges into the earth."

"What?" Williamson's eyes bulged. Simultaneously, thunder seemed to give voice to his own alarm because there was a furious sequence of bangs from overhead as the storm grew more savage. The subsequent updraft of air almost threatened to lift us from the roof.

"This grey substance," shouted Holmes, "has nothing to do with magic spells. This ..." he held out the bagful of powder. "This is nothing more than iron filings. Powdered iron. The dust of iron. And iron being the material that was used in the manufacture of lightning rods in times gone by!"

With that, he swung the open bag, hurling the powder in Williamson's direction. The man flinched, eyes wide— and for the first time I saw fear on his face. And, once again, he screeched a torrent of vile oaths.

The iron filings that Holmes had flung never even reached Williamson. The updraft of air caught the dust, carrying the cloud up toward the storm raging above our heads, where the sky was laced by fiery strands of lightning.

Holmes now ran at full speed. He smashed into the Ogre that held me captive. The force of Holmes' nerve-powered charge knocked the huge creature off balance. Holmes, the Ogre, and I—we all fell sprawling onto the thatch in a chaotic muddle of arms and legs.

Yemaya stood there—a spirit trapped in a flesh prison of Williamson's creation. Her face was expressionless, yet her eyes seemed to bleed pure sorrow at what that scoundrel Williamson had done to her: bringing her back from the grave to serve his evil whims.

Williamson, meanwhile, screwed up his face into a fierce mask of concentration. "Storm," he yelled. "I demand that you to do my bidding! Lightning, you will obey me!"

Within seconds, the two pounds or so of iron filings formed an elongated vertical cloud. The perfect lightning conductor. That's when I realized why Holmes had thrown the torn-apart ticket—he wanted to test that the updraft was powerful enough to carry the iron filings upward within the vortex of the storm. Therefore, when he hurled the iron filings in Williamson's direction, he had never intended that metal dust to strike him—no, Holmes had gauged that the iron filings would be drawn upward, creating a route for the lightning, downward to the highest point on the roof—and the highest point now was that screeching, raging individual. Indeed, just as Holmes intended, the bottommost part of the swirling mist of iron filings was just above Williamson where he stood on the roof.

At that moment, the storm discharged a colossal lightning bolt. That flash of blue sped down through the cloud of iron filings before striking Williamson's head, the resulting convulsion causing him to throw out his arms, up toward the heaven he had scorned long ago. He screamed. And as he screamed out in his fury and his pain, a column of fire jetted up from his mouth, fully thirty feet into the air, a vertical fountain of incandescence.

Strangely, there was no more thunder. There was no Williamson, either. At least, not a living one. The dead man had collapsed limply onto the building of pernicious vine.

When I endeavored to rise to my feet, the Ogre, even though it limply held onto my arm, made no serious attempt to restrain me, and I easily shrugged away those cold hands. Within seconds, therefore, I was standing upright. Holmes likewise. Sluggishly, the Ogre managed to rise to its feet also. I immediately noted that the light had gone from the creature's eyes, however. The abomination, whose face resembled that of my friend Holmes, had become a husk, or seemingly so, for there seemed to be very little substance to that tall figure with the head formed from vine leaves.

I placed my hand upon its chest and gave a gentle push. Straight away, the creature toppled as if made from nothing more substantial than paper.

Falling backward, it struck the roof. The force of the impact, which wasn't at all great, disintegrated the body. Limbs fells away, the chest deflated until flat, suggesting that the torso might have been boneless after all. At the same time, the head, now losing the appearance of Sherlock Holmes' features, as the skull softened, rolled across the thatch. The green tongue flapped loosely as it hung out between the lips. Although I could not be certain, I had the strong impression that the skull beneath the Ogre's scalp was melting, liquifying, loosing cohesion.

Then, abruptly, whatever forces had held the profusion of vines in tight compression, to create the figure of Sherlock Holmes, must have simply evaporated and that substance which resembled human flesh reverted back to Lucifer Vine—or, rather, a mushy, degraded version of the plant. Soon, all that remained was a mound of decomposing vegetable matter, which was untidily jumbled together with the purple dressing gown, white shirt (still buttoned shut and complete with bow tie) and trousers. The resultant mound now resembled a gardener's compost heap into which someone had cast a few items of male clothing.

Despite finding it hard to avert my gaze from such a horrific spectacle as the Ogre's dissolution, I did notice something else of importance. "Holmes," I said, "the storm is passing."

No sooner had I uttered those words, than the sunlight broke through the cloud to cast its brilliant radiance upon the roof where the bodies of the Ogre, Bullman, the soldier and Williamson lay.

I looked around. "Yemaya has gone."

"Indeed so, Watson. I dare say that her spirit has been released, and she has returned to whatever far-off realm she occupied before Williamson fused her spirit to that facsimile of a living woman. I truly hope she is at peace now." He took a deep breath, savoring the sunlight which broke through the clouds to paint his face with a golden glow. "Science won," he stated with such rock-solid conviction that his pronouncement still resonates within my head to this very day.

"*You* won," I corrected. "You planned this course of action after discovering that the dust Miss Dembe used was iron filings, didn't you? You knew you could use that iron powder to improvise a lightning rod in order to draw lightning down from the sky to destroy Williamson."

Holmes smiled at me. "You can read my thoughts, Watson. I swear that you really can."

Then my medical training asserted its own power over me. I swiftly checked the soldier and Williamson. "Both are stone dead," I told Holmes. A moment later, I examined Bullman. "By Jove, he's alive. The bullet didn't penetrate the breastbone."

My voice must have stirred Bullman, for he opened his eyes, sat up blinking in surprise, then he looked up at me and said in astonished tones, "Upon my soul. This isn't Liverpool."

Chapter 29

The train stood where we had left it at the end of the track. Upon our return, the stoker and engine driver immediately busied themselves lighting the boiler fire to raise steam for our journey back to New London.

During these preparations for departure, a somewhat reduced number of passengers boarded the carriages. Most of the porters had survived the battle in the jungle, and these were joined by several soldiers who had fled into the underbrush to evade Williamson's band of outlaws. Though it seemed as if the outlaws themselves were a spent force, their own numbers depleted to the point of decimation after the earlier gun battle. Moreover, if they had discovered that their leader, Williamson, was dead, they may have decided that retreat was their best option. In any event, they certainly did not appear to pose a serious threat to us now, and there was no sign of them hereabouts.

It wasn't long before Holmes and I seated ourselves at the long table in the carriage that served as our operations room. Of course, the carriage, itself, was in a decidedly ruinous state after yesterday's attack when our foe's musketry fire smashed windows, punched holes in timber walls and left plenty of lead slugs embedded in the table. Thankfully, Miss Dembe and Nolan were also seated there, none the worse for wear after being held captive by the tentacle-like vines.

Just moments after the death of Williamson, whatever spell held the vines in place released its grip. Miss Dembe and Nolan were able to brush away their constraints and step free. After that, we were compelled to leave that bizarre copy of the Baker Street building swiftly, because the entire structure began to wilt. The man known as Bullman manged to walk with us, clutching the bullet wound in his chest, while being supported by Nolan at one side and I at the other.

Back at the train, I'd treated Bullman's wound. After that, I gave him a sleeping draught to help him rest. Then, before drifting away into sleep, Bullman had spoken in mild tones, which were in stark contrast to his Goliath-like stature, explaining who he was and endeavoring, albeit with understandable vagueness, to describe what had befallen him.

"Upon my soul, I don't know what happened to me," he confessed as he lay upon the bunk, drowsiness stealing over him. "Save to say I boarded a sailing ship in New London bound for Liverpool. Alas, I have no recollection of what came thereafter until I saw your good self and Mr. Holmes bending over me on top of that strange house, fashioned from plants. That's when I felt a dreadful pain in my chest. Can you imagine my amazement when you told me that I'd been shot?"

I patted that giant of a man on the arm as I reassured him that all was well now, and that he would soon make a full recovery. My words made him smile contentedly as the sleeping draught gently gathered him up into its opiate embrace and carried him off into a deep and therapeutic sleep.

Later, as Holmes and I, together with Miss Dembe and Nolan, sat around the table, I added more information that I had gleaned from the giant who had once been our deadly enemy. "Bullman's real name is Doctor Thaddeus Spence—a Doctor of Divinity, not medicine. Apparently, he had visited New London to lecture on the letters of the Apostles. That part of his life he remembers with absolute clarity, but he has no memory of being transformed into a raging bull of a man."

Holmes nodded. "Williamson controlled the unfortunate Doctor Spence as effectively as a puppet on its strings—just as he did with the vine creature and Yemaya. I'm sure that with Williamson's demise Doctor Spence will now be free of any malign influence." Holmes glanced at Miss Dembe with profound sympathy. "I am sorry that Williamson desecrated your ancestor's tomb and, in a manner I cannot fathom yet, created that flesh and blood marionette that he so cruelly exploited."

Miss Dembe spoke with an undeniably serene composure. "Mr. Holmes. The practice of the living making ill-use of dead ancestors is well-known amongst my people. However, it is a practice that is almost universally deplored. Thankfully, the death of Williamson released my ancestor's spirit."

Nolan said: "And that is what you believe?"

"Don't we all cherish beliefs, which though they might not stand up to scientific scrutiny, do offer us at least a degree of comfort? Isn't that so, gentlemen?"

Holmes smiled. "It is indeed."

I added. "And might we imagine, fanciful though it be, that our fallen comrades, together with Colonel Maltby, are happily enjoying a tankard of some refreshing beverage in a celestial tavern?"

"Hear, hear," said Nolan, nodding vigorously.

Miss Dembe smiled, too, as she said, "And Mr. Holmes, being with you today has gifted me a valuable lesson. I watched you at work and saw how you used your knowledge of science to strike back at Williamson."

"Ah, we did fight a battle, didn't we?" Holmes said. "With science on one side and sorcery on the other."

Nolan added with satisfaction: "And your use of science, Mr. Holmes, defeated the scoundrel."

Sherlock Holmes glanced at Miss Dembe, his manner quite softly gentle for once. "My use of science? No, I can't claim credit for that entirely. It was Miss Dembe here, who realized that the use of humble iron filings was the most effective defense against Williamson."

She said, "I concluded, from many past observations, that the occult forces my own people employed appeared to be linked, somehow, to electricity."

Holmes nodded his approval yet again. "And understanding that one of the properties of iron is that it conducts electrical current suggested to you that throwing iron filings into an electromagnetic field would have a singular effect on the flow of electrons, hence interrupting Williamson's ability to use those mysterious powers he was drawing upon."

I said, "Then magic might not lie in the domain of the supernatural, after all?"

Holmes grinned. "What are you suggesting, Watson?"

"Why, Holmes. I'm suggesting that magic is merely some natural force that awaits the investigation of scientists like your good self."

My friend laughed. "Ha, didn't you scoff at Miss Dembe's words when she made the same observation just a few hours ago?"

Laudably, to spare me from embarrassment, he surged on in brisk tones: "No, my friend, I will leave the investigation of demons, clairvoyants and the spirit world to others. It is my preference that I apply scientific knowledge to perfecting my skills as a detective. And a detective I shall remain until my dying day."

My suggestion, nevertheless, had tickled Holmes. He was still laughing when the train sounded its whistle and began moving along the track—back to New London, and back to that assortment of streets, libraries, taverns, restaurants, houses, and polite society that we, in the West, loftily (and quite inaccurately) call civilization.

You, the reader, will perhaps be familiar with my accounts of my friend Sherlock Holmes' cases and the mysteries that singular gentlemen encounters. You will also be aware that so many questions are raised within my narratives that they aren't always answered satisfactorily, for the simple reason that Holmes and I are compelled to hurry away to investigate yet another case. It must be said, therefore, that there are many occasions where I fail to neatly explain what happened to the players in the drama, or what they did next, or if they went on to live happy lives.

However, during the months following the return of Holmes and myself to England, I did receive a letter here, a telegram there, a scribbled postcard, or a message passed by word of mouth from a later visitor to New London.

Therefore, please allow me to distill all those fragments of information I have gathered into what I hope you, the reader, will find to be a satisfactory conclusion to this strange tale of sorcery and danger in that faraway penal colony. The original governor of Yagomba had indeed secretly fled to a private estate in order to make his colleagues believe that he had been abducted. The man had honestly doubted his competence to rule that troubled land. Holmes remained in the role of governor for two months until he was confident that Yagomba was stable enough for him to hand over the reins of power to a very capable young man with red hair and the broadest straw hat I have ever seen. It must be added that Holmes had the outlaws who supported Williamson rounded up, arrested, and put on trial. Most confessed to their crimes and all those found guilty were imprisoned. Those men involved in the unspeakable trade in human flesh were likewise arrested and share the same prison as Williamson's wretched band of outlaws.

Miss Dembe, meanwhile, enrolled in the University of New London to study medicine. Just this week I received a letter from her, assuring me that her studies go well. I trust she is just a few short years away from being invited to swear the Hippocratic oath. The letter also included these lines, which grant us a crucial insight into Miss Dembe's wider plans:

My homeland, unlike so many others in Africa, is an independent nation. We of the younger generation wish to proudly retain that independence and, moreover, nurture a population that is increasingly prosperous and well-educated, while benefiting from medical care that is second to none in the world. And because we do not wish to become a simple facsimile of Western society, a number of my compatriots have travelled to other parts of Africa, China, India and so on where they have studied their own homegrown philosophies and science, especially medicine. You know that I am a great admirer of science as taught in Western universities; however, it is a painful truth that Western society is far from perfect, and I have learned that the provision of healthcare and a full education isn't universally available to those living on lower incomes.

My personal belief is that we all—every one of us—have the unequivocal right to decide how we live our lives. This means that we are free to reject even our own parents' cherished beliefs if they obstruct our road to a better tomorrow. It is my sincere wish that my homeland becomes a secular democracy where its inhabitants have the freedom to choose the gods they worship, or to follow the path of atheism. I will always sing my own secular hymn of praise to science, yet trust that while we embrace the life-enhancing pursuit of knowledge it is tempered with the empathy and compassion for others that should always, without fail, shine from our hearts.

Moreover, to honor the memory of my own ancestor, who was so cruelly used by that evil-to-the-core Williamson, I have adopted her name. So it is with that name I now bid you a fond adieu.

Yemaya

Yemaya's letter, as you might suppose, gave me much to think about. I know that her country will prosper and grow in the loving care of that remarkable woman and her brethren.

And as for Bullman (or rather the man we now know to be a certain Doctor Spence), he is "done with the tropics forever," he informs me. Consequently, he has joined a monastery in Dublin.

During my trip to Yagomba, Williamson inflicted distressing images of my wife upon me that suggested she appeared to be dying. My beloved wife is well, I am delighted to say. Though I keep my eye on her more closely these days, always alert to even the slightest indication of disease.

Some of you will wonder if the Lucifer Vine is now nothing more than a harmless climbing plant that adorns the walls of New London. No. I cannot state that this is the case. The plant has a certain pernicious ability to stir the thoughts of human beings and to instil madness. However, Holmes made sure before he sailed for England that the city possessed effective teams who make it their business to uproot the plant wherever it is found growing.

As for Mr. Sherlock Holmes? What is his opinion of finding himself the governor of the penal colony of Yagomba, lying in the sultry heat of the tropics, many thousands of miles south of a now utterly chilly and fogbound Baker Street? As we sat in armchairs before a crackling fire, enjoying our glasses of port wine and cigars, I said to him, "Holmes, did your time as ruler of an entire island give you a taste for political power?"

With a somewhat dry laugh, he answered, "Abraham Lincoln so wisely said, 'Nearly all men can stand adversity, but if you want to test a man's character, give him power.' I have remembered Lincoln's words many times when I investigate crimes—the majority of which have their root in those who abuse the power they wield, or the wicked people who will commit a crime to acquire power over innocent folk. Therefore, my answer to your question is 'No.' Being the Lord of Damnation has shown me what power over men and women is like, and I daresay that if I were to seek that kind of power again, it would put me firmly on the road to another form of damnation." He laughed—and this time the laugh was a warm and friendly one. "Ha, Watson! The only demonstration of power I wish to see now is the power to raise your glass to absent friends, and to wish that tomorrow brings yet another fascinating mystery for us to solve. Cheers."

THE END

About the Author

SIMON CLARK is the author of many novels and short stories, including *Blood Crazy, Vampyrrhic, Darkness Demands, Stranger, Secrets of the Dead, Bastion,* and the award-winning *The Night of the Triffids:* his adaptation of the novel has been broadcast as a five-part drama series by BBC radio.

Simon has penned many Sherlock Holmes stories over the last three decades and has edited two anthologies featuring the great detective, *The Mammoth Book of Sherlock Holmes Abroad* and *Sherlock Holmes' School for Detection,* both for Robinson Books.

About the Artist

ENnie Award-winning illustrator **M. WAYNE MILLER** still continues his quest to synthesize the perfect blend of science fiction, fantasy, and horror with his work. Primarily focusing on science-fiction and horror imagery for limited-edition book covers, lavish interiors, and numerous role-playing games, Wayne strives for constant improvement as an artist and illustrator through continuous education, training, and pushing the boundaries of his skill set.

A primary goal is to gain work for Magic: The Gathering, a client that has proven as elusive as it is prestigious. His list of clients include Weird House Press, Thunderstorm Books, Chaosium, Modiphius Entertainment, and Pinnacle Entertainment Group.

Made in the USA
Middletown, DE
27 February 2023

25473227R00175